FOR THE MAY QUEEN

"Evans' debut novel, *For the May Queen*, is a compelling coming of age story. Through a first person narrative that is as intimate and engaging as the finest memoir, Evans takes the reader on the humorous and chaotic journey of spirited Norma Rogers as she navigates her first year of college. Evans skillfully reminds us all of what it means to be young, questioning, and prone to get a lot wrong on our way toward an adulthood where we know ourselves--and those around us--- just a little better." — Jayne Pupek, author of *Tomato Girl* and *Forms of Intercession*

"In the tumultuous way of *Go Ask Alice*, so Kate Evans captures the nightmarish chaos of a young woman's attempt to find her way amid too much freedom, too much sex and too many drugs. Laced with the kind of astute detail that drops readers into that fateful freshman year of college, this story examines the hard choices that can make or break a spirit." — Martha Engber, *Growing Great Characters From the Ground Up: A Thorough Primer for Writers of Fiction and Nonfiction*

"The 80s were all about drugs, alcohol and casual sex, and Kate Evans deftly conveys the uncertainty of the era as her feisty Norma Rogers leaves a sheltered home life and dives headfirst into a series of hedonistic adventures at college, including falling in love with Chuck, who just doesn't seem to be that in to her. The clever dialogue, unexpected twists and a meticulous sense of time and place evoke the immediacy of memoir. Funny, poignant and ultimately a testament to lasting friendship, *For The May Queen* is a trip back to the not-so-distant-past without the hangover." — Collin Kelley, author of *Slow To Burn* and *After the Poison*

"Can a novel about college freshman be a page turner? In Kate Evans' capable hands, you bet! Evans' very readable coming-of-age novel transports us to that era of bad hair and worse décor between the swinging Seventies and safe sex. Readers will empathize with the engaging narrator as she negotiates her first year of college, trying to balance conflicting desires and learning to live with the consequences of her choices. Evans hooks the reader from the first paragraph with this story of love and friendship among compelling characters who grapple with the essential question we all have to face: Who are you?" — Patricia Valdata, Author of *Crosswind* and *The Other Sister*

FOR THE MAY QUEEN

Kate Evans

Vanilla Heart Publishing
USA

For the May Queen

Copyright 2008 Kate Evans
Published by: Vanilla Heart Publishing
www.vanillaheartbooksandauthors.com
10121 Evergreen Way, 25-156
Everett, WA 98204 USA

ISBN: 978-0-9821150-7-7

10 9 8 7 6 5 4 3 2 1 First Edition

First Printing, September 2008
Printed in the United States of America

FOR THE MAY QUEEN

Kate Evans

Dedication

for my mom

and in memory of Joe

Gratitude to:

My mom, Arlene, who brought a love for reading and writing into my life.

My father, Don, who didn't live to see this book published but who lives on in everything I write.

Janelle, for abiding support in all my writing—and life—projects.

Gabriele, whose early influence permeates my writing and creative life.

Collin, for loving these characters.

Ann, my unofficial agent, for great feedback and for always being a cheerleader for my writing.

Crystal, for all the support and the book party.

Nancy, oldest friend and party-thrower par excellence.

Ellen and Kathy, for reading the whole manuscript while writing their own.

The other Ellen, in whose workshop I wrote the first words of this novel and whose laugh spurred me on.

Ben, for telling me I *had* to add a dénouement.

My 20 friends who edited ten pages each.

All of my students, from whom I'm constantly learning.

Kimberlee and everyone at Vanilla Heart for believing in this book and for such a great publishing experience.

Annie, my everything.

Chapter One — Quarters

Sitting cross-legged on the orange industrial carpet, I pulled my blouse over my head. I was seventeen (eighteen in two months). And it was my first night in the dorms. I'd been invited to play Quarters, a drinking game. And Quarters had evolved into Strip Quarters. It had only been a few hours since my parents had dropped me off, had helped me bring boxes into the room and tearily hugged me goodbye, and there I sat on the floor of a dorm room with three people I'd just met, drunk and wearing only my bra and underwear.

This was the culture of dorm life, a life we created together. Yet somehow it felt like we didn't create it—that it existed before we arrived. We knew that playing a drinking game our first night was the thing to do. It would initiate us into this new life, it would mark our belonging. The university would be a place we lived and partied, and occasionally went to class. It was September 1981. The 70's were categorically over with the election of Ronald Reagan and the assassination of John Lennon. A movie star as President made perfect sense to us, even those of us who hated him. Most of us who bothered to think about politics considered Carter weak and ineffectual. The Iranian hostages had been released when Reagan was inaugurated, the waning days of our last year in high school. We were powering forward into college with a new decade before us.

The semester hadn't yet begun so we had a few days of freedom, a few days to rattle around in the half-empty dorm, parentless for the first time in our lives. The industrial quality of the dorms had surprised me. I'd lived my whole life in a comfortable suburban house with wall-to-wall carpeting, redwood decks and a swimming pool. Here were beige walls painted so inadequately that bare spots alternated with hardened paint globs. From what I'd seen so far, each boxy, pragmatic room was exactly the same as the next, holding two single beds with Denny's-orange bolsters, two identical desks, and two closets. The air smelled like hotel deodorizer, a smell that simultaneously attracted and repelled me with its resonance of dirt and exotic travel.

My roommate's side of the room was bare. She had yet to move in. As I hung up my clothes on wire hangers, I wondered what she would be like, where she'd be from, what she'd look like. I hoped for someone I could immediately befriend, a girl who at night, as we lay in the room like devoted sisters, would swap deep secrets with me. She'd sweep into the room, all energy and openness, immediately recognizing our soul-connection that would last our whole lives. We'd never forget these times, our college years. I knew this idiotic *Anne of Green Gables* fantasy was immature, yet I relished its whimsy, only to be interrupted by a guy with blond hair and an AC/DC tee-shirt appearing in my doorway, inviting me next door.

I went, and now there were four of us: the guy who initiated the game, Dan Wasserman, known as Goat, who was short and skinny with a spray of a mustache; his roommate, Billy Doan, who was so tall and lanky he reminded me of the Tallest Man in the *Guinness Book of World Records*, with an Ichabod Crane Adam's apple; and Liz Chan, who lived on the second floor and had Dorothy Hamill hair and an eye twitch.

I'd played Quarters in high school so I was familiar with the rules. There's a cup filled with beer, wine, whiskey, vodka—whatever's around. You place the cup on a table, but if you're sitting on the floor, an album cover or textbook works. You take a quarter and bounce it on the hard surface, hoping it will spring into the glass. If it doesn't, you must drink. If the quarter falls into the glass, you can choose anyone in the group to drink. You must point to that person with your elbow. If in drunken forgetfulness you point with your finger instead of your elbow, you must drink instead. Strip Quarters, I soon learned, follows all of these rules, except that the person who drinks must also remove a piece of clothing.

When it came time to remove my shirt, I watched Goat's eyes. He was wearing only his Dining Coupon book. He'd had the coupon book in his pocket and said it counted as a separate item of clothing and placed it on himself like a fig leaf. Billy was very good at the game and had lost only one sock. Liz was also down to her bra and underwear, and her eye twitch seemed to be getting worse. I didn't notice a change of expression on anyone's face when I removed my shirt and drank my shot of whiskey. Maybe they were all too drunk. Maybe I was too. I had the point-of-no-return feeling—complete freedom.

I'd felt an inkling of this sense of freedom, along with a piercing anxiety, as I'd ridden that morning in the back seat of my parents' car. Even though it was a familiar drive, it hadn't felt that way. The one-hour drive was different this time—I was going away to college. I was going away to college in the city where I'd gone mall shopping with friends throughout high school. I was going away to college in the city where I'd seen stage shows with my dad and mom—*Peter Pan*, *The Sound of Music*, *Annie Get Your Gun*.

"Norma, tell me again the classes you're taking," Dad had said, glancing at me in the rearview mirror then fixing his eyes back on the road. Mom was sleeping, her strawberry blonde hair fanned out on the headrest.

Dad knew what the classes were—we'd sat down together with the school catalogue to create my schedule. He just wanted to have a conversation, I knew, one that centered on all the possibilities that lay before me. My dad liked to futurize. So much was possible in the future. That was how I always knew him: planning, arranging, controlling, balancing the pros and cons, underscoring the bottom line. Safety and security were the goals. I could see as he asked me about my classes that he was getting vicarious pleasure imagining me taking notes in class, organizing my binder, highlighting passages in my textbooks with a yellow highlighter.

When we'd reached the San Francisco/Sacramento junction, I felt something in me contract. I had insisted on going to college in Sacramento, this brown, flat town that systematically flared up with unbearable heat. I had insisted because of Jack, who had introduced himself to me at an outdoor concert by offering me a glass of strawberry wine in a real glass, when everyone around us drank from paper cups or beer bongs. Jack, who regularly took the trip from Sacramento to my foothill town of Auburn to pick me up on

Friday or Saturday nights in his blue sports car, the car whose dashboard crevices he cleaned with Q-tips. He took me on picnics, serving me soft cheese and green grapes. He took me on day trips to Tahoe and taught me how to play Blackjack; I thought it was a sign of his sophistication that I was never ID'd in the casinos or bars we visited. We had sex every place we could — in the bucket seats of his car, in Folsom Lake holding onto an inner tube, in the supply closet of the hospital where he worked as an orderly, in my parents' bed when they were away for the weekend.

For my birthday that year, my parents had surprised me with an acceptance letter to U.C. San Diego, my dad's alma mater. They'd forged my signature on the university application. Wouldn't it be great to live near the ocean and be near my sister, Mary, and her husband Hal? Wasn't it fantastic that I was accepted into the U.C. system, which had more prestige than a state university? I knew they were trying to get me away from Jack. I'd been stubborn, unmoved.

Late that night, I'd called Jack from the princess phone next to my bed in my dark room. My father's snores rose from downstairs through the vent. It had been almost a month since I'd talked to Jack, and at least two months since I'd seen him. But as always when I called him, he stopped whatever he was doing — sleeping, watching TV, perhaps making love to someone else — and talked to me.

When I told Jack about U.C. San Diego, about what my parents had done and how I'd insisted on coming to Sacramento, he said exactly what I hoped he would: "I'm glad you'll be nearby, Babe." I snuggled in my sheets and let the "Babe" reverberate. We didn't see each other much, true. But perhaps he still loved me, I thought.

The Strip Quarters game continued, languidly. We all seemed to be moving in slow motion, our exuberant inebriation worn thin. The air in the room was stuffy and thick. At some point, Liz stumbled out of the room, clutching her clothes to her chest. And now Goat lay on his bed, passed out. Just Billy and I continued. Billy had a surprising and slow spate of misses, while I'd had a succession of drunken luck. So while I sat on the orange carpet turn after turn in my bra and underwear, he had begun to lose his clothes. His other sock, his pants, his shirt. Now he wore only his striped blue and white boxers.

Billy's long, lanky body had a paper clip quality to it, the way he sat on his heels and bent over the album cover, aiming his quarter. His Adam's apple pulsed. Carefully, strategically, he threw down the quarter. It bounced into the glass. He smiled at me, sweetly it seemed, a smile that for the first time communicated something—perhaps that he not only approved of me but liked me. I liked guys to like me, whether I liked them or not. In my altered state, it seemed I did like Billy, but I was more focused on his desire for me. Up until that moment he'd been perfectly restrained, not staring at my body even though I sat in front of him in my bra and underwear. He didn't even ask me about myself and told me little about himself except that he was from Modesto and was thinking of majoring in Mechanical Engineering. We were mostly silent, except for the times we'd sporadically sing to the songs on the radio. I sang more than he did, and he sometimes got the lyrics wrong.

As he sat, smiling, pointing his elbow at me, with the clear knowledge that now I'd have to remove my bra or underwear, he said, "You don't have to."

I took the glass and gulped a mouthful of whiskey, which by this point tasted even less like a nonentity than water. We'd turned out the overhead light long ago and left a desk lamp illuminating the room, the orange carpet creating a campfire-like glow.

"Really, you don't have to," he said again, as I reached around to unhook my bra. Unsure if he was expressing respect or regret, I paused, not unhooking it, as he stood, unfolding his body, lurching a little. His boxers bulged, betraying him, evaporating any concern I might have that he didn't want me. It was oddly poignant, and embarrassing, how men's bodies gave them away. I felt a little sorry for them. The strength and authority they were compelled to project seemed to be overcompensation for the fact that their sexual organs were in such a vulnerable position, hanging on the outside of their bodies like fruit on a tree.

Billy took a step to the corner of the room. His short dark hair exposed his defenseless neck, making him look like a gangly boy who'd just had a haircut. He turned off the stereo and then knelt down, his back to me, and I heard the snap of some latches. When he turned around, he held a guitar in his hands.

He lowered himself next to me and sat cross-legged, his bony knee grazing my thigh. As he tuned the guitar, he asked me what song I might like to hear. I closed my eyes to try to think of a song, but everything began spinning, so I opened them again.

"Do you know any John Denver?" I asked. A John Denver song seemed apt for the campfire ambiance of the room.

"God no," he said. "How about this?"

And he began the familiar opening of *Stairway to Heaven*—so familiar because I'd heard it for four years as the last song at my high school dances. Billy's Adam's apple slid up and down as he played. We sang the opening lines about a lady buying a stairway to heaven.

Goat made a noise and turned over on his bed.

Soon we got to the weird lyrics that almost no one knows. Billy stopped singing, but I continued,

If there's a bustle in your hedgerow, don't be alarmed now. It's just a spring clean for the May Queen.

I expected him to be impressed that I knew those lyrics, even while drunk. But he didn't say a word, just finished the song, set down the guitar and pulled me over onto his bed.

We didn't have much undressing to do, and I suddenly saw that I'd been wrong. When he'd stood to get the guitar, Billy's body hadn't been divulging his excitement. He hadn't been turned on then. But now he was, and I'd never seen a penis that size. I'd wanted sex as much as he appeared to, but now I wasn't so sure.

Goat's breathing was making a gurgling noise. Billy reached over and clicked off the desk lamp. A faint white glow eked through the window from the adjacent parking lot. Lying down, I was woozy. The bed felt like a car driving slowly down a rutted road.

Billy and I kissed. The kiss felt funny, as though his teeth were pressing awkwardly into my lips. I adjusted my position to try to kiss him from another angle, but the kissing still felt strange. I buried my face in his shoulder and kissed his neck to stop him from kissing my mouth. He seemed fine with that, moving his hands over me. I began to think that maybe it would be okay after all, that I wouldn't feel his huge size any differently from any other.

He bumped his head against the wall.

"Are you okay?" I whispered.

"Yes," he said, scooting down. In the weak light I could see that his legs jutted off the bed.

He kissed me on the mouth again, and I felt that same strange pressure on my lips. Again I went for his neck.

"No hickeys," he whispered.

"Okay," I whispered back.

That was when he moved on top of me, cautiously, slowly, like a cat prowling in the backyard. The pressure was not unlike his awkward kisses. He pressed on, very carefully, little by little. In spite of my earlier moment of optimism, it felt like we weren't anything close to a fit, like what he was trying to do was not anatomically possible.

"Hey, um, Billy," I said.

He paused.

"I'm not sure this is going to work," I said.

"Do you want me to stop?" he asked.

"I'm not sure."

"I can go slower."

"Maybe faster is better."

"No, I don't think so."

"Oh, okay, you should know."

"Just tell me if you want me to stop."

He persisted, slowly. I wrapped my arms around his back, feeling the notches of his vertebrae. His skin was soaked in sweat.

"Almost there?" I asked.

"No, only about a quarter of the way."

"Really, that's all?"

"Yeah. You want me to stop?" he asked again. He leaned his head back at an angle to crack his neck. His throat glistened wet. He turned his head in the other direction, cracking his neck again like an athlete preparing to take his position. "Do you want me to stop?"

"I don't think so," I said.

I tried to adjust my body to help him in some way, but I couldn't move. It seemed there were colors in the dark air, sparks of red and green. Something about this moment, imbued in alcohol, felt like the dentist—the numb of Novocain and the vaguely pleasing pinch of cardboard as you bite down on the x-ray film. The minute you don't think you can bite down anymore, the technician says release.

I needed another update.

"What about now?" I asked.

"Maybe a third."

Disappointed but in need of relief, I said, "I think that might have to be it."

"Really? Okay."

Little by little he disengaged from me then relaxed his arms and released his body down to the bed. And then he began to snore. I lay my hand on his shoulder, and he didn't flinch. In the dark, I could see the outline of his lanky limbs.

I felt myself drifting off, my head spinning, but was jerked from the edge of sleep by an upsurge of nausea. I jumped from the bed, tripping over my shoes, wrestling with my pants and shirt, trying to drag them as quickly as I could onto my body. Stumbling out of the room I was blinded by the brightly-lit hall. If I recalled correctly, the bathroom was to the right. With my eyes half closed, I limped down the hall and pushed open the swinging door, ran into a stall and knelt before a toilet. As sick as I was, I was grateful for that toilet, for the privacy of the stall. The tiny floor tiles dug into my knees.

With my stomach emptied, I pulled myself up, exhausted, and went to the sink to splash cold water on my face. This was far from the first time I'd been sick from drinking. My senior year had been filled with similar episodes—my friends and me puking out car windows, behind bushes at the canyon river beach, in each other's family bathrooms during sleep-overs. We hated getting sick and tried ways to get around it: drinking a cup of water in between every alcoholic drink, downing four aspirin before bed, drinking only one type of booze the whole night. Rarely did these tactics work. We knew that the only way to avoid getting sick was to drink less, which proved impossible.

As I lifted my head from the sink, in the mirror I saw a speck of something—maybe a shoe?—underneath the stall in the far corner. My face and hair dripping wet, I peered under the stall. Two shoes, attached to a body, lay on the tile floor—a guy's body in sneakers, jeans and a gray sweatshirt. His dark hair covered his face. I nudged his foot with mine and he yanked his foot away, curling his knees up to his chest. I couldn't tell if his movement conveyed irritation, or was merely an involuntary response.

"Are you okay?" I asked, feeling bad for the poor guy.

"Yeah," he said.

I stood there for a minute or two, the ping of dripping water echoing in my head. He didn't move. My body was weak. I had to leave, to go to my bed, or I'd be joining him on the floor.

Chapter Two — Fear of Flying

I'd always gotten mixed messages from my mother about sex, my mother who straddled two radically different decades, the fifties and the sixties. She had assimilated both Latin Mass and Vatican II; Betty Crocker and *Our Bodies, Ourselves*; *Leave it to Beaver* and *Bob & Carol & Ted & Alice*.

One weekend she had the flu and, confined to the couch, spent hours reading *Fear of Flying*. She laughed and laughed between coughing spasms. I asked her what she was reading, and she held up the book so I could see the title splashed above the arc of a woman's nude torso, exposed through a slash of silk.

"Can I read it when you're through?" I asked. We often shared books.

"Sure," she said.

The next weekend I read *Fear of Flying*, ignoring my homework, sitting up in bed all night, on fire. I was enthralled with Isadora Wing's sexual adventures but even more so by the way she broke the mold, the way she did exactly what she wanted to do when she left her husband for a jaunt across Europe with a sexy stranger, sleeping by the roadside and changing partners with people they met at campsites.

A few weeks later, Jack came to visit. When my mother saw us lying on the living room floor on our backs watching TV, our heads propped up by pillows, an afghan thrown over us, she took me aside and said harshly, "Never lie down next to a boy in this house." This from the woman who'd let me read *Fear of Flying*?

On the one hand, she explained birth control to me when I was twelve. On the other hand, she called me at my best friend's house when I was sixteen and demanded I come home *right now*. She'd found the round plastic disc of birth control pills in my room. I drove home from my friend's house, my heart in my throat.

But when I saw my mom in the kitchen, her head in her hands, I tried to act naïve. I asked her why she was so upset. "You're the one, after all, who told me about birth control," I said.

She lifted her face from her hands, her bright blue eyes flaming, and said, "I just didn't think you'd start so young."

Since she thought sixteen was young, I wasn't about to tell her I'd been having sex for a year. After the incident with the Pill, we never talked about it again, and she stopped telling me how to behave around boys. I ceased resisting most of the rules—I kept my bedroom door open when a boy came over, and usually came home by my 1 a.m. curfew without complaint.

My mother and I continued to share books. I gave her *Go Ask Alice*, she gave me *Catch 22*. I gave her *The Other Side of Midnight*, she gave me *Rabbit, Run*. And the day before I left home to go to college, I gave her *Carrie,* and she gave me *Housekeeping.*

I woke to a ringing phone. For a second, I didn't know where I was. No, not my bedroom. Not a friend's house. My dorm room, my new home. Beyond my gluey eyelashes I saw my side of the room stacked with boxes, bags and suitcases. An image came back to me from the night before: the guy with dark hair on the bathroom floor. I remembered it had crossed my mind that one of us was in the wrong place, and I realized it was me when I saw the urinals on the wall. That was the last thing I recalled. I couldn't remember how I got from the bathroom to my room, or how I got into bed.

The phone stopped ringing. My mouth was thick and dry, my head pulsing.

The phone started ringing again. I picked it up. It was my parents.

"Hi sweetheart," said Dad.

"Hi Norma," said Mom. "How are you?"

I could picture my mom on the extension in the living room, leaning back on the couch, her feet up on the burgundy ottoman. My father was probably on the phone in the master bedroom, sitting on the lavender bedspread of my parents' California king-sized bed.

"I'm fine," I said, running my tongue over my teeth.

My parents began to tell me the news of the last twenty-four hours. That morning, Dad found a dead raccoon in the pool and had a hell of a time getting it out with the leaf skimmer. Mom brought cookies to the library bake sale. Together they went for a half-hour walk along the dam overlook, and then grocery shopping. My father was still deciding whether or not to run for the school board. My Aunt Verlane had called; Grandpa had a spot of skin cancer removed from his nose.

"Has your roommate moved in yet?" asked Dad.

I looked over to her side of the room and was surprised to see a thick, white comforter on the bed and some boxes stacked in the corner. But no person.

"Not yet," I said. I told them I'd been putting away my things, and that it was pretty quiet still. Most people would probably be moving in tomorrow. I didn't have much more to say, and they had reported all their news as though to squeeze it in on a news update between commercials. After several seconds of silence, my father said, "Well, dear, have a good first week of school."

"Yes, enjoy," said Mom.

When I hung up I felt an unexpected wave of something—like I was Wile E. Coyote hit by a cannon ball, yet still upright, standing beneath a green cartoon tree with a frozen smile, but with a donut hole in my torso—a feeling I might have described as sadness, nostalgia, homesickness, but with a dash of joy. I had imagined my parents in the house, and that seemed almost as real as being there. It felt like the house would always be there, they would always be there, and now I had a chance to do whatever I wanted. A chance to create a new me, to embark on something brand new. I had a bit of my father in me, someone who believed in potential, who got a thrill from thinking about the future. I also had a bit of my mother in me, the pragmatist. My room was a mess, and I had a horrible hangover. That was the reality I had to face at this moment. But it was all temporary. The only constant, as my father always said, was change.

Flashes from the night before came to me. The quarter plopping into a glass. Billy's guitar. Billy's bony body. Goat asleep in the other bed. Billy. Goat. Billy-goat.

In spite of our aborted attempt at sex, I felt a little surge in my veins at the visceral memory of Billy playing his guitar in his boxers, of Billy's body on mine. I wouldn't mind trying again. Maybe if we weren't so drunk, sex between us might work.

My body smelled like something foreign. If I could just take a shower, I'd feel much better, I thought. I rose, rummaged through my suitcases to find some shampoo, a towel. I was aware of the aesthetics of the room, of the cinderblock walls, the cheap diner-orange décor, the tackiness of it all. The room felt like a cut-rate hotel, like the one where Jack and I had spent the night the weekend of his friend's wedding, when Jack was the best man.

I'd prepared for that weekend by perfecting an infallible lie to my parents, who never would have let me spend the night away with Jack. I'd also prepared by buying a pretty one-piece slip. I had it in my mind that a one-piece slip would make the weekend perfect. They were beautiful and grownup, those slips, very Elizabeth Taylor, the slinky material hugging a woman's hips, the lace framing her breasts. Up until then I'd only owned half-slips. Half-slips were functional and ugly, the elastic pressing into my belly, creating a little roll of fat. Many times I'd seen my mother preparing for a night out with my dad. Before dressing, she'd stand in a beige full slip, brushing out her hair in front of the mirror, the air scent-rich with perfume, lotion and lipstick. My favorite picture of my mother in our photo album was taken on my parents' honeymoon. She reclines on the bed, propped up by her elbows, in a lacy full slip.

She's smiling at the camera, at my father, a mysterious look on her face. A specific word always came to mind when I saw that picture, a word I never used in daily life, a word that would have had an elusive meaning if I'd tried to explain it to someone but which made perfect sense in the recesses of my mind. That word was "womanly."

My full-slip didn't make much of an impression on Jack. I wore it in the hotel room as we got ready for the rehearsal dinner. As I stood in front of the bathroom mirror in the slip, taming my hair with a curling iron, Jack stood behind me tying his tie. I'd felt a flush of pleasure at the scene. I'd looked at him in the mirror, willing him to look at me, to find me so irresistible that he'd run his hands up and down the silky material then take me to bed. He finally caught my eye and smiled, then finished with his tie and stepped to the toilet to pee. I looked at myself in the mirror, with my half-curled hair and cheap nylon slip. I didn't know what I'd been thinking.

There must have been water-savers in the dorm shower because the water trickled out. Even though we were in a brand-new decade, vestiges of the seventies remained, reminders of the dearth of that decade, the decade of drought, stringy hair, gas shortages, hostages. Finally it was the 1980's, the decade of possibility, of plentiful gas and water, of voluminous Farrah Fawcett hair, and a robust, apple-cheeked President who informed us enthusiastically that America was not weak. Water-savers were left over from an embarrassingly deficient era when people said things like, "If it's yellow let it mellow, if it's brown flush it down."

At least the water in the shower was warm. Steam filled the stall, and my pores opened. Dizzy and nauseous, I hoped that this shower might release the poison from my body.

After showering, I stood before the mirror, wrapped in a towel, to comb out my long, tangled red hair, which was always a challenge. That was when I saw it. I had dark marks on my upper lip. I looked more closely in the mirror, rubbed at the marks with my finger, only to realize the marks were bruises. Billy's awkward kisses came back to me. He had asked me not to give him a hickey, but he had bruised my face.

I looked more closely at the marks. Definitely bruises. It looked like I had a mustache. Tears burned angrily in my eyes. I couldn't face people like this. I couldn't start classes on Monday like this. How could Billy have done this to me?

The bathroom door swung open. In came Liz Chan, the girl who'd lost most of her clothes at the Strip Quarters party the night before. Now she was wearing Minnie Mouse pajamas and fluffy slippers, her Dorothy Hamill haircut smashed into a crooked bouffant.

"God, the bathroom upstairs is disgusting, there's puke everywhere, I had to come down here," she said, setting a cosmetic case on the sink counter. "Is this bathroom clean?"

"It seems okay," I said.

"God, what happened to your face?" She bent toward me. I whiffed alcohol and my stomach tightened.

"Is it that bad?" My eyes stung with tears. I hadn't been ashamed of my night with Billy until this moment.

"I'm sorry," Liz said, taking a step back.

"It's not your fault." I wiped my eyes with the corner of my towel. "They're bruises. I don't know what to do."

"Jesus, bruises," she said. "Let me see."

She held my chin with her thumb and forefinger, tilting my head back like a doctor examining a patient. I breathed through my mouth to avoid smelling the stale booze on her breath.

"How'd this happen?" she asked.

"I don't know."

"Yeah, I was pretty wasted last night, too." She rummaged through her cosmetic case. "Here, I think this might help." She pulled out a bottle of foundation, shook it vigorously, then began applying it to my skin. Her touch was gentle and confident, like my mother's. Liz's lips were full, her skin was olive, and her hair so shiny black it was almost blue.

"There," she said.

She had done a good job. I could barely detect what looked like a shadow of dirt on my upper lip.

"Here, take the bottle," she said. "Give it back when you don't need it anymore."

"Thanks." I went back to combing out my disobedient red hair. My freckles stood out prominently on my puffy face. I looked at Liz in the mirror, feeling suddenly safe in her robust, blunt presence—as though she could handle anything. "Where are you from?"

"San Jose," she said, extracting tweezers from her bag. She began plucking her eyebrows. "My parents really wanted me to go to school there, but Jesus, I wasn't about to stay in that town. I had to get away from all of the skanky people in my high school, and so many of them were going to go to San Jose State. It would have been like high school all over again. Are you going to rush a sorority?"

"I don't know," I said. "I hadn't thought about it."

"I think I'm going to rush Delta Gamma or Delta Omega," she said. "You know, Rush Week is the second week of school, so you get to meet all the girls to figure out which ones you get along with the best." She yanked at a last eyebrow hair then tossed the tweezers in her bag. "I smell like a cesspool. I've got to get in the shower."

As I walked out of the bathroom, she yelled through the water spray, "You seriously should join a sorority!"

I liked that Liz wanted me to be part of something with her—but a sorority? My dad had been in a fraternity. He'd told me about the hazing: getting struck with a paddle with his pants down, being forced to drink rubbing alcohol. And having to swallow laxatives before being dropped off miles from campus, at night, to find his way back on his own. I'd seen photos of him and his fraternity friends, guys with oiled hair, wearing cuffed jeans and button-down shirts. They had their arms around each other, maybe leaned against an old car. It seemed like a different, unreachable time—a foreign world.

Throughout the day, I worked on organizing my room, trying to ignore my hangover, which gradually receded. It was very satisfying to set my new electric typewriter, which had been my graduation gift from my parents, on the little desk, next to my dictionary and thesaurus. I'd always liked school, more or less. I also set out my binder, organized by class subject, and a picture of Jack and me on the Golden Gate Bridge, my red hair touching his face in the wind, his crooked smile displaying prominent eyeteeth, the sky brilliant blue behind our heads. I wondered how long I could wait before calling him. I had been tempted to call him the day before, the minute my parents left, but Goat's invitation to the Quarters game had allowed me to delay the call. I'd told Jack the date I was moving in, and secretly I'd hoped he'd show up, or do something like he used to—like put a rose in my mailbox or arrive unannounced with a bottle of champagne.

As I continued to organize my room, every so often I'd get dizzy and have to sit down. I was getting hungry but had no idea how to get food. The Dining Commons didn't open until the next day. As the afternoon passed, I kept thinking my roommate would show up, or that Billy might drop by. I hoped he would, and worried that he might. Off and on I heard noise in the hallway beyond my closed door, people moving in, dragging things across the floor, animated talk. I also heard music from next door—from what I was now thinking of as the Billy-Goat Room—a little guitar strumming, and then a stereo playing the Rolling Stones.

When I was finally putting away the last of my clothes, my door popped open and Goat's little mustached face popped in.

"Hey, we're ordering pizza. Want some?"

He didn't use my name. I wondered if he remembered it. I wondered if "we" included Billy. I wondered if he knew what happened last night between Billy and me. I wondered if he knew what I didn't know: how Billy felt now. Because I fashioned my fantasy self as a free spirit who didn't care what guys thought of me, I tried not to care how Billy felt. But my fantasy self and reality self didn't live in the same neighborhood.

"Hi. Yeah, thanks," I said.

As I dug around in my purse for a few dollars, Goat jumped into the room. He was short, just a little past my shoulder, and he was wearing stringy cutoffs and the same AC/DC tee-shirt that he'd had on the day before. Barefoot, he kept bouncing up and down on his toes, his head swiveling to scan the room. If he was a girl, I thought, he'd be a cheerleader.

"Hey, nice typewriter," he said, fingering the keys.

He moved over to the other side of the room and tipped open the lid on one of the boxes.

"That's my roommate's stuff," I said. "You probably shouldn't touch it."

"She looks pretty foxy." He held up a photo he'd pulled from the box. Two girls, one with long blonde hair and the other with long dark hair—dressed identically in jeans, white shirts, and sandals—leaned back beneath the shade of a big tree.

"I haven't met her," I said, "so how do you know which one she is?"

"Either way," he said, shaking the photo, "Foxy One. Foxy Two."

"Put that away, you're making me nervous. I don't want her to think we're going through her stuff."

"You two are going to be roomies. I doubt she'd care. Roomies share all kinds of things."

I tried to look at his eyes to see if he was getting at what I thought he was getting at—what had Billy shared with him?—but his eyes, like his feet, didn't stay in one place. He dropped the picture back in the box, and I closed it.

"Come on over when you want," he said. "We've got beer. And pizza will be here soon." He took the money I handed him and jumped out into the hall, leaving my door wide open.

The Billy-Goat Room was filled with people. They sat on the beds, the floor, in the desk chairs, and three guys stood near the back corner, smoking. The stereo blasted Van Halen. Filled with the nervous excitement I always felt at the beginning of parties—like how you feel strapped into a roller coaster right before it takes off—I squeezed in to watch a game of Quarters going on in the middle of the room. Billy knelt before the cup, aimed the quarter, and it plopped in. He pointed his elbow at a tan, blonde girl with white teeth— the most beautiful girl there. I wondered if he saw I was there, and if he cared.

I scanned the room for pizza but saw only a few crushed boxes. My stomach was sour and tight. I needed food.

"Hey Norma." Someone squeezed my elbow. It was Liz. Her face was lit up from drinking. "Here." She handed me a beer. As I took a long drink, the alcohol's dimly sexual warmth flooded my body. We watched the Quarters game; six guys and four girls were playing with beer and whiskey.

"Do you know where I can get some food?" I asked.

"What?" Liz yelled. The music was loud.

"Where can I get some food?"

She leaned toward my ear and said, "There's pizza around here somewhere."

We observed the game some more. The blonde girl was impossibly beautiful. Everyone was watching her. For some reason, she looked familiar to me. Her movements were graceful, even as she tucked her hair behind her ear or threw down the quarter or drank. She wore silky red running shorts and a white sweatshirt that accentuated her tan. She even had a beauty mark on her cheek. I thought about the dark marks on my upper lip and hoped that Liz's foundation was doing its job. The blonde's quarter went into the glass, and, to the collective disappointment, it seemed, of all the guys playing the game, she pointed her elbow at the girl next to her. And then I realized it. I was looking at the blonde girl in the photo, the photo Goat had taken out of the box. Goat had been playing with me. In my room he'd known all along which one she was. He'd met her. I bet she'd moved her stuff in when I was sound asleep that morning. Then he and Billy had snatched her up, I realized with a little pang of betrayal. I immediately chastised myself—why feel betrayed by two guys I hardly knew?

"I'm really hungry," I said into Liz's ear.

"What about the vending machines?" she said. "I'll come with."

She grabbed two more beers on our way out the door. We walked down the narrow, windowless hall. Music emanated from many of the rooms, some rock, some soul, some disco. I wondered how all of these battling music tastes would co-exist. Some doors were open, and we saw people unpacking; they waved at us, and we held up our beers, playing grown-ups at a neighborhood block party.

A guy wearing a pink Izod shirt and a sparkling gold neck chain approached us in the hall. He had big biceps, and his left nipple stood out just below the alligator on his shirt.

"Hey girls," he said. "Glad you're having a good time, but house rules, no open containers in the hall." There was something penetrating about his eyes; they were light green, like pond water struck by the sun.

"Who died and made you King?" said Liz.

"No one died, just graduated. I'm Kirk, your R.A., Resident Assistant."

"Oh," I said. "Are we busted?"

"Where are you going?" he asked.

"Just to the vending machines," I said.

"Here, I'll hold your beers for you," he said. "I'll keep them in my room. It's 146, at the end of the hall. Come get them afterward."

Liz looked sideways at me then did what I did—gave Kirk the beer. When we were feeding quarters into the vending machine, Liz said, "God, that Kirk gives me the heebie-jeebies."

The vending machines stood in the corner of the foyer, opposite the row of mailboxes. At the other corner were a few video games where two guys sat playing Space Invaders.

"Really? I thought he'd be your type. He looks like a fraternity guy."

"No, there's something about him," she said, choosing pork rinds then watching them drop. "It looks like his eyes aren't normal. Maybe he has a glass eye or something."

"Well, we don't have to go back to get our beers," I said, punching in the numbers for some chips.

"What, and let good beer go to waste? No way."

My chips inched forward on the rod but the mechanism didn't work right and the chips didn't drop. They were stuck, dangling at an angle.

"Dammit!" I yelled. "I can't believe this!"

"Here, have a pork rind," said Liz.

"I hate those things," I said. "Dammit!"

The two guys who'd been playing Space Invaders looked up. One was a white guy with brown shaggy hair, and other was a black guy wearing a "Save the Whales" tee-shirt.

"What's up?" said the black guy.

"It's stuck," I said, gesturing to the machine.

"Should we?" said the white guy looking at his friend.

"Why not?" They approached us. "Okay, girls, this is our little secret, learned last night," said the black guy. He looked both ways down the hall. "Do you see anyone coming?"

Liz laughed. "Who died and made you James Bond?" she said.

One grabbed each side of the vending machine and, with obvious effort, they pulled it forward, grunting as they did, and shook it. My chips and numerous other bags of chips and candy slid off the racks to the bottom of the machine. When they let the machine go it banged onto the floor. They high-fived each other.

"Wow, that was great!" said Liz, grabbing some M&M's.

"Thanks a lot," I said, and pulled out a few bags of chips and a candy bar, thrilled with my loot. "We don't need all of this. You guys should have it."

"Nah, just give us a few quarters, if you have them— we're running out and we want to play more Space Invaders."

Liz and I had five quarters between us and gave them to the guys.

The R.A.'s room was really a studio apartment with its own bathroom and small kitchen. A long, dark hallway led into a dimly-lit living space, with a couch, desk, dresser and small table. The place was so dark because a piece of fabric was draped over the floor lamp. The dark light softened Kirk's intense eyes, but it still felt like he was staring even when he just glanced.

Liz had told me her plan was to grab her beer, gulp it down, then get out of there to roam the halls for a good party since Kirk gave her the creeps. But as Kirk had pulled our beers out of his mini-refrigerator, he asked us if we wanted to smoke a joint.

"I'm all over that," Liz said, plopping down on the couch.

"Do you want to do the honors?" Kirk asked Liz, handing her a baggie of pot, papers and a lighter. As she began rolling the joint, Kirk put on the stereo what he told us was his favorite album. I'd never heard Al Jareau before, and the pleasing jazzy music filled the dimly-lit room. I relished the coziness—we were like lions, or ancient peoples, snug in our cave.

As we passed around one joint, then a second, then a third, we drank beer after beer that Kirk handed us from his refrigerator. Sitting on the couch next to Liz, Kirk talked about the traveling he'd done that summer. He'd backpacked alone through Europe, staying in hostels, taking trains and boats, hanging out in cafes with Europeans and Canadians and South Americans. He experienced underground clubs in Paris, wild discos in Athens, and a week-long party with a group of Italians on a beach in Malta.

For as long as I could remember, I'd fantasized about taking a trip like that—no pre-set agenda, just taking off and experiencing the world on my own. The only extended trips I'd taken had been with my parents—a Mexican Riviera cruise, a few trips to Disneyland when my sister and I were young, and a succession of camping trips in our trailer, pulled by our green Valiant station wagon. Dad wrote out an itinerary for each trip, with estimated times to get from place to place, and estimated amounts of money to spend on gas and food. Mom gave my sister and me money to spend on souvenirs: a plastic replica of a drive-through redwood tree, an Old Faithful key ring, a Grand Canyon beaded change purse.

Backpacking by yourself through Europe, or hitchhiking across the U.S., seemed liked adventures that belonged to men, the Jack Kerouacs and Jack Londons of the world. Erica Jong's Isadora Wing didn't quite count because a man accompanied her on her European trek. The closest thing I'd found was *Go Ask Alice*. I read and re-read the parts where Alice runs away from home and wanders around San Francisco.

"I'd die for a trip like that," I said.

"God, not me, you'd get so grody," said Liz. She was now stretched out on the couch, her feet on Kirk's lap. "I like hotel beds and warm showers and restaurants."

"Well, you should do it, Norma," said Kirk, his green eyes blazing, even in the diffuse light.

"Easy for you to say," I said, enjoying the role of the girl-who-can-stand-up-to-a-guy-not-caring-what-he-thinks-of-her. I reached up to take the joint from Kirk. "You're a guy. You can travel all over like that. It's safe for you."

"I met lots of chicks on my trip from all over." His gold necklace sparked as he shifted on the couch, placing his hand on Liz's ankles. "Some were alone, some traveled with friends." He took a swallow of his beer. "These two chicks in Greece, man they'd been everywhere together, had traveled through South America one time, and another time all through Asia, into Japan, Malaysia, Thailand."

"Maybe they were dykes," said Liz. There was more red than white in her eyes, and her left one twitched. She leaned back on the couch, looking like she couldn't lift her head if she wanted to.

"No, really," said Kirk. "And it's not like they were dogs or old or anything. They were hot."

"What—did you do them both?" Liz said, smiling.

"Maybe I did," he said, looking at her.

"God, I'd love another beer," she said, softly, as though she meant something else. I barely knew Liz, but I immediately recognized her coy tone.

"How about a little of mine?" he asked, leaning in her direction.

"What do you have in mind?" she asked.

He took a swig of his beer, holding it in his mouth, then leaned toward her. She didn't move. As he bent forward and put his lips on hers, it looked like he passed the liquid into her mouth. He pulled back. She swallowed, then lifted her hand to his face. He leaned into her again and they kissed.

I looked away then stood, the blood charging to my head. The Al Jareau song on the stereo must have been playing for the tenth time. My foot caught in the rug and I tripped, grabbing onto the table to keep myself from falling. Faintly disappointed that the evening in Kirk's homey room must end, I used the wall to steady me and guide me out of the dark room and into the blinding brightness of the hall.

Chapter Three — Norma Jean

I had to dial three times before I got it right. The first two times a recorded woman's voice told me I had reached a number that was no longer in service. I knew it was in service but that I was just too wasted to dial correctly. And sure enough, on the third try Jack answered the phone. He sounded groggy. I glanced at my clock radio. It was 2 a.m.

"I'm here," I said. "I've moved into the dorms."

"Ah, great, how is it?" he asked. I heard a muffled sound, like he was shifting in bed.

Toning down the thrill that buzzed through my veins at hearing his voice, I said, "It's cool. You know, people seem pretty nice and everything."

"That's great," he said.

"You sound sleepy."

"Yeah."

"Sorry if I woke you."

"That's okay."

"So what have you been up to?" I asked, hoping he'd elaborate on something, tell me a story, let me revel in his presence, the way the wires connected us, my lips to the phone, his voice in my ear.

"Not much," he said. "Just the usual, work mostly. Bought a new car stereo. And some new skis, got a good deal on them."

"I bet you're excited ski season's just a month or two away."

"You know it." I heard the muffled sound again and wondered, with a sinking feeling, if someone was in bed with him.

"You should come by," I said.

"I'd love to. Some time I will."

"I meant now," I said, my inner monitor cringing as my desire for him made a jail-break out of my mouth.

"Aw, Babe, can't do that."

"No more parents," I reminded him.

"Yeah, that's great."

"I'm drunk," I said, anything to delay his hanging up.

"Way to go. Don't waste a minute. College is supposed to be the best time of your life. Wish I'd gone."

"Why don't you? It's not exactly too late. You're only twenty-five."

"Maybe I will one day." He yawned.

"Okay, I'll let you go," I said. I always felt better if I initiated ending our calls, even though I never wanted to. "Would you like my number?"

"I don't have a pen. Would you call back after we hang up? I won't answer so you can leave your number on my answering machine."

"Wow, you bought one of those too?" I said. "You're such a technology whore."

"Yeah." He laughed.

"Okay, I'll call back."

"Okay, Babe, have a good night." He clicked off.

I called back. *You've reached Jack's. Leave me a message. Ciao.*

I left my number. It felt strange to realize that Jack could hear my voice as he lay there in his dark room. Was he alone? Was a girl with him, listening to my voice too? I hung up and sat back on my bed. I'd left Liz and Kirk in the R.A. apartment and came straight to my room, hoping to sober up a little, and to meet my roommate. But facing an empty room, I couldn't resist the temptation to call Jack. Pathetic.

There was evidence my roommate had been in the room again—the picture of her and the brunette under the tree was now pinned to her bulletin board, the contents of one of her boxes spread out on her bed. The party sounded like it was still going strong next door in the Billy-Goat Room.

I wished I had a car. I'd drive to Jack's, undress while he was sleeping and climb into bed with him. He'd be lying there, alone, dark hair on his pillow, sheet up to his waist, Tweety Bird tattoo on his shoulder. He'd reach over and pull me to him. I'd sleep, warm, in the crook of his arm.

There was no way I could sleep right now. The mixture of pot and beer in my system had me wired for some reason. Maybe it was the loud music next door. I stood and spied myself in the mirror. I looked kind of fuzzy. I rubbed my eyes and looked again. My eyes were almost as red as my hair, and the bruises were beginning to show on my upper lip again. I rubbed on more of Liz's foundation and ran a brush through my thick, kinky hair.

The Billy-Goat Room door was open, the Quarters game still going on in the middle of the room. The evening's early energy had waned; everyone looked a bit deflated, just going through the motions. I didn't see Goat, Billy, or my roommate. I didn't recognize anyone. The air was thick with cigarette and pot smoke, and a reggae song played on the stereo.

I watched for a few minutes from the doorway. A guy with glasses smiled at me and motioned for me to come join them. I went in and sat next to him, threw the quarter a few times, made it a few times, missed a few, had a few drinks of beer, a few shots of something. A guy across from me looked like he might be the guy with dark hair I'd seen on the bathroom floor the night before.

I thought about my roommate sitting here, playing Quarters with Billy earlier in the night. I wondered where she was, and where he was.

"Where you going?" asked the guy with glasses when I got up.

"The bathroom," I said. But I didn't really have to go to the bathroom. I just didn't feel like being in that room anymore.

I walked through the hallways. Some doors were shut, others ajar. Music came from some, others were quiet.

I climbed the stairs to the second floor. On the landing halfway up sat a guy and a girl, smoking cigarettes.

"Hey," they said.

"Hey," I said back.

I walked down the hallway, wondering which room was Liz's. Some people had already decorated their doors with their names, or posters, or a white board with a dangling felt pen for people to write notes. I passed one white board that had a cartoon drawn on it, the profile of a guy with an exaggerated penis. I wrote the letter "B" under the cartoon—not all of Billy's name, just the letter "B" as my own private joke.

As I approached a room with an open door, a guy with whitish-blond hair and fair skin peeked out. His face was round beneath the baseball cap he wore. He reminded me of Charlie Brown.

"Hark, who goes there?" he said.

"Norma. Who goes there?"

"Paul. Paul Fellows. Would you care for a glass of wine?" he asked, as though our meeting were a blind date.

"Yes please," I said.

His room was set up like a little apartment, with a mini-refrigerator, two floor lamps that created an ambiance the overhead florescent lights never could, and a beautiful, green velvet bedspread with soft throw-pillows. And the walls were plastered with James Bond posters, tuxedoed Bond, Bond staring down the barrel of a gun, Bond surrounded by long-legged women in bikinis.

He handed me a stemmed plastic wine glass filled with white wine from a cardboard box.

"Shaken, not stirred," I said.

"Absolutely!" He smiled, touched his cup to mine and took a drink. "Do you play backgammon? I've been looking for an opponent all night."

"I never have," I said, "but you can teach me." I hoped he'd want to. I had no desire to go back to my empty room, or to the sad remnants of the Billy-Goat party. This room felt homey, even more so than Kirk's, and I loved the idea of nestling into it.

"Are you sure you're drunk enough to learn?" He sipped at his wine.

"I've had more than enough," I said. "And I'm stoned."

"Good, very good, Norma Jean."

"Just Norma."

"I now christen thee Norma Jean," he said, raising his glass. "You know that was Marilyn Monroe's real name?"

"I'm the farthest thing from Marilyn Monroe," I said, suddenly self-conscious that he was looking at me.

"I wouldn't say that. You've got the figure."

"No." I poked at my now sucked-in stomach. "Too fat."

"I don't think so," he said. "She was a size 12."

"Really?"

"Paul doesn't lie, Norma Jean."

His playful patter was inspiring me. "Okay. If you're calling me Norma Jean, I'm calling you Chuck."

"Why Chuck?"

"Because that's what Peppermint Patty calls Charlie Brown."

"You wouldn't be the first one to draw that parallel," he said. "Damn it. If I just looked like any other cartoon character—say Clark Kent or Dick Tracy. Or Rex Morgan, M.D."

"Charlie Brown's cute," I said, reveling in my backdoor flirting. He refilled my wine glass then put two cigarettes in his mouth and lit both. He handed one to me.

"Cute? Oh well." He sighed. "Look, it's 3:00 a.m. Backgammon time."

We sat cross-legged on the bed, our shoes off, the backgammon board between us, our wine glasses within reach on the floor. I puffed at my cigarette, avoiding inhaling it.

He blew a smoke ring, then popped it with his finger. "One less virgin," he said.

"Impressive, Chuck," I said.

"Did you know that James Bond lost his virginity at 16?" he asked.

"No, I didn't."

"And that in the Ian Fleming books he has a scar on his face? Of course they can't depict him as physically imperfect in the films."

"Of course not."

After he set up the pieces, he told me the rules. We launched into playing. Whenever I started to make a bad move, he'd say, "What fresh hell is this?" and he'd move my pieces for me. In that way, I was able to win now and then.

He asked me where I was from. I told him about my town, which he'd never heard of. He was from L.A. and was surprised that Sacramento seemed like such a hick town.

He told me that Sean Connery was his favorite 007, although Roger Moore had his charms. And did I know that in 1969, an actor named George Lazenby played Bond once—in *On Her Majesty's Secret Service*?

"No, I didn't know that," I said, moving a white piece three spaces.

"You're brown," he said.

"Oops."

"So what's your favorite Bond film?" he asked.

"I liked *The Spy Who Loved Me*."

"Not an atypical choice. Have you seen any of the classics, like *Goldfinger*? Or *Dr. No*?"

"No, Doctor." Something about him made me want to assertively, and playfully, flaunt my ignorance rather than hide it. I was enjoying his cocky, jokey film connoisseurship.

"What about *From Russia With Love?*"

"No."

"We'll have to fix that," he said, capturing two of my pieces.

We played game after game, and along the way we finished the box of wine. I was having a hard time keeping my eyes open.

"Hey Norma Jean, you're falling asleep mid-play. You want to sleep here?" he asked. "I can sleep on my roommate's bed. I doubt he'll be showing up to move in"—he glanced at his watch—"for a least a few more hours."

He moved the backgammon board off the bed and stood. I stood, too, and put my arms around him.

"Would you sleep with me?" I asked, half meaning *would you have sex with me*, and half meaning *I don't want to sleep alone.*

"I think I'm too drunk to make the skunk work, Norma Jean," he said, and kissed my nose.

"That's okay," I said. "Let's just sleep."

We crawled under the covers with our clothes on. The minute he took me in the crook of his arm, I fell into a hard sleep.

I woke to voices. Several voices, multiple voices. Men's voices. I forced open my sticky eyes. My throat burned, my stomach was sour and tight. I didn't know where I was. It was bright. The curtains were open. The curtains, orange and brown stripes. A dorm room.

Chuck, wearing his baseball cap and the same clothes from the night before, was talking to a guy on the other side of the room. It took my eyes a minute to adjust. No, there were three guys, including Chuck. One leaned into the closet, putting something inside. The other set down a box. They were chatting words that my ears couldn't quite take in. My head felt like it was stuffed with straw. I inched up in the bed to sitting position.

"Look who's joined the living," said Chuck. "Norma Jean, this is Benny, my roommate—ooh, I feel a nickname coming on—Jack Benny, Benny Goodman, Benny and the Jets. Hm, need to work on it. And this is Benny's dad, Mr. Moss."

"Hi," I said, offering a half-smile. The skin on my face felt like it might crack.

"Nice to meet you," said Mr. Moss. He stepped toward me, bent down, and shook my hand. Light reflected off his bald head. Surfacing out of the depths of late-night drinking and late-morning sleeping, I felt a flash of embarrassment about being in Chuck's bed with a dad in the room. I made sure Mr. Moss could see I was fully dressed, as I threw off the covers and sat on the edge of the bed—and that helped me feel less weird. Besides, there was something about him, the way he shook my hand, kindly and calmly, that suggested he might not mind my presence.

"Where do you live?" he asked.

"Downstairs," I said.

"She's from some little town north of here," said Chuck, "a place with elm trees and Main Street and gun racks on the trucks."

"Auburn," I said.

"I know Auburn," Mr. Moss said. "We've stopped for gas there on the way up to Tahoe, right Benny?"

"Yeah, I think I remember. Maybe not," said Benny, taking off his glasses to wipe them on his tee-shirt.

"We live in San Francisco," said Mr. Moss, smiling. He looked a little like the Grinch Who Stole Christmas once his heart grew. "I think these two city boys here will have some adjusting to do."

"You know it, Mr. Moss," said Chuck. "How can the capital of the state be such a hick town? There are *cows* here."

"If you need some urban relief," he said, "come visit any time. We have room to put you up. And after dorm food, you'll think Mrs. Moss is an excellent cook."

Benny snorted out a laugh, his glasses catching the light. "Good one, Dad," he said. Mr. Moss laughed along with his son.

Chuck gave me a look. I flushed with pleasure. One night of backgammon and platonic bed-sharing, and we'd created an inner circle.

"Well, gentleman, and young lady, I need to head back," Mr. Moss said. "The wife and I have tickets for the symphony tonight. Can't miss it or there will be hell to pay. Nice to meet you all." He shook my hand, then Chuck's. He reached out to shake his son's hand, then Benny stretched out his arms and hugged him. They hugged for a few seconds, Benny's head on his father's shoulder, his glasses askew. Mr. Moss patted his son's back and pulled away.

"Okay, well, have fun kids," he said, turning quickly to go. "See you in the city, I hope."

Benny adjusted his glasses, eyes down, then turned to the closet, his back to us, and pulled some hangers off the rod. My throat tightened. I felt sorry for him. I hadn't thought a guy could get upset about separating from his father. I had no brothers, and most of the guys I knew didn't talk about their fathers, or didn't like them very much because of their controlling ways. My father never knew his father, and neither did Jack—his parents divorced when he was young, and his father disappeared.

"Well, Norma Jean, I'm ahead twenty-four games of backgammon to twelve," said Chuck. "Your honor is on the line. Don't you want another shot at me? And how about a little food? And some hair of the dog?"

He brought out some crackers, cheese and apples. Then he took a bottle of vodka down from his closet—it looked like a full bar on the top shelf—and some tomato juice from the refrigerator to make Bloody Marys. He even had celery sticks. I was thrilled that last night's events would be extended into today. I felt like I had in junior high at a slumber party when everyone else had fallen asleep and my best friend Suzy agreed to stay up all night with me. Over and over we played the board game where you spin the handle and open the plastic door, hoping one of three cute guys would appear—and screeching in euphoric horror whenever the one ugly guy did.

"Your dad seems really nice," I said to Benny, who had set up his television and was disentangling wires of video game controls.

"Yeah," said Benny. "He's okay."

"That must have been cool, growing up in San Francisco," I said. "I like Fisherman's Wharf."

"It's just tourists who go there," he said. "No offense." He looked at me, his glasses flashing. "Wow, you've got a lot of hair."

I patted my head. "Is it that bad?"

"No, you're pretty, and you just woke up," he said. He worked at the wires for a moment, then looked at me again, then shifted his gaze to Chuck. "Did you two know each other before, or what?"

"We knew each other in a past life," Chuck said, handing us each a Bloody Mary. "She was Marilyn Monroe, and I was Joe DiMaggio. Wait, he's not dead. I was James Dean. Who would have imagined that dorms in Sacramento would throw us back together again? Cheers."

We lifted our glasses and drank.

Chapter Four — The Bob Game

My mother had been engaged three times before she married my dad. All three engagements took place between the time she was seventeen and nineteen. The first engagement was to her high school sweetheart. The second to a sailor. And the third to the T.A. in her college chemistry class.

"Why did you break off all your engagements before you met Dad?" I asked her one evening, when I was a senior in high school as we sat alone in the living room.

She looked up from her book. "I don't know."

"Really? You don't know?" I sipped my cocoa. My mother and I both liked strong, dark hot chocolate, which we'd sometimes drink together in the evening after dinner. "What about the high school sweetheart? Why'd you break up with him?"

"Well, I suppose it's because I wanted to go to college, and he didn't want me to."

"He didn't want you to go to college?"

"Nope. You know, Grandma wasn't too thrilled about it either. She worried I wouldn't get married if I went to college."

"Geez, how ridiculous," I said.

"Don't rush to judgment, Norma. Times were different. Of course later she went to college herself to become a teacher. People change."

Stung from her rebuke, I took a drink of my cocoa. I flipped through a magazine, hoping to regain through silence our snug sense of intimacy. After a few minutes I said, "What about the sailor? Why'd you break it off with him?"

She looked up from her book again. "He got shipped out."

"Yeah, so?" I said.

"Well, I—" the corners of her mouth lifted in a little smile. "I fell for the T.A. in my Chemistry class."

"Mom!" I said in mock horror. "You fell for someone while you were engaged to someone else?"

"Yes, I actually did."

I could see by her eyes that she drifted off, transported to a whole world I knew nothing about. I was intrigued at the glimpse of a stranger in my mother. I waited, took a few more sips of my hot chocolate, and pet my cat Silly who lay curled next to me on the couch.

"So what happened to the T.A.?" I asked.

"Well, it turned out he wasn't Catholic."

"So? Neither was Dad."

"But your father converted."

"And the T.A. wouldn't convert?" I asked.

"Well." She paused for a moment, pushed back a cuticle with her thumb. "I didn't ask him."

"Why not? Is it because you met Dad and fell in love with him?"

"No. I'm not sure why I didn't. Maybe because it didn't seem right to ask a Jewish man to convert."

"Oh, he was Jewish? Did Grandma know that?"

"No, and don't you ever say anything," she said, sharply.

"God, Mom, I wouldn't. But you must have known he was Jewish when you got engaged."

"It wouldn't matter to me now," she said. "But then, well . . ." She drifted off again, gazing at the dark window. Soon she went back to her book. I pet the cat some more, turned a few more pages in the magazine. I had another question I was dying to ask, something I'd wanted to ask her for a long time, but I was scared to. It had been a year since our horrible fight about my being on the Pill. I thought that now she might actually answer the question.

"Mom, were you a virgin when you married Dad?"

She closed her book on her finger and looked at me.

"Why do you want to know?"

Her question took me aback. "Geez, I don't know . . . you were Catholic and everything, and it was the 1950's, and I know that people didn't have sex as much then as they do now . . ."

"Oh you know that, do you?"

I flushed. "God, that was a stupid thing to say," I said.

She burst out into a laugh. I laughed, too. We didn't laugh together that often, so I laughed a little longer than I needed to because it felt so good. When our laughter died down, I sat and waited, my question to her lingering in the air.

"Well?" I asked.

"Yes, I was." After a pause she added, "Technically."

I heard a chair scrape across the floor in the kitchen.

"Technically!" I heard my dad yell. He came charging into the living room. "What the hell does that mean?"

Because we were sitting, he towered over us, his arms hanging down as though paralyzed. At first I'd thought he was joking, but now I could see there was something else going on. I flushed, my heart racing.

"Exactly what it means," said Mom, calmly. "I was a virgin."

"But you said 'technically.'" He almost whispered the word, as though trying to erase it.

"Yes, I did," she said in the same tone of voice she used when telling me to do my chores. "And this discussion is over." She rose and left the room.

My dad stood there, his arms dangling at his sides.

I navigated gingerly down the stairs, trying to keep my footing. I was drunk and nauseous after too many Bloody Mary's to count in Chuck and Benny's room. We'd taken turns playing backgammon against each other and, to my disappointment, Chuck had fallen asleep as Benny and I played. The sun had gone down, the windows blackened, but I was unsure of the time. I said goodbye to Benny, and the minute I slipped out of the room, fatigue swept my body.

In spite of my weariness, in the foyer downstairs I checked my mail hoping there might be something from Jack, but there wasn't. I knew it was pathetic to think he might send me a letter when he lived in the same town. But when we were first together, he used to mail me notes all the time even though we saw each other almost every weekend.

I went to the restroom. Two girls leaned into the mirror, applying layers of mascara so that their eyelashes looked like spider legs. In a stall, I knelt at the toilet. My stomach lurched, but I couldn't throw up. I went to the sink to wash my face.

The bathroom door swung open.

"Norma!" The explosive energy of Liz's entry startled me. "Where the hell have you been?"

"Upstairs, hanging out with Chuck, I mean a guy named Paul."

"Oh, the James Bond guy?" said Liz, abruptly blasé, looking at herself in the mirror and pinching her cheeks. "Is he your type?"

"I don't know," I said. "I think he's cute. What's going on with you?" I splashed cold water on my face, and ran my wet hands through my hair to try to tame it. The bruises surfaced through the diminishing foundation.

"There's a party in the Billy-Goat Room," she said. "A big one."

I dried my face with rough paper hand towels and asked, "What happened to the R.A.?"

"He has one nipple that sticks out and one that sticks in." She wet her finger with her tongue and smoothed out her thin eyebrows. "Ugh. I'm onto bigger and better things."

I almost made a crack about Billy being a bigger thing but decided against it. Even though I didn't explicitly describe myself as an emancipated sexual free-spirit, deep down I wanted to be one. But something held me back from expressing that desire to others, especially a girl I just met, as much as I liked her.

"I need to get into bed," I said.

"What? It's our last night before classes start. And it's only 10:00!"

"No, really. I don't feel too good."

"Listen," said Liz. "Go take a nap. I'll come get you at 11:00. You'll feel better by then."

"You think so?" For some reason, I wanted her to persist, to convince me.

"Yes." She rubbed her lips with lip gloss. "You'll be ready."

The door to my room was open. In the dim light, I could see that Billy leaned back on my roommate's bed, his long legs sprawled out. As irritated as I was at the way he'd bruised me, his gawky little boy quality revived some tenderness in me. I was glad he was finally there to see me. But then I realized my mistake. Sitting next to him was my roommate—the tan, blonde girl with the very white teeth. They each held a bottle of beer and were watching T.V. He was there for her, not me. I tried to tell myself I didn't care, and part of me—about the size of my ring finger in relationship to my whole body—was convinced.

I knew I looked terrible; fortunately the lights were off, the room illuminated by the blue T.V. glow.

"Hey Norma," said Billy. He tilted his long neck side to side to crack it. I remembered that gesture from two nights before, in his bed. I lay down on my bed and didn't answer.

The blonde girl stood and walked over to me, bent down, and hugged me, her shirt falling low and revealing a lacy bra.

"Hi roomie! We finally meet! I thought you were a ghost or something! Norma, I'm Stacy," she said, all exclamation points. She smiled broadly, and I was glad to see she had something dark lodged between her front teeth.

"The commercial's over," said Billy.

"Oops, excuse me! *The Bob Newhart Show* is on. We're playing 'Bob,'" she said. "Each time someone says 'Bob,' we have to drink! I'm a little looped because the secretary just said, 'Oh, Bob, Bob, Bob, Bob, Bob!'" Stacy laughed, and again I saw the stuff in her teeth.

"Emily just said 'Bob' again!" exclaimed Billy energetically, obviously influenced by Stacy's exclamation point voice and body as she flounced next to him on her bed. He clinked his bottle against hers and they drank. She flipped her long hair off her shoulder, and it clung to Billy's tee-shirt.

I saw she had claimed both Billy and her side of the room. Her boxes were gone, all of her things now set in place: books, a jewelry case, stuffed animals. A framed print of pink and blue flowers hung on the wall over her bed, which was strewn with pink and green pillows. A guitar leaned against the corner of the room.

"Do you play the guitar?" I asked Stacy.

"What? Oh no," she said, gesturing to the guitar. "That's Billy's."

I'd figured it was. I wanted Billy to know I noticed.

I closed my eyes. My body felt unconnected to me, the room swaying like a boat. The canned laughter of the sitcom audience echoed in my head.

Just as I drifted off, I heard Stacy say, "Your phone rang. Sorry, I wasn't thinking, and I answered it. A guy named Jack."

Liz kept her promise and woke me in an hour. The room was dark; Billy and Stacy were gone. I told Liz I needed to make a phone call. She turned on the light then flipped through my binder while I called Jack's number.

You've reached Jack's. Leave me a message. Ciao. I hung up.

"God, you're Miss Organized," said Liz, shutting the binder. She grabbed my towel and shampoo and steered me to the shower. She waited until I was done, walked me back to my room, and handed me my hairbrush, then my mascara, then the foundation to cover the bruises.

"Here, wear this." She handed me a lavender blouse from my closet. I put it on with jeans. I could hear the party next door—laughter, a yell now and then, loud music. In spite of myself, I felt a flutter, imagining the possibilities of the night.

"That looks great," she said, smoothing down the back of the blouse after I put it on.

"Thanks," I said. "You look great, too." She was wearing white pants and a white shirt. I thought she looked a little like a dental hygienist.

"Here." She handed me her lip gloss.

"So did you meet Stacy?" I asked, as I rolled her lip gloss on my lips. "My roommate?"

"Yeah," she said. "God, what a ditz."

I laughed, taking refuge in the fact that I wasn't the one who said it.

The Billy-Goat Room was filled with smoke. A game of Beer Bong Quarters was going on—same rules, except the drinking involved a beer bong, a plastic contraption with a funnel that forced a full beer down your throat in a matter of seconds.

"Norma!" Stacy staggered over to me. Drunk, she was even more beautiful, her eyes wet, her lips red, her hair silky. The stuff between her teeth was gone. "I'm so glad you're my roommate!" she enthusiastically slurred, draping her arm around me.

Even if she didn't mean it, I was a sucker for a compliment. And there was something pitiable about seeing someone simultaneously drunk and gorgeous. Her vulnerability flipped a switch in me from irritated and resistant, to benevolent and curious. She was, after all, going to be my roommate for a year. I knew I'd been swiftly judgmental, just because of her looks. Who knew what she was really like? She could turn out to be a great friend— even if we weren't immediately soul mates. If, with her arm around me she had whispered in my ear, "Norma, you're a jerk," I wouldn't have argued. But she didn't seem like the type to put someone else down. So Billy was after her. Who could blame him?

"Thanks," I said, getting a whiff of the beer on her breath. "I'm glad you're my roommate too."

Liz frowned at me. I read her thoughts: *Norma, are you disloyal, or just a liar?*

I smiled and shrugged, my look attempting to send back a message to Liz, *Let's give her a chance.*

"You've got such beautiful hair," Stacy murmured. "Really, really pretty. So red."

"Thanks."

"And you, what's your name again?" she said, pointing her finger at Liz's chest, her "what" sounding more like "wash."

"Mata Hari," said Liz. I had the feeling Liz wasn't into giving people a chance, especially someone so pretty who was probably given a million chances a day.

"Oh, is that Chinese?" said Stacy.

"She's kidding," I said, "It's Liz."

"Liz?" By now Stacy was hanging on me, her arm tight around my neck. She was surprisingly heavy for such a slender girl.

"Why don't you sit here for a minute?" I moved her over to the bed, lowering her down next to a guy who was smoking a joint.

"Thanks, Norma," Stacy said. She leaned against the guy with the joint. He held it up to her lips, and still leaning on the guy she inhaled, the ash burning red. The look on his face suggested he couldn't believe his luck.

Liz had found the drinks and handed me something in a plastic cup. I took a sip—maybe rum and coke.

"You're being awfully chummy with Miss America," Liz said. She gear-shifted her voice into a faux beauty queen: "I believe we can create world peace by distributing cute, pink stuffed animals to all the world's leaders."

In spite of myself, I laughed. "Seriously, Liz, she seems okay. She can't help it that she looks the way she does. Maybe she's cool. Let's give her a chance. She's my roommate, after all."

"Lucky you," she said, grinning and delivering a stinging pinch to my arm, then walking over to sit in the drinking game circle.

Billy came up to me. I ignored him until he said, "Hey Norma." The whites of his eyes looked like a red roadmap. Standing next to me, he was so tall I could see his nose hairs. "I need to talk to you."

"Okay, talk," I said cavalierly. But my heart thumped hard at the *I'm-the-man-and-you're-in-trouble-young-lady* tone in his voice.

"I mean in private. Could we go into the hall for a second?"

From the drinking circle, Liz lifted her eyebrows at me as I turned to walk out with Billy. We squeezed through the crowd and found a quiet spot at the foot of the stairs. Billy's long legs folded up to his chest as we sat. Wrapping his long arms around his legs, he reminded me of a spider. I took a drink of my rum and coke, then held the cup out to him in a pre-emptive peace offering. Clearly he was upset for some reason. He drank and handed the cup back to me.

"Why didn't you tell me you have something?" he said, his red eyes searching my face.

"What are you talking about?"

"I have two sores. They just appeared this morning."

My stomach dropped. "What do you mean?"

"You know," he said softly. "Down here."

"We barely did it," I said.

"You should have told me."

"There's nothing to tell," I said more firmly than I felt. Tears threatened to well up in my eyes. "Whatever your problem is, it has nothing to do with me." I stressed *your problem* to fortify myself.

"They appeared this morning. Just appeared."

"That doesn't mean anything," I said, thinking about the bruises on my face that also just appeared. "It could be anything."

"I've never had anything like this before," he said.

"Neither have I."

"Come on, Norma. Tell me the truth."

"Billy. I'm telling you the truth. Honest to god."

We sat there in silence. I drank from my cup and offered it to him again. He took it and drank, then handed it back.

"Well you better get checked out." He pushed up from the step, unfolding his body to stand. As he walked down the hallway, away from his room, I wondered instinctively and irrationally where he was going. I shouldn't have cared. While I felt the inequity of his blame lodge in my body at a cellular level, I couldn't have articulated what was wrong with how he'd just spoken to me.

I knew I wasn't at fault, but my body burned with shame. I finished my drink then stood up and went back to the party, as though to claim my rights to the Billy-Goat Room, even though I couldn't prove anything to Billy since he'd disappeared down the hall.

From the edge of the circle in the Billy-Goat Room, I watched the drinking game. Liz's quarter made it into the glass, and she pointed her elbow at Goat. He jumped up from the floor and held the funnel in one hand and the long tube in the other. Liz poured a beer into it. Everyone shouted "Go, go, go, go!" and Goat put the tube to his mouth while Liz held the funnel up high. Aided by gravity, the whole beer rushed down Goat's throat. He did a little jig, moving his feet to the music, then sat back down to take aim with the quarter.

His quarter plopped into the glass. He jumped up and pointed his elbow beyond the circle of players and right at me.

"Come on, Norma!" he shouted.

"Nor-ma! Nor-ma! Nor-ma!" chanted the people in the circle, their endorsement a Billy-antidote.

Goat handed me the beer bong tube and held up the funnel, filling it with a full beer.

"Okay, go!" he shouted, his little blond mustache twitching.

I put the tube to my mouth, and he held up the funnel. In just a few seconds, I had swallowed a whole beer.

In that way, I joined the game. Sitting cross-legged next to Goat, all of us drinking and drinking, I fuzzily watched events unfold like movie scenes.

A guy played air guitar in the corner of the room.

A girl stood on top of Goat's desk, twirling around and around.

Two guys removed the shirt of a guy who passed out on the bed and wrote *I'm a fag* all over his chest in black marker.

Someone threw a bottle against the wall and it bounced off, leaving a dent.

Kirk, the R.A., appeared, his green eyes flashing. He asked us to turn down the music then drank a beer bong before leaving.

I lost track of time. I lost track of beers. I lost track of people. At some point Liz had drifted away. Stacy had been there but now was gone, too. Billy had never come back. Only Goat remained a constant, sitting next to me, pouring me rum and cokes, handing me the quarter to throw, smiling his funny small smile at me. *He likes me*, I thought.

The next thing I knew, the room was dark, and I was lying on Goat's bed, under Goat. He was kissing me, his mustache grazing my face. I was very, very drunk, but it seemed that he was a good kisser, thank god. I wanted good sex, real sex.

He pushed his body against mine. I pressed mine into his. I could feel my body responding, wanting more, but it didn't quite feel like my body.

It was quiet. No music on the stereo, no noises from the hall.

In the midst of my drunken arousal, Billy's accusation flicked in my mind. *You better get checked out.*

"Do you have a rubber?" I whispered into Goat's ear.

He rolled over. In the silver light from the streetlamp, I could see his skinny, pimpled back. I heard the tearing of paper, watched his back move, snake-like.

He turned toward me again and whispered, "Okay."

It felt like I was floating, somehow not quite on the bed. I pulled him to me, moving with him, willing him to move the way I wanted him to move, and he responded. His hands were in my hair, pulling at it in a way that might have hurt could I completely feel.

He didn't say a word, and neither did I. We quietly moved together in the dark, and soon I edged toward my peak, and then it hit, the explosiveness, the waves, the concurrent gripping and letting go.

I could have kept going, wanted to keep going, but too soon Goat's body slackened and he rolled away from me. The blanket scratched my skin. In a minute I realized he wasn't awake anymore. Asleep in the dark, he was a blue-skinned stranger.

I disentangled myself from the bed to put on my clothes. The light from the streetlamp illuminated Billy's side of the room. He wasn't there.

I slipped on my shoes and went next door to my room. I expected to see Billy in Stacy's bed with her, but she was sleeping alone, her blonde hair fanned out on her pillow.

Chapter Five — Girl Stuff

My parents told and retold their stories to my sister and me around the dinner table—how they were both the first in their families to go to college, how they met in an English class, how my mom helped my dad by typing his papers, how he helped her with her math homework. My father had so much test anxiety that he'd often be absent on the days of tests so he could take make-ups. Something about not being surrounded by other test-takers made it easier for him. Once he went to talk to a history professor about taking a makeup for a test he'd been especially dreading. He was worried because he was about ready to graduate, and without a passing score on this test he might not make it.

As my father told the story, the professor looked up from his desk and said, "I suppose you're here about the test."

"Yes, sir."

The professor opened his grade book and looked up and down the columns. "Rogers, right?"

"Yes sir."

"You got a B."

At this point in the story, my dad would always grin and say, "The gods must have been with me. For some reason that professor had a grade in his grade book for me. I didn't correct him, just said, 'Thank you, sir,' and walked out."

And then my mom said, "Stan, that was cheating."

"No, it wasn't, Barbara," he responded. "Besides, you wrote some of my English papers for me. Wasn't that cheating?"

"I didn't write them," she said. "I heavily edited them and typed them up."

"Your definition of 'heavily edit' might be someone else's definition of 'write.'"

And then they'd launch into a lengthy discussion about ethics and education while my sister and I looked at each other over our dessert, pretending to condescend to their passionate discussion of a pointless topic while secretly relishing the peek into their pasts, into a hazy world when they were young, unmarried and childless.

My parents would always end the discussion agreeing to disagree. Mom would be a little heated by this point, and Dad would be terse.

And then, Dad would lean across the table and hold out his hand. Mom would reach over reluctantly, and then she'd warm a little as he squeezed her fingers.

The professor wanted us to call her Linda. She wanted us to write about things that mattered to us, things we cared about, things we were passionate about that were in the news. What did we think about equal pay for equal work? Abortion rights? The Equal Rights Amendment? The appointment of the first female U.S. Supreme Court Justice? What did we think about the Middle East? The release of the hostages? The Air Traffic Controllers' strike?

I opened my binder to the "English Class" section and fished a pen out of my purse. I was sitting in the back row because I'd been late to class. I'd slept through my alarm, and then I had a hard time finding the classroom. When I first exited the dorms, I wasn't even sure where the main campus was. The dorm buildings were positioned in a circle around a well-manicured lawn. I didn't know which direction to walk to get out of the circle, so I followed two guys with backpacks who looked like they knew where they were going. Rounding the corner of Dorm Four they took a cement walkway, lined by pink and yellow flowers, to the central campus.

The air was hot and the sky lake-blue. The campus seemed huge, with cluster after cluster of identical-looking white and red-brick buildings. Students lay on patches of grass in the sun or beneath huge shade trees. Other students walked purposefully, backpacks slung over a shoulder. After glancing at my class schedule, I was about to ask someone the location of Riley Hall when I looked up and saw that I was standing right in front of it.

"Your first writing assignment," said Linda, "is to write about something in the newspaper that interests you. Spend some time looking through each section—read a variety of headlines, scan different stories, until you find something that grabs you."

I wrote "newspaper" and "grabs" on the lined paper. I reminded myself I was sitting in my first college class, and I felt a tinge of excitement rise in me—but my head was fuzzy, my chest tight, my stomach sour. Images of the previous night played in my mind, a strange feeling running up my spine: holding the beer bong to my mouth, a girl spinning around and around on top of Billy's desk, Goat's mustache grazing my face, Stacy's long blonde hair, Billy's words, *you better get checked out . . .*

Linda held up a newspaper, pointing out the sections: News, Lifestyle, Opinion, Business.

A guy in the front row raised his hand. "Can we write about sports?" he asked.

"Yes, for this first assignment, choose anything at all. After this first assignment, though, I'm going to ask you to stretch beyond what's familiar."

I wrote "stretch" on my paper.

As Linda talked, she walked back and forth across the front of the room, wet patches blooming under the arms of her silky pink blouse. Large gold earrings hung heavily from her elongated earlobes. She was plump, fleshy in a solid, yet feminine, way. Whether she wrote on the board, brandished the newspaper, or distributed the syllabus, her movements seemed decisive, streams of words flowing effortlessly from her mouth.

It was hot in the room. I wished I'd worn shorts like the girl sitting next to me. She had long legs, recently shaved by the looks of it. My legs needed to be shaved, but I didn't even have time to shower this morning. I'd pulled back my unruly hair with a rubber band, washed my face, and quickly applied foundation to my bruises, which were, fortunately, fading. And another fortunate thing was that someone had cleaned the bathroom. It didn't take long to learn that the dorm bathrooms were cleaned only during the week—meaning, on the weekends, we'd have to suffer whatever havoc we wreaked.

"Right now," said Linda, walking down the rows toward the back of the room. "I want you to write down something about yourself. Just a few paragraphs describing where you've come from, what your interests are, and your goals."

She stood next to my desk, her arm in pink silk gesticulating near my face. Her body emitted a spicy perfume—flowers and gingerbread.

"So now please take ten minutes to write."

I wrote my name on the paper. Linda had circled the class and ended up once again at the front of the room. Leaning against the board, she surveyed the students. She caught my eye and smiled at me. I smiled back, then looked back at my paper, wondering if my hair looked crazily out of control in its rubber band, if I looked as messy as I felt.

I picked up my pen and thought about where I was from. Auburn, in the Sierra Nevada foothills. The air smelled different there, the light was different too. Oak trees, ghost pines, the owl who perched out my window at night. Our house of windows, redwood decks, wall-to-wall carpeting, blue swimming pool. My friends who went away to college, my friends who stayed behind, two who were engaged, including my best friend. My parents, alone in the house now that my sister and I were gone.

I couldn't write about any of that. I didn't know what to say. I began to write about my interests instead. I liked movies and music and books, I wrote. My favorite book when I was a kid was *Harriet the Spy*. I'd loved *Heidi*, too. Books about girls on adventures. Adventurous women. *Go Ask Alice. Fear of Flying.*

That sounded childish. I tore the paper out of my binder and crumpled it up. A guy with a sunburned face looked at me, then back to his paper.

I'm from Auburn, a small town, I wrote. *I like to read and go to the movies and hang out with friends. I always had a goal to go to college, and here I am, fulfilling my goal. I want to be educated so I can get a good job and travel. I think my major will be Communications.*

I didn't really know what Communications was, but it sounded good because I believed it didn't require math and science.

Or maybe I'll major in Spanish. I'd like to learn another language.

I didn't know where that came from; I wasn't even signed up for a Spanish class.

Or maybe I'll major in English, since I like to read.

As I wrote, I became more and more aware of a huge gap between what I really wanted to say and what I was able to write down. I didn't know why I couldn't say what I meant.

And maybe one day I'll get married, I continued to write. *But I won't stay at home, cooking meals, cleaning the house, and raising the kids. Everything would have to be fifty-fifty.*

I was developing a headache, and the room was so hot. I knew that after class I'd need to traverse the huge campus to find the health center so I could, as Billy said, get checked out.

I don't believe that men should work and women stay at home.

I re-read my paragraph. It sounded like something written by someone else.

"Please finish your sentence," said Linda. "Then pass your paper up front. Don't forget to write about a newspaper article. Two to three pages, typed, double-spaced. And I'll see you all on Wednesday."

"Norma Jean!"

It was Chuck, coming out of the classroom next to mine. His face grew even more round as he grinned at me under the brim of his baseball cap. He bumped his shoulder against mine, his playful touch flushing me with warmth. His presence felt immediate and sure, as though we'd known each other much longer than a weekend. Maybe he was right—that we'd been linked in a past life. What a funny thought: me, the reincarnated Marilyn Monroe; him, the reincarnated James Dean.

"How are you doing, Norma Jean, Norma Ray, Norma Desmond?"

"Norma who?"

"I'm ready for my close-up Mr. DeMille." He framed his face with his hands and bugged his eyes out at me. "Don't you know *Sunset Boulevard*?"

"No, what is it?"

"1950, Gloria Swanson, William Holden."

"I'm not too into old movies," I said. "I do like Elizabeth Taylor with her violet eyes. But her movies, I don't know. I like newer ones. Did you see *Raiders of the Lost Ark*? *Rocky*? *Ordinary People*?"

"Yeah, yeah," he said. "But they don't hold a candle to the classics, film noir, Billy Wilder, Alfred Hitchcock. I'm assuming it's a sad fact that you've never seen *Vertigo* or *Rear Window*?"

"You'd be correct," I said.

"And we know you haven't seen Sean Connery as 007. We have some work to do. There's a great theater downtown that shows old movies. Let's go now."

"I have another class," I said. "And I need to go to the Health Center first."

"What for?"

"Girl stuff," I said, trying to sound carefree.

"Oh, the elusive girl stuff," he said. "The magical mystery tour of girl stuff."

"Do you know where the health center is?"

"I think it's over by the Student Union. Shall I escort you?"

I shielded my eyes against the bright sun with my hand as we walked across campus. I was grateful not to have to navigate the campus alone, but the last thing I wanted was for Chuck to be privy to my problem. Oblivious, Chuck pattered on about how Alfred Hitchcock sometimes made cameos in his own films, about Doris Day singing *Que Sera Sera* in *The Man Who Knew Too Much*, about the shower scene in *Psycho*.

As he pulled open the door to the Health Center for me, he told me he was majoring in film and that one day he wanted to make great movies.

He followed me into the Health Center. Thankfully, though, he seemed sensitive to my need for privacy and said, "I'll wait here" as he took a seat with other students in the waiting room.

I told the woman behind the counter that I needed to see a doctor for a gynecology checkup.

"Okay, there are some appointments available next week," she said, clicking her pen.

"I really need to see someone now," I said.

"Is it an emergency?"

"I'm not sure. I think so. Maybe."

"Well in that case, sign here." She pushed a clipboard toward me. There were six names on the list.

"How long will I have to wait?"

"Probably two to three hours." She clicked her pen again.

"But what if I'm in pain?"

"Are you in pain?"

"I don't know. Maybe. Kind of."

She looked at me, narrowing her brown eyes.

"Just sign in," she said.

I felt my chest tightening and tears welling up in my eyes. I had never been alone at the doctor's before. Once I'd been to the free clinic to get my birth control pills, but my best friend, Suzy, had come with me. Other than that, my mother had always made my doctor and dentist appointments—and had taken me to them, dealing with the receptionists, asking the doctors questions, getting my prescriptions filled, and always taking me out afterward for cake or ice cream. Even with Chuck waiting for me, I felt an irrational upsurge of loneliness, of abandonment.

"Are you okay, hon?" asked the woman, her tone softening. She put down her pen and handed me a tissue.

I wiped my eyes. "I don't know."

"I'm sure everything's fine. Now, take a deep breath and tell me if there's anything I can do for you," she said in a concerned psychotherapist voice.

"Do I really have to wait until next week for an appointment?" I sniffled then blew my nose.

She flipped through the spiral notebook in front of her. "I can squeeze you in tomorrow at 2 p.m."

"Really?"

She nodded.

"Okay," I said. "Thanks."

In the waiting room, I found Chuck reading *Cosmo*.

"Here are ten ways to make your man happier in bed," he said. "And ten ways to get that nasty cellulite off your thighs. What is cellulite, anyway? It sounds like something an astronaut would drink. And why is everything a list of ten?" He looked up at me. "Oh. Have you been crying?"

"Is it that obvious?"

"Red puffy eyes. You could pass for stoned. But I doubt you smoked out with the nurse, did you?"

I blew my nose in the tissue. "I have an appointment tomorrow."

Chuck stood and grabbed my hand. "I have something that'll make you feel better. Let's get the hell out of here."

And so it was that I took my first Quaalude on the day I cut my first class. Instead of going to the opening session of Cultural Anthropology, I bought a diet cola so Chuck and I could swallow the pills. Then we went downtown to see *The Postman Always Rings Twice*. While Lana Turner lit up the screen, Chuck and I sat in the cool, dark womb of the theater, flying on Quaaludes, eating popcorn, and sharing a bottle of peppermint Schnapps.

Chapter Six — Princess

The summer before I went to college, Prince Charles married Lady Diana Spencer. My best friend, Suzy, and I had stayed up all night at her house to watch the wedding.

"I really don't know why in this day and age it should matter if a prince marries a virgin," I said, pulling my sleeping bag up over my legs.

"I know," said Suzy, popping open a diet soda. We were both on diets, so the fare for the night was diet soda and air-popped popcorn. "I mean, you can lose your hymen riding a horse. Don't those royals ride horses all the time?"

"Good point," I said, as Lady Di rode to the church in a glass coach, which struck me as romantic yet juvenile. "Wow, that is so Cinderella."

"I really don't get it," said Suzy. "She's got such a big nose. Makes me think I could marry a prince if I wanted to." Suzy had her father's nose, a prominent, beaky thing with a large bump. But she was pretty, with her big blue eyes, full breasts and thick brown hair that conformed perfectly to the feathered Farrah hairdo. She never lacked for a good boyfriend. And now she was engaged to Sammy, who had been her boyfriend all senior year.

"She's taller than he is," I said. "I read that in their engagement photos, Prince Charles stood on a step."

"I'm so glad Sammy's taller than me." She grabbed a handful of popcorn. "This shit tastes like packing material," she mumbled through a full mouth.

Lady Di emerged from the coach in a cloud of white dress. As she walked down the red-carpeted aisle, her long train dragged behind her like a deflated sail. Her face was softened by the veil. I didn't mind her nose, or her height. I thought she was beautiful.

"I wonder if she's really a virgin," Suzy said.

"Maybe she's just one technically," I said.

"What do you mean, *technically*?"

"You know, has done everything but."

"Can you imagine being one of her ex-boyfriends?" said Suzy. "You'd be like, 'I had my tongue in that Princess!'" She shouted out a laugh.

"You'd be like, 'That Princess blew me!'" I said.

We laughed hard. Then we laughed harder and harder, holding our stomachs, falling down in our sleeping bags, pounding at the floor with our heels, while Diana's father, Earl Spencer, gave her away to Prince Charles.

It was 3 a.m., and my English homework was due the next day. I spread out the newspaper on my bed and smoothed it down. I turned the pages, looking for something to jump out at me, as Linda, the professor, had said to do.

In the quiet of our room, Stacy lay in bed, her side of the room dim, her blonde hair spread out on her pillow. Slowly turning the pages of the newspaper, I envied her deep sleep. I was so sleepy I was beyond sleep, residing in the jittery world of over-caffeination. I had planned to do homework that afternoon, after my morning classes. But instead I'd spent hours with Chuck, Liz and Benny drinking wine, smoking cigarettes, and playing backgammon. When Chuck realized it was past midnight, he made coffee for everyone. We all had homework to do.

As we'd walked down the hall from Chuck and Benny's to Liz's room, she'd said, "God, I bet Benny's a virgin."

"Really?" I said. It seemed funny to think of a guy as a virgin.

"Yeah, look at him, with those glasses, such a Mama's boy. And he couldn't stop staring at my boobs." Liz was wearing a tight scoop-neck tee-shirt that hugged her breasts. "He's so adorable."

"You think so?"

"Yeah, there's something about him."

We reached her room that had a poster plastered on the door of David Bowie, all bleached blonde shaggy hair, pink tights and rainbow platform shoes. She opened the door. As usual, her roommate, a girl named Brenda, wasn't there. I'd never met Brenda because she used the dorms as a front. In reality, she lived with her boyfriend in his off-campus apartment, but she didn't want her parents to know. Liz told me Brenda came by once a week to get her mail and phone messages.

"It's too damn bad our classes get in the way of our college experience," Liz deadpanned. "Want to come hang out?"

I did, but I clutched at my last shred of self-discipline. "No, I really should go do my homework."

"Okay, maybe I'll organize my binder like yours," she said. "You're a good role model." She laughed.

I wished I had a retort, something funny to say back, but I was anxious and preoccupied. I had gone to the Health Center that day after class, alone, and had my checkup. Stern and efficient, the doctor's cool hands swiftly performed a pap smear and breast exam. An equally efficient nurse had taken my temperature and drawn my blood, capturing its swirling darkness into three elongated tubes. I'd left with a card in my hand. Written on the card was another appointment in a week to get the results.

And now, as I sat on my bed thumbing through the newspaper, it appeared that the world was a mess. Assassinations, military actions, a mine collapse leaving 65 dead. Gay men were getting some strange disease. A test-tube baby was about to be born in England.

I turned to the style pages. The new trend was to bring to your hairstylist a photo of Princess Diana and request her cut, which to me wasn't much different than the Dorothy Hamill cut.

On the T.V. page was a long story about the soap opera *General Hospital*. Everyone anticipated the wedding of two characters, Luke and Laura, just six weeks away. I decided to write about that.

As usual, I felt a prickly resistance as I began to write, but soon my pen flowed across the paper. I wrote about how people all over the nation were planning Luke and Laura wedding parties, about how I had watched *General Hospital* most days during my senior year, rushing to my house, or Suzy's, to catch it. We'd seen Luke and Laura meet. We'd seen her work for him as a waitress at his disco. We'd watched Luke pull Laura to the floor of the disco late one night, after all the customers had gone. We watched him rape her. Then, after Laura went to rape crisis counseling, she fell in love with Luke. Their love affair—and it was an affair, for Laura was married to Scottie—was passionate, rocky, and strewn with obstacles. And now Laura had divorced Scottie and was marrying Luke. Everyone eagerly anticipated the revealing of Laura's wedding dress—would it be like Diana's? Would Luke wear a tux or a suit? What would be their color theme?

I wrote and wrote. I was on a roll, even though I half believed, half doubted my words. There was something magical about weddings, I wrote, something that got everyone excited and optimistic, that made us all hope that true love, authentic love, everlasting love might find us one day.

Stacy's alarm rang at 6 a.m. while I was trying to decipher my handwriting to type up the last paragraph of my paper. With her eyes half closed, she got out of bed and pulled on running shorts and a tank top.

"Wow, have you been up all night?" she asked.

"Yeah, I had a paper to write. I hope my typewriter didn't wake you."

"I could sleep through a bomb." She pulled her hair back into a ponytail. "I've always been that way. Once I'm out, I'm out."

"I'm not that way so much anymore," I said. "But I used to be. When I was a kid, a train exploded in our town, blowing out windows of houses down the street. It woke up the whole neighborhood, but I slept through it."

"Sounds like something I'd do." Stacy put her face close to the mirror to clean the sleep sand out of the corners of her eyes.

"Who's that girl in the picture?" I asked, pointing to her bulletin board, to the photo of her and a dark-haired girl sitting on green grass under a tree, the one Goat had pulled out of one of Stacy's boxes before I'd even met her.

"Tabitha," she said. "My step-sister." Something about the way she said "step-sister" and "Tabitha" made the words sound exotic. That was Stacy's aura: exotic combined with girl-next-door.

"Oh, your parents are divorced," I said.

"No. My mom died."

"She did?"

"Yeah, three years ago, when I was fifteen."

"Oh." I almost added, *That's terrible*, but it didn't seem like a nice thing to say. Stacy was nice. So nice that she made me interrogate most of what I said for its niceness factor. She made me kinder than I really was.

"And then my Dad married the florist who prepared the flowers for my mother's funeral. It was weird. He's really into her. It seems like he loves her more than he loved my mom." She sat on the edge of her bed, pulling on her socks. When she looked up, I glanced at her eyes to see if they had tears in them. They didn't.

"But," she continued, "the good thing about the Flower Lady—her name's Tina, really—is that she brought Tabitha to live with us." As though Stacy heard a mosquito buzz of criticism in her words, she backpedaled. "Actually, Tina's not bad, it's just hard for me to see someone else with my dad. But I'm happy for him, that he found love."

I wondered how her mother died, but it didn't seem okay to ask. Stacy took the picture off her bulletin board and brought it over to me.

"See, we look like sisters, even though we're not."

"Yeah, you really do." The two girls looked like photo negatives, with the contrast between Tabitha's dark hair and Stacy's light hair.

"You'll get to meet her soon, I hope," said Stacy. "I think God gave me Tabitha so I could deal with my mom's death." She took the photo and pinned it back on her bulletin board. "She's a senior right now, but next year she'll be coming here. We're going to get an apartment together."

"That sounds good." I tried to imagine what would have happened to me, my sister, and my dad if my mom had died. I thought about the one day, a few years back, when Mom had the flu and lay on the couch all day reading. I had never known her to do something like that before. She never got sick. I couldn't imagine her in bed, ill—much less in the hospital, dying. Had Stacy experienced something like that? Here she was, just being normal, being nice, living in the dorms, taking classes, partying with us as though we were all the same.

Turning around to face me, she suddenly looked different. It seemed there was something mysterious and dark around her eyes.

With her hand on the doorknob, she said, "My mom had breast cancer." She shut the door quietly behind her. A minute later I saw her jog by the window, her blond ponytail bobbing.

After English class, Chuck met me as I came out of the classroom like he had before.

"Professor Sominex put me to sleep again," he said, bumping my shoulder with his in greeting. "I think he missed his calling as a hypnotist."

"I'm sure he'd be grateful if you set him straight," I said. "Maybe you could have 'career counselor' as a backup plan to 'filmmaker.'"

"Nope, no backup plans. It's all or nothing. I'm either the next Alfred Hitchcock, or I'm drinking out of a paper bag on the street. Where're you going, Norma Jean?"

"To my class I missed on Monday because you drugged me and dragged me to the movies." I smiled, filled with the pleasure of our flirtatious playfulness. It niggled at me, though, that I was more witty around Chuck and more nice around Stacy. Did that mean I had no personality of my own?

"Wanna do it again?" asked Chuck. "They're showing *The Country Girl*, 1955. Grace Kelly won the Oscar."

"Is she the one who married that prince?" Maybe this was my personality—a question-asker.

"Yes, Prince Rainier of Monaco. Tragic, really, that she'd leave a movie career to sequester herself in some vague country no one but Catholics have ever heard of."

"Was she a good actress?"

"Good? She was great. Hitchcock put her in three of his films, which wouldn't mean anything to you, but we will fix that."

"But not today," I said. "I really have to go to my class." As much as I would have loved to go to the movies, it felt good to be firm. Maybe that was it, my personality profile: Norma is a firm question-asker.

"I'll escort you, Madam."

As we walked across campus, Chuck talked about the Sunbeam Alpine Sports Roadster that Grace Kelly drove in *To Catch a Thief*, the fact that she turned down Bing Crosby's marriage proposal, and that in 1953 she lost the Best Supporting Actress Oscar for her role in *Mogambo* to Donna Reed in *From Here to Eternity*.

"Jesus Christ," he said as we turned the corner of the bookstore.

"What?"

"Is it my imagination run amok? I'd swear that's the young Grace Kelly walking toward us."

It was Stacy, holding her books in the crook of one arm, waving at me with the other.

"Hi Norma," she said.

"It's just too unbelievable," said Chuck. "I have the chills."

"You'll have to excuse him," I said to Stacy. "He doesn't have any manners. Chuck, this is my roommate, Stacy."

"Your roommate? Unbelievable."

"Chuck—I mean Paul—lives on the second floor," I said.

"You look just like Grace Kelly," he said. "The resemblance is mind-boggling."

"Quit staring, you're making her nervous," I joked in an effort to disarm my budding jealousy.

"It's okay," she said, smiling. She was perfection. I felt sloppy and fat and petty by comparison. I flashed on our talk this morning, her dead mother. How could she be standing here, so perfect and nice, and have a dead mother? Or maybe a tragic aura contributed to her flawlessness. It didn't matter that I'd seen her drunk, or with food between her front teeth. She transcended flaws.

"Are you majoring in Theater?" asked Chuck.

"No, Biology."

"You should be an actress. You should be on stage, and in films," he said. "My films!"

"Chuck, knock it off, you're drooling," I said. "And you're walking me to class." I pulled him by his shirtsleeve toward me.

He tripped over his feet as I pulled at him, then he turned his head toward Stacy. "Hasn't anyone ever told you that you look like Grace Kelly?" he said.

"No, I don't think so," she said. "People always say I look like Cheryl Ladd!"

"Good God," he said, "don't let people diminish you so."

"Chuck, let's go, I'm going to be late. Bye Stacy." I smiled, trying to project a magnanimous warmth when I felt a jagged iciness.

"Bye," she said. "Nice to meet you, Paul. See you later, roomie!"

"Stay away from princes!" Chuck shouted over his shoulder.

On the way to my class, Chuck talked the whole time about how remarkable and serendipitous it was, that we'd just been talking about Grace Kelly, and then she miraculously manifested. I nodded, doing my best impression of impressed.

The Cultural Anthropology professor was tall, his hair so perfectly twisted into tight little curls that he reminded me of Mr. Brady from *The Brady Bunch* post-perm. It had always been a puzzle to me that one season Mr. Brady and his sons had straight hair, and the next they appeared with curly hair. No mention had ever been made on the show of their perms, as though their transformation to poodle-heads had been a natural occurrence.

As the professor lectured, he used terms I'd never heard before, like "ethnography," "habitus," and "acculturation."

I stayed after class to talk to him. He was fastening his briefcase to the back of his bicycle, which leaned against the chalkboard.

"Excuse me," I said, "I'm enrolled in this class but you didn't call my name. Norma Rogers."

"Were you here on Monday?" he asked, pulling a bike helmet onto his head.

"No, I couldn't make it."

"Then you've been dropped."

"Dropped?"

"Yes, it's an automatic drop if you're a no-show on the first day."

A series of lies jumped into my head: that my parents didn't bring me to the dorm until yesterday, that my grandmother had died, that I couldn't find the classroom.

"Can I re-add?" I asked.

"Okay," he said, surprising me with the ease of his agreement. I was relieved I wouldn't have to use one of my lies after all. "But if you have more than two more absences, it's highly unlikely you'll pass the class." He pulled fingerless bike gloves onto his hands with a distracted, superior air.

"Thank you," I said, resisting the impulse to genuflect.

As he pushed his bike out of the classroom, he said, "Bring me an add form on Monday, and I'll sign it."

The pneumatic door sucked shut before I was able to ask where to get an add form.

I spent the next two hours wandering campus, seeking out the Admissions Building, standing in lines, being sent to other offices by the impatient pointing of long red fingernails attached to the abrupt hands of various harried administrative personnel, until finally I held an Add Form, in triplicate, in my hand.

Chapter Seven — Tweety Bird

The problem with the food in the Dining Commons was that everything tasted the same. The pizza, the Mexican casserole, the Sloppy Joes, the spaghetti. Ditto for the desserts—close your eyes, and you couldn't tell whether you'd taken a bite of a cupcake with pink frosting, a chocolate brownie, or a peanut butter cookie that lacked essence of peanut butter, much less cookie. The pale vegetables and cut-up fruits, floating in gray water, didn't taste like much at all. Some dorm residents lost weight, while others gained. Those who gained piled their plates high then ate like zombies in the vain hope they might catch some flavor through quantity. Those who lost weight tended to be on speed.

The speed supplier lived on the third floor in a single room. Other than the R.A.'s quarters, there was one single room on each floor, and the oddest people tended to live in them. The speed supplier was known as the Meteorologist because you could give him any date—say July 7, 1963, or November 23, 1834—and he'd tell you what the weather had been like in Sacramento on that day.

"Let's see," he'd say, "November 23, 1834. That was a Wednesday. Partly cloudy." He spoke with such authority that no one bothered to check his facts.

He wore Dad-pants that were so tight the inner white pocket material poked out. At age 23, he was one of the oldest dorm residents. He never let anyone inside his room. If you wanted to ask him a Weatherman question or to buy some speed, you'd have to catch him in the T.V. room. Or you could knock on his door. If he was there, he'd say, "Step back," then quickly open the door and step out, closing it behind him like an unintentional parody of a paranoid drug dealer. He always had speed in a baggie in his shirt pocket in anticipation of making a sale.

Sometimes he'd have other drugs to sell, too—Qualuudes, hash, codeine, shrooms, yellow jackets, blue devils, red devils, pot, and the occasional hit of acid.

"Hi Norma, it's Mom."

"And Dad."

The ringing phone had awakened me. My clock said 11 a.m. A hangover gripped my head and gut—the night before, a group of us had snuck beer into the T.V. room to watch a rerun of *The Bob Newhart Show* and play The Bob Game, drinking each time a character said "Bob." We stayed up late, through Johnny Carson (drinking each time someone said "Johnny") and a late-night showing of *The Blob* (drinking each time a character screamed). We'd laughed and laughed at the surprise of each "Bob" or "Johnny" or "Helllllllllp!"—and it had crossed my mind that all my fun these days was alcohol-induced. I wasn't sure how I felt about that. Yes, I loved the playfulness, the camaraderie, the laughter that seemed to open up internal dark caverns to the light. No, I didn't like waking up sick most mornings and not always knowing exactly what had happened the night before.

"Hi Mom and Dad." I tried to sound upbeat and awake.

"How are you?" asked Mom. I could hear birds chirping in the background. She had probably stretched the extra-long phone cord out to the deck and was sitting on a chaise lounge near the pool.

"I'm good, how are you guys?"

They told me that Dad was still deciding whether or not to run for the school board, that Mom took the cat to vet for his shots, that Grandma and Grandpa came by for lunch, and that deer had gotten into the garden, eating the last of the tomatoes.

"What are you reading in your English class?" asked Mom.

"So far, just the newspaper."

"The newspaper? What kind of English class is that? If I remember correctly, in my freshman English class we read *Middlemarch*, *King Lear*, *Moby Dick* and *Crime and Punishment*."

"I think I'd shoot myself if that was my required reading," said Dad. "So what's your roommate like, Norm?"

"She's nice." I sat up in bed and looked over to Stacy's side of the room. She wasn't there. I had caught a glimpse of her sleeping last night before I fell to my bed, drunk and exhausted. Her bed was now made, pillows and stuffed animals neatly in place. "Her name's Stacy."

"Where's she from?" asked Dad.

"The Bay Area. She looks like Grace Kelly."

"She must be pretty," said Mom.

"She is. And her mom died."

"That's too bad," said Dad. "Tragic for a young girl to lose her mother."

"Yes," I said. "Really."

We paused for a minute. The line crackled. Chatting about mortality was not our forte.

"Well, is there anything you need?" asked Mom.

"No, I'm okay."

"Call collect any time," said Dad.

"Okay," I said. "I better go. I have to get to class."

"Bye sweetie," said Dad.

"Bye Norma," said Mom.

When I hung up the thought of going to tennis class then to the Health Center to get my test results filled me with dread. And I had stacks of homework—chapters to read in a muddle of a Psychology text, and a thick article on cultural taboos for my Cultural Anthropology class, and another paper to write based on the newspaper for English class. On the one hand, the image of myself doing that work was appealing—I could see myself in the library, immersed in ideas, surrounded by stacks of books, taking thoughtful, organized notes in my binder. Yet as I dressed in my tennis clothes, I felt a buzz of restless pleasure as I imagined myself in another scenario: withdrawing my savings and buying a plane ticket to Europe, securing a EurRail pass and backpacking country to country.

My door swung open.

"Hey Norma, guess what I have," said Liz, throwing her tennis racket on Stacy's bed, knocking over a stuffed monkey. Liz had added tennis to her schedule so we could be in a class together.

"What?"

"Pot." She shook the baggie she held in her hand.

"Where'd you get that?" I asked, pulling a brush through my hair.

"Kirk."

"I thought you hated him and his inverted nipple. I thought you were onto bigger and better things."

"And turn down free pot?" She pressed some of the pot into a pipe she'd pulled out of her purse. "Don't you think it'd be fun to play tennis stoned?"

"Why not?" I said.

She giggled and lit up. As she inhaled, her cheeks puffed up. Holding in the smoke, she passed the pipe to me. We sat on the bed, passing it back and forth.

"I'm going to a Delta Theta party tonight. Want to come?"

"No thanks."

"Don't you want to rush a sorority?"

"I don't think so," I said. "Sororities—I don't know. Why do you want to?"

"The guys!" she said. "My god, there's an endless supply of guys in fraternities."

"But so are there in your classes, and here in the dorms."

"It's not the same." She leaned back on the bed, smoke drifting from her nose. "When you're part of that world, it's just different, that's all. And it's not just the guys. The girls are cool. They become your friends for life."

"That's so strange to me, that they haze you then become your friends." I flicked the lighter over the pipe bowl. "For life." I took a hit. "I wouldn't want to be hazed."

"That's no big deal. Especially in a sorority. They just make you play Pin the Dick on the *Playgirl* centerfold and force you to drink a disgusting concoction of ten different kinds of booze, things like that."

I didn't say so, but it all sounded unnecessarily humiliating. I was learning, though, that Liz wasn't the type to be easily humiliated. I admired the way she wore her skin like a suit of armor.

"Who's that guy?" asked Liz, pointing to the photo of Jack and me on the Golden Gate Bridge.

"A friend. Kind of my boyfriend. Sort of."

"What the hell does that mean, 'kind of, sort of'?"

I told her the story—that Jack and I had met over a year ago, the summer before my senior year, and had been together a lot the first few months but not much since. That I had decided to come to Sacramento to be near him but we hadn't seen each other since I arrived.

"Call him right now," she said, handing me the phone.

"What?"

"I can tell you want him. You can't be too passive about these things. Go out and get what you want."

"It doesn't quite work that way with us."

"Do it anyway."

"But—"

"Sometimes you have to break the cycle."

I liked being forced to call Jack—that way I didn't have to fully admit to myself that I was chasing him. My mom would be appalled. She didn't believe in girls pursuing boys.

I dialed. I knew he was off Tuesdays and would probably be home. I was right.

"Hey Babe," he said. "I've been thinking about you."

"Me too." I told him I was a bit high, that I was sitting there with my friend Liz. Disingenuously I added that I'd called just to say hello.

Liz elbowed me.

"And," I said, "I was wondering if you're doing anything right now. Want to get together?"

"Sure. You want to come by?"

"I don't have a car." Cool sweat was blossoming in my palms and armpits.

"I do!" shouted Liz at the phone. "You can borrow it."

"Well, why don't you have her come along," said Jack. "Bull's here." Bull was Jack's best friend and occasional roommate whenever he and his girlfriend were fighting.

When I hung up, Liz high-fived me. We replaced our tennis outfits with jeans and blouses. We reapplied our makeup and brushed our hair.

As I sat in the passenger seat of Liz's car, speeding over the river bridge, James Taylor singing *how sweet it is to be loved by you*, I couldn't believe I was finally going to be with Jack. And to have Liz along was such a bonus. Tough Liz, Liz who didn't take no for an answer, Liz who powered through the world like a steam train, as though inside her lived a team of muscular men, shoveling coal into her internal, raging fire.

Jack opened the door wearing cut-offs and no shirt, his blue Tweety Bird tattoo displayed on his muscled shoulder.

He kissed me on the lips, just a basic kiss, but my whole body lit up as it always did with him. His hair looked a little longer than usual, but otherwise he seemed the same.

Bull stood in the kitchen, making margaritas. He was only twenty-five, but his dark hair was thinning. Like Jack, he lifted weights, but he was much bulkier and stockier and had almost no neck like the Incredible Hulk.

We sat in the sun on the apartment's concrete balcony in plastic chairs, drinking margaritas in glasses with salted rims and smoking Liz's pot. The balcony overlooked the empty balconies of other apartments in the complex. Children splashed in the pool below, young mothers in bikinis stretched out on beach towels.

"Why Tweety Bird?" asked Liz, handing the pipe to Jack and taking a cigarette out of her purse.

"Because Tweety Bird is cute but crafty." He smiled at her, showing off his crooked eyeteeth. I loved the endearing shape of his mouth, those teeth.

"So is Wile E. Coyote," she said. Bull held the lighter in front of her cigarette, and Liz lit up, distracted, as though Bull were merely performing his duty as her servant.

"Nope. Wile E. Coyote may be crafty, but he's not cute," said Jack.

"What about Goofy?" she asked.

"Cute but not crafty."

They talked for a few more minutes about cartoon characters, and then the conversation trailed off. We looked out to the pool, silent for a minute or two.

Liz broke the silence by asking Bull, "Do you have a tattoo?"

"Yep," he said. "On my back."

"When did you get it?"

"A while ago. I woke up one morning with my back sticking to the sheets. I couldn't figure out what the hell was going on. I looked in the mirror and saw the tattoo. I swear to god, I can't remember getting the damn thing."

Liz lifted her thin eyebrows. "Really? You can't remember at all? I think you're shitting me."

Bull smiled, not ruffled by Liz's challenge. He leaned toward her, his nose almost touching her face. She didn't flinch. "Guess what it is?" he asked.

"Mickey Mouse," she deadpanned, taking a long drag on her cigarette.

"Ha!" laughed Jack, reaching over to take my hand in his. My hand sparked with electricity.

"Not quite," said Bull, leaning back, his face slightly shifting. Was he blushing? I felt a little sorry for him at the same time feeling admiration for Liz's power.

"I know," I said, "I bet it's a bull."

"Wrong again," said Jack. "Show 'em, Bull."

Bull stood, turned, and pulled his shirt up. A multicolored dragon, all smoky curlicues, spanned his impressive mountain of a back.

"That's amazing," I said.

"I don't believe for a minute that you don't remember getting that tattoo," said Liz, taking a drag of her cigarette, her eye twitching. I thought she was feigning being unimpressed—and that Bull's body had electrified her. "Tweety I could believe. But that thing?"

"It's good luck," he said. "And it worked that night because I must have driven home after I got the tattoo, but I don't remember driving, and I didn't have one little dent in my car." He sat and took the pipe as Liz handed it to him.

"What other good luck have you had?" she asked—and then I knew I was right about her interest in Bull. She was using the same tone of voice she'd used that night in Kirk's room, her feet on Kirk's lap. It seemed that Liz chose guys rather than waiting for guys to choose her. I could learn from her, I thought.

"Good luck? Well, let's see," said Bull. "For instance, you're sitting here in my house. I'd say that's pretty good luck."

"Damn right it is," she said, smiling at him for the first time. Her eye twitched again.

"Play that Funky Music White Boy" came on the stereo, and Liz grabbed Bull's hand. They danced on the tight balcony then he pulled her into the living room. Jack and I joined them, dancing and dancing, dizzy, and laughing. When Liz moved Bull's hands onto her breasts while they danced, Jack took me into his room.

My missed doctor's appointment to find out my test results flashed through my mind as Jack removed my shirt. I pushed the thought away as I unbuttoned his cut-offs. We always undressed each other.

"I'm off the Pill," I lied.

He led me to the bed. "I'll pull out."

"I'm not sure that's the best idea. Don't you have a rubber?"

He ran his hands up and down my arms and kissed my mouth, softly. I was crazy ready for him, even though on the way to his room I'd seen several framed photos of nude women hanging in the hallway. The photos looked amateurish, as though he or Bull had taken them of girls they knew, which wouldn't have surprised me. But I didn't ask. I just wanted him. If he didn't have a condom, I didn't know what I'd do.

"No, really, I'll just pull out," he said. We lay down on the bed and kissed some more.

After a minute, I asked again, "Don't you have a condom?"

He lay back away from me.

"Babe, condoms just don't do it for me. Maybe you could just, you know . . . ?" He put his hands on my head and gently pressed down so my head rested on his stomach.

I kissed his stomach then looked up at him. "That wouldn't do it for me," I whispered, seriously meaning it while trying to sound light and playful.

A knocking noise filled the air. It sounded like something crashing against the wall from the other room, over and over. Then Bull's voice shouted, "Yes! Yes!" Silence, then "Yes! Yes!" again.

Jack smiled. "Well, I guess something's doing it for Bull."

I laughed. Jack lay his body on top of mine and kissed me some more. I was drunk and stoned, but not too high to know exactly where I was and what I was doing. It felt a little surreal, but I knew it was true. I was finally with Jack again. *Jack, Jack,* I thought, *Jack. I love you.* And then I let him move into me.

Chapter Eight — Ado Annie

My parents smoked pot once. At least that's what my mom told me. We were driving to Sacramento to buy my senior prom dress when I asked her if she'd ever done drugs. That's when she told me that she and my father had once gotten some marijuana for Grandma Faye, my dad's mother, when her cancer was really bad.

"Where'd you get it?" I asked.

"I don't know," she said. "Someone your father knew."

"So if it was for Grandma Faye, why did you and Dad smoke it?"

"She insisted we try it too." Mom's eyes were on the road, and she had a small smile on her lips.

"And did Grandma Faye really smoke it?"

"Oh yes. She seemed happy to be able to smoke again."

Grandma Faye had lung cancer. She'd been a big smoker. Dad constantly tried to talk her into quitting, but she'd hide her cigarettes in her shoebox of hair curlers and continue to do what she liked. She quit on the day she coughed up blood.

"And you smoked it too? And Dad?" I tried to imagine the three of them passing a joint around, the blue curtains in Grandma Faye's bedroom drawn shut.

"Yes, we all took a few puffs."

"And?"

"Not much happened. I just felt a little more relaxed. Like having a glass of wine."

"Would you ever do it again?"

"I doubt it," she said. "There doesn't seem to be much point."

"Hi stranger," said Stacy when I came into the room. Books and papers were spread out all over her bed, where she sat, legs crossed.

"Hey Stacy," I said, dropping down to my bed. Liz and I had spent the night at Jack and Bull's. In the car on the way back to the dorms, we cranked up the music and laughed and laughed, giddy from good sex and little sleep. Exhausted and exhilarated, I ached all over.

"Everyone was wondering at the Billy-Goat party where you were," she said. "You don't look too great. Are you okay?"

"I'm great, actually." I felt myself stiffen. I didn't like someone so beautiful telling me I didn't look good. I lay back on my pillow and closed my eyes.

"Well, something happened that I need to tell you about," she said.

I opened my eyes and turned on my side to face her.

"What?"

"Well, I don't know how to say this. It really sucks. But someone taped this to our door." She reached over and grabbed a piece of paper, unfolding it to its full size then turning it to face me.

NORMA IS A SLUT it read in thick, bloody red ink.

I sat up, my heart pounding.

"I almost threw it away," she said, softly. "But I thought you might want to know."

"How long was it on our door before you took it down?"

"I don't know. I had classes all day. It could have been there for hours, or minutes."

Nausea stirred in my chest, and my heart was racing.

"Fuck," I said. "What a fucking asshole."

"Do you know who did it?" she asked.

"Yes," I said. "Fucker."

"Who?"

"Billy."

"How do you know?"

"I just do."

"But why would he do it?"

"Never mind," I said. "I need to get some sleep." I turned over and closed my eyes, willing myself to drift off. I could feel Stacy's stare burning into my back, her questions lingering, but I just couldn't deal with her at that moment. I felt a stab of guilt for treating her that way. She'd been nothing but nice to me. She seemed to be trying to help. But I was too ashamed and angry and disgusted with Billy and myself to talk to Stacy.

I couldn't fall asleep. After a few minutes, I got up and changed my clothes, avoiding looking at Stacy. She didn't say a thing as I grabbed my backpack and slammed the door on my way out. I walked through the lobby and went to the mailboxes, fishing my little mailbox key out of my pocket. When I put my key in and opened the little door, a glob of dorm spaghetti fell out and onto my shoe. Someone had stuffed my mailbox with gluey red-sauced spaghetti.

"Fuck!" I yelled. "Fuck!" Tears burned my eyes.

The white guy and black guy who had tilted the vending machine for Liz and me a few weeks back looked up from their Space Invaders game.

"What's wrong?" asked the white guy.

"Are you okay?" asked the black guy. It seemed that more people had asked me if I was okay in the past few days than ever before in my life. The question felt like an affront to what I liked to think of as my generally happy nature. I wanted to be okay. But I wasn't.

"Sure, I'm okay." My voice came out in a hoarse whisper, belying my words. I began to cry, and my backpack slipped off my shoulder and fell to the floor.

The black guy came over and picked up my backpack. The white guy peered into my mailbox.

"Bummer," he said.

With someone else confirming the appalling nature of the crime against me, I cried harder.

The black guy ran down the hall and came back with a handful of paper towels. Carefully he extracted my mail, wiping it with the towels. He handed me three envelopes stained pink.

"I think the janitor will get this if you just leave your mailbox door open," he said.

"Thanks," I whispered, wiping my eyes with my shirtsleeve.

When the white guy handed me my backpack, I shoved the envelopes into it and ran out the door, crying as I walked to class.

Late to class, I slipped in quietly and sat in the back. Linda, the English professor, paused briefly, smiled at me, then continued talking about our essays she was returning to us. She held the stack in her hand.

"Some of you merely summarized your articles," she said, stepping forward, her large gold earrings swinging. "But I don't want mere summary. What's the point? I can read the article myself. What I want is opinion and analysis. What do you think of the issue you're focusing on? Why is it significant? Or not? How does it connect to other issues?"

My head was spinning. It was hard to focus on her words. I watched her pink lipsticked lips moving, her large pearly teeth.

"Now this one, by Norma Rogers—Norma, where are you?"

It took me a moment to register. I raised my hand. Everyone turned around and looked at me.

"Oh, okay, you're Norma. Is it okay if I read your piece aloud to the class?"

My throat clenched. I nodded my head yes.

"So this piece not only describes the article, but it comments on why it's significant in a sophisticated way."

Linda read aloud my essay on Luke and Laura's wedding, pausing every few sentences to express admiration for the way I'd—as she put it—cogently, and satirically, analyzed the irony of the media's celebration of a marriage between a rapist and his victim.

I hadn't realized I'd done that. If I'd felt better, I would have been elated, figuring if she could find it on the page somewhere in me I had the thinking and writing abilities she praised. But instead of basking in the attention, I wanted to shrink down in my chair, to run away, to disappear, to buy a one-way ticket to Europe and wander around old cities, anonymous.

"What fresh hell is this?" said Chuck, greeting me with a shoulder bump as I walked out of class. "Norma Jean, you look like shit. Are you okay?"

"I'm horrible," I said, feeling a little less horrible the minute I said it. "Thanks."

"What's wrong?"

"I don't want to talk about it."

"No problem-o," said Chuck, linking his arm through mine. We walked along the quad in the hot sun, in silence. Students lay on the grass, talking and laughing, thumbing through books, or sleeping.

"I came looking for you yesterday," said Chuck, "but you weren't anywhere to be found. I have a surprise for you. It's bound to make you feel better."

"Oh yeah?"

"Yeah. I got something special from the Meteorologist."

"What?"

"Two hits of acid. One for you, one for me."

"I've never done it before," I said, a ticklish apprehension crawling up my back like a spider.

"I have and it's brilliant."

"Isn't it a little scary?"

"Not if you're contained in a safe space. We'll have my room to ourselves. Benny was missing home, so he's gone for a few days. We'll lock the door. And I've picked out some great tripping music—all 60's and 70's rock of course."

He wanted us to experience something together. And he was concerned for my comfort, my safety. At that moment I knew I was falling for him in a way I'd thought had been reserved solely for Jack. A new Norma Jean Baker love, a fresh one-piece slip of desire.

"So what are we waiting for?" I asked.

The thumping strains of *Inna-Gadda-Da-Vida* played on Chuck's stereo. We sat on his bed, leaning against the bolster, drinking white wine, waiting for the LSD to hit. The walls were covered with white posters—the backside of the James Bond posters. Chuck had turned them around to face the wall because the expressions of James Bond might freak us out, he'd explained.

"Why would James Bond freak us out?"

"No particular reason," he said. "You just never know. The less visual stimulation while tripping, the better, I've found."

While he poured us more wine, I sang all the lyrics to *Inna-Gadda-Da-Vida*.

"Oh, Norma Jean, you surprise me—you know this song?"

"Yeah, I heard it a couple of weeks ago, at a party," I said.

"You're amazing. You memorize the lyrics after hearing the song once?"

"You'd never guess how many songs I have in my head," I said, pleased to be praised as an expert at something by Chuck, the expert on so many things.

"Don't all those lyrics crowd out other more important things?" he teased.

"Look who's talking," I said, taking a sip of wine. "The guy who knows every detail of every James Bond movie, and who knows all that trivia, like that Grace Kelly won the 1963 Oscar and drove an MG convertible in such-and-such movie."

"1953. Sunbeam Alpine Sports Roadster in *To Catch a Thief*."

"Right."

We listened to the song's extended drum riff, bobbing our heads to the beat.

"Nothing's happening," I said.

"I know, sometimes it takes a while."

"Are you sure it's the real stuff?"

"I don't think the Meteorologist sells substandard shit. He'd get a bad reputation and lose too many customers. The dorms are a drug dealer's paradise."

The song ended. The stereo arm lifted then set back down at the beginning of the album to play again.

"I've always been good at remembering songs," I said. "I was in musicals in high school. I played Ado Annie in *Oklahoma*."

Chuck jumped up and faced me. "Oh god, that's great!" He turned down the stereo, spread out his arms and sang in Ado Annie's twang, *I'm just a girl who cain't say no*.

I picked it up from there:

I'm in a terrible fix!
I always say "come on, let's go."
Just when I orta say nix!
When a person tries to kiss a girl,
I know she orta give his face a smack.
But as soon as someone kisses me,
I somehow sorta wanta kiss him back!

"Priceless!" shouted Chuck. "Holy shit, Norma Jean! It's just too much." Laughing, he turned the stereo back up to the thumping of *Inna-Gadda-Da-Vida*. I started to laugh too. Soon we were both doubled over, laughing until tears came to our eyes. My tears felt strange, gelatinous, almost like honey. My head was buzzing.

I wiped my eyes with my shirtsleeve. My hand moved slowly, more slowly than I willed it to.

"I'm feeling something," I said.

Chuck got up and turned out all the lights except for one desk lamp, which he draped with a dark tee-shirt.

"Whee!" he laughed. "Here we go. Welcome to the other side, Norma Jean."

He lit two cigarettes and gave me one. I set mine in the ashtray, watching the white smoke crawl up the wall. Crawl and crawl. When Chuck moved his cigarette to his mouth, a red trail twisted through the air and lingered there.

"Wow," I said.

"Yes," he said.

I sat back and watched the air. Everything pulsed. Everything was rich, thick. Everything breathed—the walls, the desk, my hands. My pores opened, letting everything in.

My heart pumped melodiously, my chest moving up and down to the beat of my pulse. A red glow spread under my chest, my heart growing and growing. The warm glow flowed down my shoulders, through my arms to the tips of my fingers. I moved my hand up and down. The red life-glow overflowed into the air.

Everything was good.

Beautiful.

Fine.

I had so much, so much.

"Yes," said Chuck.

The letters of his words flew into the air, the Y, the E, the S. Everything was goodness, was YES. His letters dripped into my hair, down my body. My spine, my bones, were filled with Chuck's YES. Chuck was it. He was it. Not Jack. No, not Jack.

No Jack.

Yes Chuck.

All love, all love.

I moved through the air, the thick, thick air. I saw it, the air. I swam toward him, to him. Everything connected us, swirled in and out of us. My lips moved toward his, on his, into his. We kissed. Once. One gem. One perfection. The one kiss was everything. Every Thing. We'd never need anything more.

One was it, it was the world, it was yes.

Chapter Nine — A Kiss is Just a Kiss

As I was growing up, my parents took my sister, Mary, and me to Sacramento and San Francisco to see musicals on stage, productions of everything from *Fiddler on the Roof* to *The Music Man*. And when a musical came on T.V. we'd watch it together. I wasn't a big fan of old movies, but musicals were different. When a character broke out in song, you learned what was in her heart. When a character danced a few steps, he expressed more with his body than he could with words. I thought as a family we all felt that way, but at age 15, Mary had had enough.

"Musicals are idiotic," she said one night at dinner. She was refusing to go with us to see Sandy Duncan in *Peter Pan*. Mary was like that. She changed quickly, like someone walking for miles who suddenly takes a quick left and steps off a cliff. When we were little, we'd spent hours playing with Barbies—Barbie and Midge working at an advertising agency, Barbie and Ken having sex under the bed, Barbie getting pregnant with a green-haired troll. And then one day, with no warning, Mary handed me two shoe boxes. Inside laid her Barbie dolls as though in coffins, their painted eyes blank. After that, it was hard for me to see them as anything other than cadavers.

"Just because you don't enjoy musicals, you don't have to ruin other people's enjoyment," Mom said, slicing the pot roast.

"Whatever." Mary dropped her head into her hand, propped up by her elbow on the table.

Mary was four years older than I was. We had the same reddish hair, but hers was straight. I knew she went to parties at her friends' houses and listened to Carole King and drank red wine and smoked pot. I knew she was having sex with her boyfriend, Mario. She didn't tell me any of this, but I read her diary, which for some reason she kept unlocked in full view on her bedside stand.

"I thought you liked *The Sound of Music*," said Dad. "At least you did last year."

Mary frowned and didn't say anything, just stared at the chunks of potato and pot roast on her plate.

Cutting into his pot roast, my dad said, "I love Julie Andrews, spinning around on those green hills, the swell of music, the panoramic shot of the snow-topped mountains."

"Me too," I said, taking a bite of potato. "I like those puppets singing *The Lonely Goatherd*, Yodda-lay-hee-hoo."

"Gross," Mary said.

"That's fantastic," said Dad, grinning. "Yodda-lay-hee-hoo."

"What's your favorite part, Mom?" I asked.

She pierced some carrots with her fork, thought for a minute, then said, "I like the nun singing *Climb Every Mountain*." Even though she was a lapsed Catholic, my mom admired and respected nuns.

Mary's face was getting red.

"And *Edelweiss*," added Dad. "You've always loved *Edelweiss*."

"That's true," Mom said.

Looking right at Mary, Dad sang the first line: *Edelweiss, Edelweiss, every morning you greet me.*

Mom joined in, her voice off-key in an attempt to harmonize: *Small and white, clean and bright, you look happy to meet me.*

"You guys are such jerks," Mary whispered, pushing back her chair and leaving the room. Through my parents' singing, I heard her tromp down the hall to her room and slam the door shut.

"Tabitha's coming next weekend!" Stacy spun around the room, her hair flying.

"Who?" I was sitting on my bed, sorting through the mess of my backpack and binder.

"My step-sister!" She pointed to the photo posted on her bulletin board, of the two of them—dark hair and light hair—sitting side-by-side on the grass.

"Oh, yes, right. That's great."

"Her boyfriend was going to come, too, but he can't."

"Do you have a boyfriend?" I asked, looking up from a mass of crumpled papers that had been crushed at the bottom of my backpack. I'd been wanting to ask that question for a long time, but I was hesitant to invade what felt like her carefully-guarded privacy. Now that she'd brought up Tabitha's boyfriend, however, it seemed like the perfect moment to slip in the question.

"Well kind of. Sort of." She flushed a little, as though sensitive to opening the door on her love life, as I thought she'd be. "His name is Ted." She said that Ted was her boyfriend through senior year. When he went to a school on the East Coast, they decided a long-distance relationship wouldn't be a good idea.

"We may get back together one day," she said. "But for now we're focusing on school. So we're kind of together, kind of not."

"I can relate," I said. I told her a little about Jack.

"It sounds like you love him," she said, tucking her hair behind her ear. "Oh, no, is it really 3:30? Sorry, Norma, I have to take off to class." She grabbed her backpack. "See you later. Tell me more later, okay?"

"Sure," I said, as she shut the door behind her.

Talking about Jack to Stacy sparked my familiar yearning for him. It had been a month since the acid trip. A month since the amazing kiss between Chuck and me. But nothing else had happened between us since, sexually. We continued to hang out, to party together, to play backgammon. But we acted like the kiss never happened. And the epiphany I'd had—that Chuck was the one for me, not Jack—drifted around in my mind, unanchored. I still recalled my connection to Chuck in a bodily sense, like a lump in my throat. I could still feel that amazing kiss on my lips. But my feelings for Jack had not evaporated. I couldn't just will them away. Was it possible to love, to desire, two people equally?

I went back to my task of sorting through my schoolwork. In a pocket of my backpack I found the three envelopes, stained pink, that had been in my spaghetti-stuffed mailbox. One was from the Health Center. My heart began racing. I had avoided thinking about the appointment I'd missed. I never did find out my test results. I had shoved the whole business aside, into a little dark cave inside, so deep I had almost forgotten it. And now I was faced with this envelope.

I tore it open. At first I didn't understand what it said in its little typed script. Pap results. Blood test. All negative. All fine. I had a clean bill of health.

"Ha!" I yelled. "Ha! So there, Billy!"

I jumped up and spun around the room, like Stacy had moments before, elated.

I grabbed the phone and dialed Jack's number.

"Hello?" said a female voice.

I hung up. Maybe it was Bull's girlfriend. I dialed again.

"Hello?" said the female voice. "Who's there?"

"Is Jack there?" I asked.

"Well, he can't come to the phone right now. Who's this?"

"Who's this?"

"Peggy."

No, not Bull's girlfriend.

"Tell him Norma called."

"Okay," she said abruptly and hung up.

My face burned. What did she mean he couldn't come to the phone?

I looked at my pile of homework and my letter from the Health Center. Good news, I reminded myself. I had good news. Don't let some Peggy, or anyone else, spoil it.

I couldn't be in my room another second.

Passing the open door of the Billy-Goat Room, I saw Billy tuning his guitar. He looked up at me, then quickly back down. Trying to talk to him right now would spoil my elation. I kept walking, up the stairs, around the corner, to Chuck's room.

"It's 4:00, backgammon time," I said, walking into the room. Benny was playing a video game on his T.V. Chuck was flipping through the channels of his.

"Oh my god!" he said. "Look, *Casablanca* is just starting!"

"Black and white," I said, sneering.

"Don't be so uncouth, Norma Jean. It's a classic."

I sang: *A kiss is just a kiss, a sigh is just a sigh, the fundamental things apply, as time goes by.*

"You know the song—now you need to know the movie."

"Okay, okay," I said.

Chuck went to his closet and pulled down a bottle of vodka. The playful presence of him, and the warm sanctuary of his room, swept over me joyously.

"Screwdriver, Miss Norma Jean?"

"Absolutely."

"Benny, care for one?"

"No, that's okay," he said.

Chuck made one for Benny anyway while I set up the backgammon board. Chuck angled the T.V. so we could all see it.

As we played backgammon, and Benny played Missile Command, we drank screwdriver after screwdriver and watched *Casablanca*, a secret celebration of my good news.

Chuck told us when to listen for the best lines.

Peter Lorre: "You despise me, don't you?"

Humphrey Bogart: "Well, if I gave you any thought, I probably would."

"Ha!" laughed Chuck. "That's the best."

Rick to Renault: "When it comes to women, you're a true democrat."

"What a classy way to call someone a whore!" laughed Chuck.

My face flushed, the blood-red words on white paper calling me a "slut" flashing through my mind.

"He's not calling him a whore," I said, indignant, doing my best impression of a strong, knowledgeable woman. "He's calling him a lady's man. No one calls a man a whore."

"You are quite the astute feminist, my dear Norma," said Chuck.

I wasn't sure how he meant that. I didn't say anything, just captured two of his backgammon pieces.

In synch with Rick, Chuck said,
"I stick out my neck for nobody," and
"Here's looking at you, kid," and
"We'll always have Paris."

In synch with Ilsa, Chuck said,
"Play it once, Sam, for old times' sake," and
"Kiss me. Kiss me as if it were the last time."

And with Renault,
"Round up the usual suspects."

And finally with Rick,
"Louis, I think this is the beginning of a beautiful friendship."

The door flung open.

"There you are," said Liz.

"Lizzy Borden, welcome," said Chuck.

"Lizzy Borden my ass," she said, plopping next to Benny on his bed. "What are you doing?" She took some pot and papers out of her purse and began rolling a joint.

"Playing Atari," he said.

"Ugh. So I have great news," she said, leaning against Benny. He reddened, looking both pleased and alarmed. "I'm now officially a Delta Theta."

"Do you have to take an antibiotic for that?" asked Chuck.

Benny snorted out a laugh. "Good one," he said.

"You guys are hopeless," she said, passing the joint to Benny. He took a hit and passed it back. "So is everyone just hanging out here playing dumb games? Anyone want to play a real game, like Quarters?"

"Well, I might as well try to win at something," said Chuck. "Miss I-Just-Learned-Backgammon-But-I-Kick-Ass is killing me here."

So Benny put on the music, Chuck clicked off the T.V. and pulled out another bottle of vodka and some beer, and I found a cup and a quarter on Chuck's desk.

After we'd played a few rounds, it was Benny's turn again. He aimed, and the quarter plopped into the cup of beer. He pointed his elbow at Liz. She drank the beer down and pulled her shirt off over her head, stripping to her pink bra.

"It's time to raise the stakes," she said.

Benny looked down and pushed his glasses up on the bridge of his nose. Chuck grinned. My whole body glowed. Maybe tonight would be our night.

Liz took a shot and made it. She pointed her elbow at Benny. He drank then removed his glasses. He squinted.

"Listen, honey," said Liz, "I really think you want to be able to see."

Benny flushed. "I think you're right." He put his glasses back on then took off a shoe.

After what must have been hours of drinking and stripping, we turned out the lights and paired off. Me with Chuck, Liz with Benny. I slipped into Chuck's bed with him, excited yet filled with a calm sense of comfortable familiarity.

Chuck lay on his back, naked, breathing deeply. I wondered if he was passed out. I curled up next to him and lightly touched his chest with my hand. The hairs were sparse and wiry. I kissed his neck and moved my hand down to his stomach. Sparks of red and blue shot through the dark whether my eyes were open or closed. I moved my hand down further and further then put my hand around him. He was limp.

"Chuck," I whispered in his ear. "Paul." I moved my hand on him, up and down. He made a squeak of a noise. He began to move a little.

I kissed his neck some more then kissed his mouth. He kissed me back, softly, weakly.

"Chuck," I whispered, "are you awake?"

"I don't know," he whispered back.

I moved my hand on him, over and over.

"Are you drunk?"

"Were George and Martha?"

"Who?"

"Whose Afraid . . . Virginia Woolf . . . Taylor . . . Burton . . . 1966 . . ."

"Shh . . ." I quieted him and continued to move my hand.

He began to respond. I moved on top of him, maneuvered myself onto him. We were finally fully connected, in the deepest most intimate way. Exactly what I wanted.

"Norma Jean," he said.

As we moved together, there was a sensation of something familiar in me—something from my childhood, like being on a swing or a bicycle. The colors in the air sparked past my eyes.

I heard noises from the other side of the room, Benny and Liz's whispering, followed by a sharp exhalation or a sigh.

Chuck and I moved together some more, then things began to slow down. His whole body seemed to deflate. He slipped out, softened.

"Sorry, Norma Jean, sorry." His voice was thick, drifting.

I didn't care, not really. We'd be less drunk next time. It was all okay—better than okay. Wonderful. We were here together in his bed, warm and safe. I moved off him and curled next to him, feeling his skin against mine.

"Chan! Where are you Chan?"

"Oh shit!"

The light burst on, flooding my sleeping brain.

"Chan! Chan!"

I opened my right eye to Chuck's jaw. He lay completely still. I propped myself up on my elbow.

"Oh shit!" said Liz again. She was hopping around in the middle of the room, tugging on her bra and underwear.

"We know you're here!" shouted female voices from the hallway.

"Liz, what's going on?"

"Delta Thetas," she whispered hoarsely.

I opened my other eye. Stuff floated in my vision like pond water through a microscope. Chuck let out a snore. Benny lay on his bed, a sheet up to his waist, his bare back toward us.

"There's a light on in here," said a female voice on the other side of the door. The doorknob turned. Liz stuck her foot in her pants, almost toppling over as she struggled desperately to pull them on. The door swung open.

"There you are, Chan. Freeze!" A group of girls ran into the room, squealing. Chuck shot up in bed, wide-eyed.

"What the hell?" he croaked.

With her jeans twisted around her ankles, Liz was surrounded by girls wearing matching flannel pajamas. Someone slapped handcuffs on her, and they dragged her out.

The next morning, when Benny woke with a horrible headache and an empty bed, we explained with glee what had happened.

"I thought once you were officially in a sorority there was no more hazing," I said.

"Maybe that's their way of celebrating a milestone," said Chuck.

"I can't believe it," Benny said, holding his head in his hands. "I just can't believe I missed out on seeing Liz handcuffed in her underwear."

Chapter Ten — Somebody to Love

My English teacher, Linda, asked to see me after class.

"Norma, what's going on?" She leaned against the chalkboard, her big gold earrings swaying.

I looked down at my feet and flushed.

"You started out the course so strong. You're really a terrific writer. But now you're not turning in your work."

"I know," I said, mortified. "I'm sorry."

"Don't apologize to me," she said. "It's your education. You're paying for this. Is there something going on?"

"No. I know I can do better. I will. I promise."

"Don't promise me," she said. "Promise yourself. But is there anything I can help you with? Is everything okay?"

"Everything's fine. I promise I'll do better. I'll go work right now on the next paper."

"Okay," she said. "Just let me know if there's anything I can do to help."

I couldn't meet her gaze. I threw my backpack over my shoulder and left the room, humiliated. I had always done well in school, especially English class. I had never been reprimanded by a teacher before, and it felt worse than terrible. As I walked outside, I expected Chuck to greet me as he almost always did, but to my disappointment he wasn't there.

Clouds passed over the sun, dimming the bright day. I walked back to the dorm along the flower-lined path, imagining myself writing the next paper, sitting down and organizing my binder and all my notes, leafing through the newspaper and finding an issue that shocked and surprised me, one that engaged me and prompted me to write a passionate, deep paper. I was so wrapped up in this fantasy that I was surprised when I looked up and found myself at my room.

Something smelled funny when I walked in. Stacy wasn't there. I threw my backpack on my bed, sniffing the air. That was when I noticed it. My typewriter was gone. My desktop was bare. My heart started to race. Could someone really have taken it? I looked under my desk, threw open my closet and scanned the shelves. I did the same with Stacy's closet.

Stacy walked in, holding books, her hair in a pert ponytail.

"Did you borrow my typewriter?" I asked, hysteria piercing my voice.

"What?" she said, dropping her books on her bed.

"It's gone!" I shrieked.

"Really? Are you sure?" She walked to my desk and put her hands on it, as though to test the reality of my claim.

"Fuck!" I yelled, tears forming in my eyes.

"Ew, what's that smell?" She sniffed the air. "It's coming from over here . . . oh, Norma, look!"

She lifted my backpack. A yellow stain spread out on my bedspread. Urine. Someone had peed on my bed.

"How awful," she said, softly, as though to avoid upsetting me further. "It's sick, really."

I picked up my backpack and threw it across the room. It burst open at the foot of Stacy's bed, papers and books scattering.

"Norma, Norma," she said, putting her arm around me. I was shaking and crying. "Norma, it's okay. Come on, we'll take care of it. And we'll report this to Kirk. He'll find out the jerks who did this. Really. Here, sit down."

With her arm around me, she sat me on her bed and handed me some Kleenex.

"Now, just relax," she said.

She stripped the bedding off my bed and stuffed it into her laundry basket, along with her box of laundry detergent and bottle of bleach.

"Now, you just relax. I'll go wash this, and I'll talk to Kirk."

"Oh Stacy, you don't have to do this," I said, grateful but degraded. I didn't like her seeing me like this.

"No, I don't mind. Now you just take it easy." Her arms full, she bumped the door open with her hip and left.

I blew my nose into a tissue and sat in a daze. Stacy was right, it was sick. Who else could be doing this other than Billy? No one seemed to have any reason other than Billy, who thought I had given him some kind of venereal disease. Maybe it was time to show him my letter from the Health Center, to let him know that his penis problems had nothing to do with me. But the thought of explaining myself to him infuriated me. He had blamed me for something that wasn't my problem. He had humiliated me, and now I had to go explain myself to him?

I blew my nose again then went to examine my mattress. Fortunately there was just a little stain, not much urine had soaked through. I sprinkled baby powder on the spot then picked up my phone.

"Hi Mom," I said, when she answered.

"Hi Norma," she said. "Just a second. Stan! Norma's on the phone."

I heard him pick up an extension.

"Hi sweetheart," he said.

"Hey Dad." My voice broke, and I started to cry.

"Norma, what's the matter?" asked Mom.

"Someone stole my typewriter!" I wailed.

"Oh no, I'm sorry honey," said Dad. "When did it happen?"

"Today when I was in class."

"Don't you lock your door?" asked Mom.

"No one locks their doors."

"Well maybe you better," she said.

"And report this to the authorities," said Dad.

"My roommate's doing that right now." I sniffled.

"Good," said Dad. "That's good. And don't worry. I can get reimbursed from the insurance, I think. No matter, we'll get you another one."

When we hung up the phone, I dialed Jack's number. I knew I was being childish with Stacy taking care of me like a mother, and then needing to call my parents and now Jack. But I felt an insatiable need for assurance that I was a better person than my secret attacker thought I was.

"Hey Norma," Jack said.

"Hi. What are you doing?"

"Not much. What's up?"

I tried to ignore his rushed tone that told me he didn't want to be on the phone. I tried to swallow the lump in my throat that felt like a big, hard vitamin that wouldn't go down. "Nothing's up, really," I said, realizing I didn't want to tell him the horrible things someone was doing to me—it might make him think less of me. "I'm just calling to say hi. Just been doing homework, and things like that."

"That's good. Hey Babe, I was just walking out the door. Can I catch you later?"

I paused, hoping he'd read something into it.

"Babe, are you there? I said I have to go. Sorry."

"Sure, okay," I said. "Bye. See you later."

"Ciao."

I sat on the floor, buried my face in my hands, and sobbed.

Chuck and Benny sat on my bed, Chuck smoking a cigarette, Benny eating a dining commons hamburger. Liz and I stood in front of the mirrored closet doors, applying the finishing touches to our makeup. We were all wearing bed sheets, wrapped around us like togas, and drinking beer. Tonight was the toga party, a traditional event, or so said the fliers that appeared the previous week, taped to our doors and signed "Kirk, Your Friendly R.A."

"I love this song," I said, as Queen's *Somebody to Love* came on the radio. I sang into the mirror,

I just gotta get out of this prison cell — one day I'm gonna be free —

Liz, who was already a little drunk, came up behind me in her Minnie Mouse-print toga, singing with me into her brush like a microphone,

Anybody find me — Somebody to love!

Liz linked her arm in mine and we danced around the room as the rest of the song played out, singing and laughing, until we fell down on top of each other on Stacy's bed.

"Ooh, dyke action," said Chuck. "I'll watch, I'll watch!" he laughed, raising his hand like a nerdy student.

Benny giggled, his glasses flashing. He was wearing a toga made from a striped brown and green sheet.

"Where's Stacy?" asked Chuck.

Liz sneered, her usual response when someone mentioned Stacy. I'd tried to tell Liz that Stacy was a good person, but I'd had to be vague. I couldn't tell her how Stacy had been so kind and non-judgmental as I faced the actions of my anti-secret admirer, my secret hater, as I was now thinking of him. I didn't want Liz, or anyone else, knowing what he was doing to me. They knew about the typewriter—a benign and random robbery, as I presented it. But the SLUT sign, the urine, the spaghetti. No one but Stacy knew. On the one hand, I was convinced that whoever was doing this was a pervert with a problem. On the other hand, the judgment of me—both explicitly stated and implied—somehow felt real and deserved. Maybe I was different from other girls in the dorm. Maybe I was worse. Or maybe we were all harboring secret haters in silence. It was too hard to think about at length, too painful, a sunburn raw to the touch.

"Stacy went to the airport to pick up her step-sister," I said.

Liz rolled her eyes again and said, "God, let's get out of here and get some real action."

"First we need to make a toast," said Chuck, adjusting the laurel wreath on his head then holding up his beer. "Here's to the Greeks."

We clinked our bottles.

The party was in full force in the common room, cleared of its usual couches, TV, and air hockey games to make room for the D.J. and dancing. The rules about drinking outside our rooms were lifted for this event, and kegs lined the wall beneath the darkened windows. A disco ball shot shards of light all over the room, sprinkling everyone's faces with light and dark.

K.C. and the Sunshine Band played. Mirroring the song's lyrics, Chuck said into my ear, "I'm your Boogie Man."

I smiled at him, relishing that he called himself my something, my anything. I leaned into him, and he placed his hand on my back. We were standing with Liz and Benny, drinking beer, watching the dancers. Suddenly Stacy came pushing through the crowd with a tall brunette in tow, both stunningly beautiful in their togas.

"Norma! Everyone!" she exclaimed through the loud music. "This is Tabitha!"

Tabitha smiled at us, a bright white smile. She wore big gold hoop earrings and Cleopatra eye makeup.

"Good to meet you!" I yelled. "Stacy's told me a lot about you!"

Two guys squeezed by me and asked Tabitha and Stacy to dance.

"Oops!" shouted Stacy, being pulled to the dance floor by a tall, bulky guy who was looking at her in the way most guys did. "Talk to you later!"

I waved.

"That girl bugs the shit out of me," said Liz.

"Stacy? Why?" I said.

"She's just so — I don't know."

"She's really okay," I said, for what seemed like the hundredth time to Liz. "More than okay, she's cool."

"Why do you keep defending her?" growled Liz. "She's such a ding-dong cheerleader. Worse than most of my sorority sisters."

"I know she seems that way, but she's not, really. Give her a chance," I begged.

"I think she's nice," said Benny.

"Of course you do," said Liz dryly. "Hey, before I forget." She reached down the top of her toga, into her strapless bra and pulled out some Quaaludes. "All the power of drinking without the calories."

"Where'd you get those?" I asked before taking one and swallowing it with my beer.

"Kirk."

"Kirk, the R.A.? The R.A. gave you drugs?" said Benny.

"Quaaludes aren't exactly heroin, Benny," said Liz. "Here, take one."

"I know they're not heroin." He sounded a little offended. "Give me two." He stuck his hand out with bravado.

"You got it, big man."

"Hey, me too! Me too!" said Chuck, mimicking a little kid begging for candy.

Liz handed out the pills then pulled Benny onto the dance floor. She bumped her hip to his, knocking him off balance. She tried it again and this time, with some concentration, he got into the rhythm of it.

"With Liz's help in every way, Benny will become one of the most coordinated guys around," said Chuck.

I laughed and was just about to pull Chuck onto the dance floor, ala Liz, when Stacy reappeared, a sparkle of sweat on her forehead.

"Hey, Paul, want to dance?" she asked.

Chuck grabbed my hand, squeezed it, then followed Stacy to the dance floor. I felt a pang of jealousy. I watched Chuck smiling and leaning in to talk to Stacy, both of them laughing as they danced. When had they become friends?

I went to get another beer, passing a group in a dark corner snorting coke. Goat stood at the keg, dispensing beer in his cup. Ever since we'd had sex that one night, I always felt weird when I saw him—a little off-balance, like when you step off a roller coaster. He was always eyeing me, it seemed. But I found that playing his friendly buddy made me regain my balance.

"Hi Goat," I said.

"Hey Norma." He looked up at me, his sparse blond mustache lighting up in the disco ball light. "Beer?" He moved his body back and forth like a feinting boxer before filling my cup.

"Thanks." I smiled. "Nice toga." An AC/DC logo decorated the front of his white sheet, which hung just so to reveal his skinny legs.

"Can't leave my individuality behind on a night I'm forced to dress like everyone else," he said.

"You're always an individual, Goat, no matter what." I smiled and took my beer.

"Do you want to get together later tonight?" he asked, looking at me then quickly looking away, his eyes scanning the room. I didn't know what to say. I knew what he meant, and I didn't like thinking about it. The last thing I wanted to do was to make a decision like that in advance, before I knew if I could be with Chuck.

Fortunately, at that moment Kirk squeezed in next to me, asking me to dance. Without looking at Goat, I let Kirk lead me to the middle of the room. A piercing white strobe light began to flash making everything look like something else.

"So what's up with Liz?" Kirk yelled into my ear. His breath smelled sharp.

"What do you mean?"

"Does she like me?"

"I don't know," I said, feeling a little sorry for him, as I did when guys got eager.

He fell silent, dancing, his lake-green eyes glittering. His toga was draped over the shoulder that allowed him to hide his sunken nipple. He leaned toward my ear again.

"Hey, I'm working on finding out who stole your typewriter."

"Thanks," I said.

I could feel the Quaalude settling into me, spreading looseness and warmth all over my body. Instead of pulling me down, though, the warmth pulled me up, like helium surging into a balloon, the stirrings of elation. My body felt free, like it was a flying kite.

I scanned the room and saw Billy, leaning against the wall, talking to a girl I didn't know.

"Excuse me," I said to Kirk, surprised at hearing my words slur, not fully able to control my tongue.

I floated toward Billy, bumping into people as I went. As I stepped up to Billy, the girl talking to him puckered her lips in surprise.

"You went over the line," I said, my face close to his.

"Hey, back off, Norma," he said.

"You went way too far," I said.

"What the hell are you talking about?" His face flushed red.

"You know exactly what I'm talking about," I said, channeling Liz's vigor. "I want my fucking typewriter back. I'm clean. I have documentation."

"Norma, get away from me. You're crazy." He took the hand of the girl and turned, walking away with her in tow.

Watching him slink away, I felt omnipotent and high, so high that I felt I could shoot up into the sky like a rocket. I scanned the room and saw Chuck smoking a joint with Kirk.

I ran up and grabbed Chuck's hand. He dashed with me onto the dance floor.

I jumped and jumped to the music. Chuck laughed and jumped with me. We bounced higher and higher, as high as our legs would take us, like two kids home alone, jumping with a frenzy on their parents' bed.

"To the moon!" I yelled through the raucous music.

"To the moon, Alice!" yelled Chuck.

"To the moon!" I screamed.

"Do you want the moon Mary?"

"Mary?" I shouted, laughing.

"It's A Wonderful Life! Jimmy Stewart as George Bailey! Donna Reed as Mary Hatch! Do you want the moon, Mary? If you want it, I'll throw a lasso around it and pull it down for you!"

Still dressed in their togas, Benny and Chuck lay passed out on their beds.

"God, it's only 3 a.m., what's wrong with them?" asked Liz.

"Yeah, some fun they are." My head was buzzing. Music and shouting voices from the night echoed in my ears. I was so tired I was wired, past sleep. It seemed Liz was in the same state, my fervent twin.

"Aren't you starving?" she said. "I am."

"Famished."

In bare feet, Liz and I raced downstairs to the vending machines, our footsteps reverberating in the empty halls.

"Do you have any change?" she asked.

"I don't even have pockets! Don't you have some change in that bra of yours, or does it hold only Quaaludes?"

"Neither at this point," she said. "Crap. Too bad those two guys aren't here, they could shake the machine for us again."

"We can do it." I was so energized and jittery, I was bouncing foot to foot.

"You think so?"

"Absolutely! I am woman, hear me roar!"

I grabbed one side of the machine, Liz the other.

"Okay, go!" I shouted.

It didn't budge.

"Okay, more muscle-power," I said. "Try again. Go!"

With all our strength, we pulled at the machine. It began to tilt forward, just a little. I shoved my whole body into it.

"It's working!" Liz shouted, as a few bags of chips slid down their rods.

And then I felt the machine come alive and take over, its heft like a tsunami engulfing a rickety boat. My hands and arms were useless in the face of this overpowering strength.

And the next thing I knew, the monster slipped from my hands, falling forward in a deafening roar and crash. A new sound rose in the midst of the shattering machine— Liz's agonizing scream. The machine had fallen on her right leg. She lay on her back, trapped like a ghastly character in the movie *Jaws* who is slowly being eaten alive by the great white shark.

"Help!" I screamed. "Help! Help!"

"Get this fucking thing off me!" screeched Liz. "Help! Help!"

People came running, some in togas, some in pajamas, gathering around Liz, shouting, "Call an ambulance! Call the fire department!"

A group of guys grabbed the machine and pulled it off Liz's leg. She moaned, her skinny eyebrows sharp dark slashes on her increasingly pale face.

The door to Chuck and Benny's room was ajar, but the room was pitch black. Shaking, I felt my way in and over to Chuck's bed. I felt for his arm, shook it, tried to wake him. He wouldn't budge. He was snoring, heavily.

"Chuck, Chuck," I said. He just continued to snore. I tried again to wake him, but he was out.

Without removing my toga, I climbed into bed and curled up next to him, my heart pounding in my ears. I was dying to tell him what had happened. I was hoping he'd calm me and convince me to trust the logic of the ambulance attendants. As they'd fitted Liz's leg with a splint and then lifted her onto the stretcher, they assured us that she'd be fine. I asked them if I could come with her, but they said no—they'd contact her parents right away, and I could call the hospital in the morning.

I had a hard time sleeping. As soon as I'd begin to drift off, I'd jolt awake. Images flashed through my mind. Liz lying infuriated and helpless under the vending machine. Billy glaring at me, telling me I was crazy. Benny and Chuck taking two Quaaludes each, swallowing them with beer. Chuck's lips near my ear: *I'm your Boogie man. Do you want the moon?*

Finally, light began to leak into the room through my eyelids. I was glad it was morning. It was hopeless trying to sleep anymore.

I opened my eyes. Something looked strange about Chuck's head. I reached out and touched it then recoiled in shock. His head was slick, soft. Completely bald. Was this a dream? How could this be? I shot up in bed. Clumps of Chuck's blond hair lay on his pillow and on the floor. I shook him awake.

"Chuck, Chuck, there's something wrong."

"Huh?" he grumbled, his eyes still closed.

"Wake up. Something's wrong!"

He rolled over onto his back. He still had some hair on the other side of his head, but one side was definitely bald.

"Chuck!"

His eyes creaked open.

"Norma Jean, let me sleep."

I took his hand and moved it up to his head. "Can't you feel this?" I asked.

His hand slowly lifted, and he touched his head. "What the hell?" He rolled out of bed and stumbled to the mirror. Without most of his hair, he looked even more like Charlie Brown.

"Holy shit!" he said. "What—?" He flicked on the light, looked around the room, and at the same time our eyes locked on a can of shaving cream on the floor. Then, as though synchronized, our eyes moved to Benny. Clumps of his dark hair littered the floor and his bed.

"No way!" said Chuck, erupting into laughter. He looked at himself in the mirror again and laughed and laughed.

Benny stirred.

"Oh, god," I said. "Benny. Benny."

"What?" said Benny, his voice thick.

Chuck bent over Benny. "Look, we've been freed from our hair! No more worries, no more hours under the dryer in hot rollers, no more agonizing bad hair days!"

Benny opened his eyes and blinked. I handed him his glasses. When he put them on, Benny said, "What? What happened?"

"Feel your head!" Chuck laughed, a little maniacally.

Benny sat up, bits of hair falling to his shoulders. He felt his head, and his hand shot away as though electrocuted.

"Oh no!" he shouted, jumping from his bed to look in the mirror. "Oh no! What happened? What happened? How did this happen? My parents are going to kill me!" He slumped on his bed and put his face in his hands. Tears dripped down, smearing his glasses.

"Who did this?" I asked, sitting next to Benny, putting my hand on his back.

"How should we know?" said Chuck. "We were too fucked up on Quaaludes to appreciate that someone was giving us a complementary haircut. Geez," he said, looking at himself in the mirror again. "I look like a nuclear holocaust victim. So do you, Ben, hate to tell you."

Benny's back shuddered. I rubbed it in little circles with my hand, feeling as I consoled him that I was emulating Stacy comforting me.

Chuck picked up the can of shaving cream and shook it. He sprayed the white cream on his head and then, with his own razor, carefully shaved off the rest of his hair.

"Ah, free at last!" he said. "Your turn, Benny."

As Benny, shivering, let Chuck shave his head clean, I told them about the vending machine falling on Liz. As I described what had happened, Benny got so agitated I said I'd call the hospital right away, so I picked up Chuck's phone and dialed.

"Norm, I have a fucking cast crotch to toe," croaked Liz into the phone. "But these painkillers—wow, they're fabulous."

I felt horrible. I hadn't slept all night, and all the beer and the Quaalude weren't helping much. I felt dizzy, dirty, disconnected from my body—as though I were a floating Macy's parade balloon, casting a large shadow. I needed to get out of my toga, take a shower, and sit down and do some homework. I looked forward to the prospect of feeling normal for the day.

Stacy and Tabitha lay on Stacy's bed, still in their togas, talking, when I walked in the room. Even though they'd been through the same crazy night as me, and obviously hadn't yet taken showers, they looked like Greek goddesses posing for a painting.

"Hi Norma, where were you all night?" asked Stacy.

"With Chuck, I mean Paul," I said. I was glad she asked. I wanted her to know that I lay claim to him, as petty as that seemed. How shitty of me, I thought, at the same time taking refuge in admitting to myself my limitations.

"The guys we were with, from Dorm 5, they just left," Tabitha said. "I'm glad you didn't come in last night, if you know what I mean." She giggled.

I thought about Tabitha's boyfriend, the one who couldn't come this weekend. But I didn't say anything.

"Who were they—the guys from dorm 5? Would I know them?" I asked.

"No. No one special," Tabitha said. I decided not to pry, to let them revel in the pleasure of their little secret.

I told them what had happened to Liz.

"Is she okay?" asked Stacy.

"Yeah. She's got a monster cast, and her parents are with her. She'll be back in the next day or two."

I went to take a shower, and when I came back, Stacy and Tabitha were gone. I sat at my desk and rummaged through my binder, trying to organize the chaos by writing a list of all the assignments I thought were due the next week. My head spun, and I was nauseous, but I did my best to try to focus, to pull my attention back to my tasks every time my mind wandered or my body reminded me of everything

I'd ingested the previous night. I thought about Liz's joke—how school would be great if it weren't for the classes.

I heard a tap at the door, and then it swung open. Chuck and Benny entered, both wearing baseball caps.

"Don't we look suave?" said Chuck.

Benny looked like a bug, his face so tiny under the hat, his glasses so big.

"We're going on a raft down the river," said Benny. "Want to come?"

"Oh, guys, thanks, I can't. I have too much to do."

"Come on, Norma Jean," said Chuck. "We'll be like Huck, Tom and Jim. Except with ganja."

"I can't, really," I said.

I must have said "no" ten times. But, to my delight, they weren't satisfied with my refusal.

Soon, wearing my bathing suit, I lay on a rubber raft with Chuck and Benny, in the hot, hot afternoon, the water cool on my fingertips, the pungency of drifting pot smoke, the sky an eternal stretch of blue. The river was translucent and calm, and we floated dreamily along, drifting under the bridge into its cool, dark shadow and then out again into the sizzling sun.

While Chuck pattered on about James Bond obscurities, I closed my eyes and wrapped myself in the comfort of his familiar voice, punctuated by the sweetness of Benny's lilting interjections. The sweet freedom and camaraderie of the moment nestled into my mind, and heart.

Chapter Eleven — Staying Alive

"Happy Birthday!"

I walked into my room, to Chuck, Benny, Stacy and Liz singing "Happy Birthday" standing in a group except for Liz who lay on Stacy's bed, cast-engulfed leg propped up on pillows, her crutches leaning against the wall.

"Wow, hey you guys. How'd you all know?" I said.

"Ve half our vays," said Chuck, rubbing his hands together.

I set my backpack on my bed, next to a big box. "What's this?" I opened the card attached to the box. It read, *Happy Birthday. Love Mom & Dad.*

"My parents were here?" I asked.

"They said they wanted to surprise you," said Stacy. "They were on their way to something here in town, some event, I forget, and couldn't stay, but they said they'll see you next week anyway for Thanksgiving. They seemed really nice."

I opened the box. Inside was a new electric typewriter. A lump pinched at my throat.

"Wow, that's so cool," said Stacy.

"Here's to Mom and Dad," said Chuck, handing me a beer and clinking his against mine.

"Time to party!" said Liz. "Light the candles, Benny."

Benny flicked a lighter and lit the candles on a platter of brownies with chocolate frosting that filled a platter on Stacy's desk.

"Wow, you guys did this for me?"

"Liz made them," said Benny.

"You baked?" I marveled. "Where? And how?"

"It wasn't easy with this damn cast on. But Benny bought the ingredients and helped me make them in Kirk's apartment. We had a deal. We made two batches and gave him one."

"They have a special ingredient," giggled Benny.

"I'm sure she figured that out already, Ben," Chuck said.

I smiled knowingly. But I'd honestly not thought about it because I was so surprised, so pleased. Of course if Liz made the brownies, they had pot in them. That was nice, but it didn't really matter to me one way or the other. I felt so happy that my friends cared enough to throw a surprise birthday party for me.

"Okay, Norma Jean," said Chuck, "make a wish and blow, before the wax ruins our special treat."

I closed my eyes. I didn't know what to wish for. At that moment, I felt so happy, so grateful for my friends—I felt like I didn't need anything more. I wished that everything would stay like this, all this fun and love among us. I opened my eyes and blew out the candles.

While we ate brownies and drank beer, Liz said, "Sign my cast, Norm."

With a red felt-tip marker, I drew a little stick figure, its leg crushed by a rectangular square. I signed it, "Friends forever. Norma."

Stacy put on disco music and, while Liz watched from her perch on the bed, Stacy, Ben, Chuck and I danced wildly in a circle to the *The Hustle*, to *Boogie Fever*, to *It's Raining Men*.

Stacy cut more brownies and walked around, feeding bites to everyone.

We danced to *Boogie Oogie Oogie*, to *I Will Survive*, to *Staying Alive*.

An elation began building in me, like I'd been swimming underwater, holding my breath, and was about ready to break through the surface. As we continued to dance and dance, the feeling grew and grew, like it had the night of the toga party. I was a rocket on a launch pad, engines roaring, seconds from take-off. If I stood at a cliff, I'd jump, certain I could fly.

"I love you all!" I shouted, breaking into a spin.

"I love you all too!" said Stacy. "I love you Liz! I love you Norma!"

She wrapped her arms around me, and we whirled around together. When we let go, she spun around and into Chuck. He grabbed her, and they danced, cheek to cheek, her long blonde hair spread across his shoulder.

"I love you Paul!" she shouted, grabbing his hands and turning around and around, her hair flying. She let go and threw herself into Benny.

"I love you Benny!" Radiant, she grabbed his hands and spun with him. He grinned, his glasses flashing.

She hugged him close, moving her body against his.

"Quit being such a prick tease!" yelled Liz.

We all stopped, stunned, the Bee Gees moaning, *Staying aliiiiive . . .*

"Why do you have to be such a prick tease?" said Liz, slurring her words, her eyes red and glassy.

"Why are you saying this to me?" asked Stacy.

Liz pushed herself off the bed and hobbled over to her crutches. She shoved them under her arms.

"Fuck this shit," Liz said, maneuvering herself on her crutches across the room. "Benny, open the goddamn door."

He did.

"Bye," he said in a small voice. "Happy Birthday, Norma." He waved meekly and followed Liz out.

"What just happened?" I said, stunned. I sat on my bed next to the typewriter in its box.

The record screeched as Stacy angrily yanked the arm off and slammed it down.

"I don't need this," she said, tears in her eyes. "I just don't need this."

"Stacy, I'm sorry, I don't know what happened," I said, shocked. I'd never seen Stacy angry before, and it frightened me.

"Don't apologize for Liz, Norma," said Chuck. "And Stacy, come on, don't take it so personally. Liz is just jealous of your gorgeous self, can you blame her?"

Chuck's jokey compliment didn't sway her. "I'm out of here," she said, grabbing her purse and running out the door.

"I'll be right back," said Chuck, running after her.

Bewildered, I stared off into space. The Bee Gee's harmonies echoed in my head. I tried to focus on my shoe, the curtain, something, but everything was blurry. Wasn't I elated just a moment ago? And now I sat alone on my bed, on my birthday, baffled and distressed.

Moments later, Chuck came back into the room, picked up the typewriter box and placed it on my desk, then sat next to me.

"Is she okay?" I asked.

"She'll get over it," he said, taking my hand.

"Everyone left," I said softly, dejected. "You don't want to go, too, do you?"

"What, and leave my Norma Jean on her birthday? Hardly." He ran his thumb across the palm of my hand and lifted it to his lips to kiss it, a move so sweet and sexy in its near-chasteness.

I looked at him. He put his arm around me. I put my arms around him. We kissed. He was no Billy. His kisses were perfect, as though our mouths were molded by the same sculptor and belonged together. My body flooded with wet warmth, a feeling not unusual but always welcome—especially since Chuck was, for the first time, the instigator. I wondered how much he had drunk, or if he was stoned. We were kissing, quietly. He wasn't making jokes, or cracks about the "skunk" not working like the first time I'd asked him if he'd sleep with me. He didn't seem wasted like the night of the Strip Quarters game. He was kissing me, touching me, pulling his shirt off over his head then helping me with mine.

Soon we were naked. He lay down on the bed, facing me. As I moved on top of him, stretching above him for full effect, he welcomed me, pulling me onto him, the best birthday present ever.

Later, past midnight, Chuck and I weren't asleep, just lying in my bed talking, and he was smoking a cigarette, when someone knocked at the door.

"It's got to be Stacy," I said, getting up and wrapping a blanket around me. "She probably forgot her key."

I opened the door to Jack, wearing tight jeans and a tank top, his arm muscles bulging. My first instinct was to slam the door shut, but my arms were weak, useless. I shrank back. He held out six blood red roses, wrapped in cellophane.

"Happy Birthday, Babe," he said, leaning over to kiss me on the cheek then pushing past me into the room. Panic surged through me.

Leaning back in the bed against a pillow, Chuck took a drag on his cigarette and eyed Jack. "Who's the brute?" he said, calmly. For a brief, irrational second I thought maybe we could work all this out, have a beer together and—what? All climb into my bed?

"Hey, what the hell's this?" said Jack. "I come here on your birthday and find this? Some bald dude?" He dropped the roses on my desk.

"Jack," I said, my throat raw and dry. "It's nothing, really. It doesn't mean anything." When I heard those words coming out of my mouth, I froze. My hair and fingernails ceased to grow, my heart to pump, my eyes to blink. I was a freeze frame of fear and shame. Had I really just said what I thought I said?

"Is that so, Norma Jean?" said Chuck. "Nothing?"

He pulled the sheet aside and climbed out of bed, displaying his chunky Charlie Brown nakedness. As though he had all the time in the world, he bent to the floor and picked up his clothes, then pulled on his jeans, tee-shirt and baseball cap. His movements were so slow and controlled that I thought he might be giving me a chance to retract my words.

But that was impossible. I was granite, my limbs a burden, my mind igneous rock. Watching Chuck dress, I wanted to call out to him, to tell him he meant so much to me, to tell him how I felt so loved and safe with him. I wanted to tell him I didn't mean what I'd said. But wanting something, anything, in my current state was futile. I could as much change what was happening as a mannequin could jump off the display floor and run for her life.

I didn't—couldn't—move as Chuck walked past me and out the door, quietly closing it behind him.

Jack opened the mini-refrigerator and took out a beer. He drank the whole thing in a few gulps then opened another.

"Hey Babe," he said, "no hard feelings. It's okay."

I was now a block of ice, my muscles shivering, my heart petrified.

He kissed me, and I let him, hoping the heat would melt my body of ice. He unwrapped the blanket from around me and kissed my breasts, moving his hands up and down my body. I shivered and shivered.

"Ooh, you're warm," he said.

He pulled his tee-shirt off, and I saw he had a new tattoo, a little Sylvester right next to the little Tweety. I didn't say anything, just numbly let him push me onto the bed and throw his body over, onto, and into mine.

Chapter Twelve — Reader

I sat in the back of the car with my eyes closed, pretending to be asleep. When I had my eyes open, my parents wanted to talk to me about my classes and about my friends—but I couldn't talk about the disastrous truth, and I didn't have the energy to concoct a bunch of ingenuous-sounding lies. We were driving to San Diego, to my sister's house, for Thanksgiving.

It had been almost a week since my horrid birthday. Jack had stayed with me for an hour after we had sex, and the minute he left, I ran to the bathroom and threw up. I stayed on the bathroom floor for hours, dry heaving when there was nothing left in my stomach, the tiles digging into my knees.

For three days, I lay sick in bed. Stacy brought me 7-Up and saltine crackers. But she was aloof, not saying much. I tried to ask her why she seemed to be punishing me for Liz's awful comment, but I felt so sick it was hard to say—or even pinpoint—what I felt. Silent, Stacy placed a cold washrag on my forehead and added ice to my 7-Up, then took off to class or to who-knows-where. She just didn't hang around the room.

I watched Luke and Laura's wedding on Stacy's little black and white T.V. Laura, with her puffy veil and huge teeth. Luke, an unlikely heart-throb, with his Bozo-the-Clown hair. As soon as they said *I do*, I wept.

When I finally felt able, I got out of bed and went upstairs to see Chuck. Benny looked up from his video game and said, "I don't know where he is, Norma, sorry."

"When was the last time you saw him?"

"Yesterday."

"He didn't come back last night?"

"Nope. He hasn't been around hardly at all. But his stuff's all here, so I know he didn't leave for Thanksgiving yet, like Liz."

"Liz is gone?"

"Yeah, she went home early. Her leg was bugging her. Her parents came to get her. Want to play Space Invaders?"

"No thanks," I said. "But is it okay if I sit here for a little bit?"

"Sure," he said, turning back to his game.

I sat on Chuck's bed, then lay back. His pillow smelled like him. I turned around and buried my face into it for as long as I could stand it, and when I felt tears coming, I pulled back and lifted my head. James Bond, in a tuxedo, pointed a gun at me. I sat up and went to Chuck's desk. My hands shaking, I pushed aside packets of matchbooks to find a piece of paper and a pen.

Chuck, I wrote. *I came looking for you. I've been sick. Really, really sick about this whole thing. I miss you. Are you okay? Do you hate me? I feel terrible. Worse than I've ever felt about anything. I want to beg your forgiveness. Can I do that? Will you let me? Can we play backgammon? Please forgive me.*

Please, please, please.   Love, love and more love, Norma, who wants the moon.

By the time my parents came to pick me up, I had gone by his room several more times, but each time he wasn't there. And Stacy was nowhere to be found, either. I didn't say goodbye to anyone.

I opened one eye and saw we were just a few miles from my sister's house.

"She's exhausted, huh?" said Dad.   "She must be burning the candle at both ends."

"I wonder," said Mom.

"Don't you remember? That's what we did in college."

"I suppose," she said.

I closed my eye and kept them both shut until we drove up to Mary's house.

We ate Thanksgiving dinner—turkey, stuffing, mashed potatoes, cranberry sauce—in the backyard at the picnic table.

Mary and Mom had cooked the turkey, while Dad and Mary's husband, Hal, watched a football game and I slept, or pretended to sleep, on Mary and Hal's bed.

"Norma, time to eat," said Mary, poking her head in the room. She untied her apron and pulled it off, standing there with her hands on her hips. It was strange for me to see my sister—who I often still thought of as a critical, rebellious teenager—as a married woman who did things like make Thanksgiving dinners.

"I'm not hungry," I said.

"You have to come. It's Thanksgiving."

So I sat on the redwood picnic bench, with my sunglasses on, picking at my food. It was a hazy afternoon, the air sticky and humid.

Mary, Dad and Hal talked about mortgages, retirement plans, car loans. Mom put in her two cents now and then. When the financial conversation waned, Hal, running his hand through his hair bleached white from the sun, asked, "So, how's college life, Norma?"

"It's fine," I said, dismissively. I took a bite of turkey.

"Do you like living in the dorms?" asked Mary.

"Yeah, it's fun."

"Are you meeting nice people?"

I took a deep breath, exhaled. I knew I'd have to conjure up some energy to answer these questions. "Yeah. My roommate Stacy's really nice. Mom and Dad met her last week when they brought my birthday present to my room."

"Yes, nice girl," said Dad. "And we met another of your friends. Can't remember her name. Chinese or Japanese girl?"

"Liz? You met Liz?"

"Yes," said Mom. "She walked in with a plate of brownies for your birthday. She gave one to each of us."

My chest tightened. I was mortified. How could Liz have done such a thing?

"I had an intuition, though," said Dad, eyeing me. "In the car, we broke one open and saw, well, we saw green . . . fibers . . ."

Mary burst out laughing. "Oh my god! Can you imagine if you guys had eaten them?"

"Sure, Mary," said Mom, stiffening. "It would have been hysterical to have your father driving, stoned."

"Stoned!" Mary laughed some more.

Hal shifted in his seat, straight-faced. "Mary, it's really not that funny," he said.

"Yes it is!" Mary was in hysterics.

As lousy as I felt, I couldn't help it—I cracked a smile.

"All's well that ends well," said Dad. "So did you have a good birthday?"

"I guess she did!" Mary hooted.

Mom stood and began clearing the plates.

"Barbara, please sit down," said Hal. Mom looked at him, set down the plates and took her seat. Mary's laughter had subsided, but her eyes were sparkling. "We want to tell you all the good news," Hal said. "We're having a baby."

"Really?" said Dad.

"Mary!" said Mom, leaning over and squeezing her hand.

"We wanted to tell you all together, here today," Hal said.

Dad held up his coke, the ice chiming in his glass. We all followed suit and made a toast to the baby.

"I can't believe you're pregnant," I said to Mary as we walked along the wide beach. The water and sky were gray. There was no horizon line.

"Yeah, pretty amazing, isn't it?" She tapped her flat belly with her hand. A breeze jostled her long hair. A seagull pecked at something in the sand. Whenever I thought about the ocean, I thought about peace and beauty.

But the reality was that the beach always made me a little anxious—that long stretch of nothing.

"Norma, is everything okay?"

"Yeah, why do you ask?"

"You look . . . different. I don't know."

"I am different. Moving away from home makes you different." I wanted to say more but didn't know where to start.

"That's true." She stopped and pulled off her sandals. I did the same. We continued to walk. The rough sand on the soles of my feet kind of hurt and kind of felt good.

"So what's it like—college and living in the dorms?" To my parents' disappointment, Mary had never liked school and didn't go to college. She worked for a rental car company. "I mean, what's it really like? I can't believe a friend of yours gave Mom and Dad pot brownies."

"Liz. She's crazy. I swear she joined a sorority just so she could be hazed. At least that's what it seems like."

"How often do you get to see Jack?"

"Every once in a while. I'm really busy with school work."

My words rang such a false note that I couldn't stand still in my body anymore. I dropped my sandals and ran toward the water. The remainder of a wave lapped at my feet. The water wasn't too cold. I splashed a little. A yacht floated by with people on deck holding wine glasses. I thought about how I was looking out toward Europe, and then I realized, no, I was looking out toward Hawaii. But if I kept going West, past Hawaii, all the way around the planet, I'd eventually end up in Europe. I wanted to fly there, to fly away, rather than back to the dorms, back to the mess I'd made of my relationship with Chuck, not to mention the mess of my classes and the mess of Liz and Stacy.

I turned and saw Mary seated on a large piece of driftwood. I went and sat next to her.

"Norma," she said. "If anything ever happens, or if you get bored, or for whatever reason at all, you could come live with Hal and me, you know."

Something took over and shook me inside out. Maybe it was the concern and love in Mary's voice. I burst out crying. My back heaved with sobs. Mary sat and waited until I was finished. It took a while, as though my dried-out spirit needed to be watered by my tears.

"I feel terrible," I said, wiping my eyes on my sleeve. "I don't know why." Oddly, those words felt true. I didn't truly know why I felt so bad. It seemed there was something else going on—something beyond Chuck, Jack, Liz, Stacy, homework, hangovers, and my secret hater. Or maybe it was the unique combination of all of the above. "I don't know what's wrong. I feel horrible. Maybe I'm anemic. Maybe I should get a checkup."

"Maybe," Mary said. "I'm always a little borderline anemic. I've had to take a lot of iron for this baby."

"Maybe I have low blood-sugar," I said. "I'm really not eating right. I should start eating better. And I get no exercise at all. Maybe I'll buy a bike. Sacramento's flat, it's great for bike-riding."

"But hot," said Mary.

"I think if I eat better, drink less, and get some exercise, I'll be able to think straight. I mean, I'm having a hard time focusing, a hard time thinking."

"A little too much partying, huh? I feel a little fuzzy-headed, too," she said. "Maybe it's in the air."

"You're pregnant. You have an excuse."

"That's true." She reached down and grabbed a fistful of sand. We both watched it slowly drizzle from her hand like an hourglass.

"Do you like living with all those people?" she asked. "I think it would make me claustrophobic."

"It's mostly fun," I said, realizing that most of my fun, my true joy, came from hanging out with Chuck, Liz and Benny. I wondered with a sinking feeling if we'd ever all be together again. "There's always a party going on," I added.

"Sounds like it."

"But it's distracting. I don't think my grades will be too hot this semester." I knew I was minimizing everything. But I didn't know how else to talk to my family, even my sister who I doubted would judge me. Other than being upset about specific events—like the theft of my typewriter—I was hesitant to portray myself around my family as anything other than happy or optimistic or together. Maybe I felt they wouldn't know me anymore if I showed my darker side.

"Bad grades, really? You were always so good in school. Sometimes I wish I was more like you."

"You do?" My older sister envied me? I was flattered.

"Yeah, you know, your nose in a book all the time, like Mom. Reading has never been my favorite thing. But I think it's such a good thing."

It struck me that I hadn't read one book since I started college. Just the newspaper and some textbook chapters.

"But," she continued, "I'm going to get a ton of kids' books, and I'll make this baby a reader if it kills me."

"I think that's what Mom thought about you," I said.

She smiled. "Probably so. Holy shit. What if my daughter is as rebellious as I was?"

"Well," I said, "just pray for a son."

That night, as I lay on the fold-out couch in the living room, I wondered if Chuck would ever forgive me. I wondered if Stacy would warm up to me again. I wished I'd had the chance to talk to both of them before they disappeared for Thanksgiving break.

It struck me that they both seemed to vanish the last few days before break. I hadn't been able to find either one of them. Did they go off together? I remembered them dancing together at the toga party, talking and laughing with a familiarity that surprised me. And then, at my birthday party—Stacy throwing herself into his arms, telling him she loved him, and him looking at her, moving with her, her long beautiful blonde hair and perfect skin. My stomach lurched, my whole body tightened. I played these scenes over and over in my head, and it took me hours to fall asleep.

Chapter Thirteen — Taboo

Chuck and Stacy were sitting on Stacy's bed, talking quietly, when I entered the room. I was so happy to see them both that I forgot to be jealous that they were huddled together, clearly engaged in a private conversation.

"Hi guys!" I grinned, trying to emanate an upbeat friendliness. I dragged my suitcase to my side of the room.

"Hey Norma," said Stacy. She stood and gave me a hug. She felt warm, soft.

"I have to go," said Chuck, his eyes shielded by his baseball cap. "See you later, Stacy."

He brushed by me and left the room.

I ran out and caught up to him in the hall.

"Did you get my note?" I asked.

He continued to walk straight ahead, silent, not looking at me, as though I were the ghost of nothing. I followed him.

"Chuck, please. You don't know how terrible I feel. I'm a mess. Please, please talk to me."

When we got to the staircase, I stopped and watched him take the steps two at a time then turn to the right and disappear. I tried to take a deep breath but my chest was clenched and I could sip just a little air. I turned and looked at the long, empty hallway, with the sunk feeling that I'd done irreparable damage to Chuck. And myself.

Back in my room, I sat on my bed, my feet on my suitcase, my head in my hands.

"What was that all about?" asked Stacy, reaching into the fridge and taking out a diet soda. She held one out to me, but I waved it away.

"It's because of our fight. He's not talking to me." I was sure Chuck had told her all the gory details.

"What fight?" Standing by her desk, she flipped open the soda and took a sip.

"Don't you know? You mean, he didn't tell you?"

"Tell me what?"

"That he and I were in bed together and got in an awful fight?"

"You were what?" she said, sinking to her desk chair. Her face suddenly seemed a little thinner and whiter. She looked disturbed. Was she upset that I had sex with Chuck? Maybe I was right. Maybe she had a thing for him—and he for her. If that was so, I was secretly, guiltily glad to be able to reveal this intimacy to Stacy.

"Yes, it happened right here, in bed, here, in this room. Right here." I slapped my quilt. I fully expected waves of sadness to take over as I told this story sitting on the very bed where these events unfolded, but instead, I was numb. It seemed like someone other than me was talking, someone who wasn't intimately involved in the whole thing—like I was a news anchor reading from a teleprompter. "The night of my birthday. After you all got in that horrible fight, Chuck and I got in one of our own."

"We all didn't get in a fight," said Stacy, pulling her hair back into a knot. She grabbed a pencil off her desk and stuck it through the knot. "Liz went off on me for no reason."

"She was jealous," I said. "Stacy, Liz and Benny are kind of together. You told Benny you loved him."

"I did?"

"Yes, you told us all you loved us."

"I was high! We were all high! And I do love you all. Well, not Liz. She's horrible."

It was the first time I'd heard Stacy say something blatantly negative about another person. For some reason, I felt the need to defend Liz—like I defended Stacy around Liz. Part of me still craved the *Anne of Green Gables* vision of college—the 1980's dorm version of laughing and rolling down green hills, of intimate youthful connections prefiguring lifelong friendships.

"She's not that horrible, really," I said. "She just has, well, fits. Think of Liz like an epileptic. Can an epileptic help having seizures?"

"Well, no," said Stacy. "But I'm not sure that comparison works."

"If Liz apologized, would you accept her apology?"

Stacy pulled the pencil out and her hair cascaded down her back. "Maybe. Probably. I don't know. She'd have to mean it."

"Well, I apologized to Chuck. I wrote him a note, begging his forgiveness, and you saw him, he won't even talk to me."

"You must have really hurt him."

"Thanks a lot."

"I'm sorry, I didn't mean it that way. But what did you two fight about?"

How could I tell her without revealing what a monster I was? What kind of woman kicks the man she's falling in love with out of her bed when her kind-of boyfriend—who rarely displays love for her anymore, and who probably has other girlfriends—shows up, unannounced? There was something gravely wrong with me.

Stacy must have seen an awful look on my face. Maybe she was worried I'd throw my backpack across the room again and she'd have to pick up the mess—the mess of my scattered books and papers, the mess of my scattered brain and heart.

"Don't worry, Norma," she said. "Keep trying. Chuck will forgive you in time."

"You think so?"

"And grovel," she said, smiling her broad, white-toothed smile. "He'll forgive you if you grovel enough, I'm sure."

I wasn't in the mood to laugh, much less smile. You have to be generous with yourself to be self-deprecating—and right then I was a callous *Scarlet Letter* judge, sentencing myself to the stockade.

A party blasted loudly through my wall from the Billy-Goat Room. All I wanted was to be playing backgammon with Chuck, drinking white wine, while on the other side of the room Liz handed a joint to Benny and he stared down her shirt, like he always did, even after they'd slept together.

But in the past weeks, every time I went by Chuck's room, either he wasn't there or wouldn't see me. He'd literally walk out the door if I tried to talk to him. But more often than not, he was gone.

Benny always said, "Sorry, Norma, I don't know where he is."

And Liz was gone a lot, too, hanging out with her sorority friends. If I wanted to see her, I had to go upstairs; she wouldn't come to my room because she didn't want to run into Stacy. She probably wouldn't have, though, because Stacy, too, was hardly around. She said she was at the library studying, but I wasn't sure I believed her. It made me sick to think about it, but perhaps she and Chuck were sneaking off together somewhere. And when I thought like that, I was reminded what a terrible person I was for continually suspecting Stacy, Stacy who had been nothing but nice to me. More than nice. She'd taken care of me. Besides, after the way I'd acted, she deserved Chuck's company, even Chuck's love, more than I ever would.

Bass notes thumped at the wall like *The Telltale Heart* heartbeat. I read through my notes from English class. I had another paper due the next day, the last paper of the semester. We had to write about an issue from our own lives, something we had experienced that had, as Linda put it, "larger implications."

"Write about anything," she'd said. "There is nothing too taboo. The more real you are, the likelier you are to write something worth reading."

Real. Taboo. Worth reading.

The first time and only time I took LSD, I wrote, *I thought I understood the meaning of the universe.*

I stopped and looked at that line. It felt like a good first line. Something crashed in the Billy-Goat Room, and laughter erupted. The music stopped.

People are always wanting to discover the meaning of the universe. They read the Bible. They study philosophy and science. They walk on the moon, or dive down to the bottom of the ocean.

The music started back up again, the bass vibrating the wall.

They work for world peace. They bomb each other.

But no one, not even Einstein, not a girl on LSD, not the priest in the confessional—no one has discovered it yet.

Sometimes they shout "Eureka!" Sometimes they think, "I've found it!" But each discovery has one of two possibilities: It either falls flat after the initial excitement, or it leads to new questions.

That's what happened what I dropped acid. I don't have answers, only more questions.

"Liz, will you please, please, please, please apologize to Stacy?"

"Why should I?" She took a bite of quivering macaroni and cheese. It looked like an orange brain. I was eating some kind of meat in a weird white sauce. We had hit the tail-end of dinnertime, so the food was lukewarm and the dining commons was almost empty. Liz was mastering moving about in her new walking cast and had maneuvered her way to the dining commons in half the time it had taken her just a few days before.

"You should apologize to Stacy because it would be a nice thing to do," I said.

"A nice thing. Well, it would have been a nice thing if she didn't throw her body all over Benny. Did you see him? I swear he was getting a woody."

"It wasn't his fault." I took a drink of orange soda.

"So it was hers."

"No, it wasn't hers, either. We were all stoned. And Stacy was being—I don't know, high. She was being high. Come on, Liz. She's my roommate. I want you guys to be friends."

"Friends? I don't think so." Liz gingerly crossed her legs.

"Please, please, please, please, please."

"God, that meat stuff looks disgusting," she said.

"Do you think your mac and cheese looks any better?"

She threw her fork down and pulled a black film canister from her purse. After prying off the lid, she shook several little white pills into her palm. Cross-tops, speed.

"Want some?"

"Okay." I needed a boost.

We each took two.

"Liz, please apologize to Stacy."

"For god's sake, Norma, you don't give up, do you?"

"I'll do something special for you," I said.

"Like what?"

"I don't know. Score you some pot or something?" I thought I sounded convincing even though I'd never scored pot before. In fact, I'd never used "score" as a verb before. I suppressed an urge to giggle.

"How much?"

"A lid?" I wasn't sure how much a lid was, or how much it would cost.

"Okay."

"But only if you mean it," I said. "You'll have to mean it with Stacy, or she'll know."

"How can I mean it if I don't?"

"I don't know. Have sex with Benny first, give him a blow job or something to calm yourself down, to remind yourself that he's into you, not her. He doesn't want her, he wants you. And so does Kirk. You are one desired chick."

"Yeah right. I don't have a chance against Cheryl Ladd."

"Grace Kelly."

"Whatever."

My scalp started tingling, a sign the speed was kicking in.

"A lid," I said. "A whole lid, and a new roach clip, one of those pretty ones, with dangling feathers and glass beads."

"Okay, okay," she said, standing up and picking up her tray. "I'll do it. I'll apologize to the little bitch."

I gave her a look.

"I mean to your lovely blonde roommate."

Liz wrote Stacy a letter. I would have preferred a face-to-face apology, but Liz said she could sound more sincere in a letter.

"Liz wrote me a letter," said Stacy, from the darkened side of her room. She lay in bed. I'd thought she was asleep. My Cultural Anthropology final was the next day, and I was anxiously planning to pull an all-nighter to read 200 pages of the textbook I hadn't read all semester.

"She did?" Feigning ignorance, I picked up my yellow highlighter.

"Yeah. She apologized. She said she was sorry for calling me a prick tease, that it was a horrible thing to say to someone as kind and wonderful and perfect and beautiful and gorgeous and fabulous as me."

"Oh." I swallowed hard. Damn that Liz. She wasn't getting the pot I'd planned to buy from the Meteorologist, no way.

"It was a bit much," said Stacy. "In fact, it was a lot much. Way, way too much." She bunched up her pillow and shifted in bed. "You put her up to it, didn't you, Norma?"

"No. I did not tell her to write a letter." Adamant in my half-truth, I was awed at Stacy's intuition.

"Well, at any rate, if I've been counseling Chuck to forgive you, I suppose I should forgive Liz."

I looked up at the profile of her face, her graceful nose. "You've been counseling Chuck to forgive me?"

"Yes."

"Thanks," I said, meaning, *you are a goddess.* How could she be so generous when I'd been so small-minded in my suspicions of her, thinking she was sneaking behind my back to seduce Chuck?

"No problem," she said.

I wanted to ask if her counseling of Chuck was working, but she said "good night" and turned over to sleep.

In English class, I got back my paper about my acid trip. An *A.* At the bottom, Linda wrote, "This is a beautifully written meditation on life's big questions, all centered on one very personal, very honestly-conveyed experience."

It looked like I'd save my course grade in English. Next I had to do the same in Cultural Anthropology. As I left my English classroom, I looked for Chuck, out of habit, even though he hadn't met me after class for more than a month. All I saw were unfamiliar faces, shrouded by sweatshirt hoods and umbrellas. It was raining. I held my backpack over my head and made my way to class.

I arrived dripping wet. The Mr. Brady-look-alike professor stared at me like I was a stranger. I was. I had rarely attended class. But he handed me the final anyway, a thick packet—10 pages, stapled together.

Rain beat at the roof. Windows clouded, the stuffy room smelled like a dirty sock. I thumbed through all the pages, reading questions on each page. *Give an example. Diagram this. Fill in the blank. Essay Question 1. Essay Question 2.*

Not one multiple choice. Not one True-False.

I put down my pencil and stared at the gloomy sky, rain streaking the windows.

I flipped through the pages again. Then, mortified and defiant, I stood up and walked out, leaving behind the blank exam.

Chapter Fourteen — Jump

"Here, what do you think about this one?" Suzy turned the magazine to a dog-eared page. The dress was dusty pink and had puffy sleeves.

"That's pretty," I said. She'd shown me so many bridesmaids dresses they were all beginning to look the same.

"But which one do you like better—this one, or the one with the spaghetti straps?"

"I guess the spaghetti straps."

"Me too! But my mom thinks they look slutty."

She took a sip of her Manhattan. She'd never had a Manhattan before. She'd ordered one because she always thought a "Manhattan" sounded classy, especially since it came with a shiny cherry. We sat in a booth at The Cellar, a bar in Auburn. I was home for winter break. For the first time, we both had fake ID's. Mary had given me her old driver's license over Thanksgiving, and Suzy had borrowed one that belonged to an older friend.

"What about this one?" She turned the page to a dress that looked pretty much like the one she'd just shown me.

"I don't know. It's kind of cute, I guess."

"Hm," she said, gazing at it. "I just can't believe how much work a wedding is. It's fun, but it's hard. Sammy's oblivious. My mom and I are doing all the work. All he has to do is get his tux, and he's bitching about that."

"So you're really going through with it?" I took a sip of my wine, amazed that my best friend, a girl my age, felt ready to get married. I half understood the appeal: you immediately became an adult, it seemed, at least in others' eyes. And then you could be autonomous, making decisions like, *I think we'll go on a European trip this fall.* That is, if you had the money. That is, if you had the time. That is, if your spouse agreed. That was a paradox in my mind: through marriage you gained adulthood, while you also created a dependence on someone, someone who might have veto power over you.

"Yes, I'm going through with it. I mean, I've had second thoughts, but there's always divorce."

I laughed. She sipped at her drink, daintily.

"You're joking, right?" I asked. "I mean, you're not going to walk down the aisle thinking you can get a divorce?"

"Why not?"

"I don't know. It seems weird. I mean, what if Diana was thinking that as she walked down the aisle toward Prince Charles?"

"Maybe she was. Who knows?"

I waved at the waiter and asked for another glass of wine.

"It just seems weird, that's all."

"Divorce is a reality, Norma." She took a little mirror out of her purse and ran lip gloss over her lips. "So is this nose. This honker of a nose. I'm seriously thinking of getting a nose job before the wedding."

"Really? What does Sammy say?"

"He's all for it. He says I can do whatever I want." She slipped her mirror back in her purse. She took the cherry out of her drink and slid it in her mouth. As she chewed, her eyes grew distant.

"What are you thinking?" I asked, feeling a surge of tenderness for my oldest friend, the girl I'd met in fifth grade. On that first day of class, we'd bonded immediately, being the only two girls in the room wearing beaded moccasins. Later, in high school, we'd go clothes shopping together and deliberately buy the same jeans or blouse.

"Norma, I'm dying to tell you something. But you have to swear you won't tell anyone else."

I moved closer to her, relishing her words. I loved it when Suzy told me secrets. They were always juicy. "I promise," I said.

Suzy paused while the waiter set down my wine.

"Well, you're never going to believe this, but I slept with someone else."

"Oh my god, who?" My words belied my heart. For some reason, I wasn't surprised. Something about Suzy's enthusiasm for the wedding details failed to fully mask a restlessness I'd sensed in her.

She looked down, then back at me, with her glassy blue eyes. "Ty Villanueva."

"That black guy who was a year ahead of us?" My question was spiked with the thrill of the forbidden.

"Half black, half Mexican. It just happened. I didn't mean for it to, but it did. And it was wonderful." Her eyes lit up, and I could tell she meant it. "Oh my god, my Mom would kill me if she knew I slept with a black guy. She'd kick me out of the house! She'd disinherit me."

I sipped my wine and looked at her, waiting for her to say more. She'd fallen silent, lost in her thoughts.

"Suzy, do you love Sammy?"

She dropped her eyes to her engagement ring, twisting it on her finger. It shimmered in the dim bar.

"Yes. Yes, I do. But I just couldn't imagine getting married having had sex with only one guy. Well, two, if you count Chip Smith."

"Why wouldn't you count Chip Smith?"

"Because I was only a freshman and didn't have an orgasm."

I laughed, but then I noticed her eyes were brimming with tears.

"Suzy," I said in my *I've-known-you-for-a-long-time* voice. "Maybe you should postpone the wedding a year or so. Why do you have to get married this June?"

"My mom would kill me. She has everything all planned out."

"So? She'd get over it."

"The invitations are printed. The flowers ordered. And I love Sammy. I do. I love him. I do. I love him. So much."

That night, I lay in the dark in my bed, in my old bed in my parents' house, in my bedroom, or my old bedroom, or whatever it was. The bed seemed extra soft, and the window extra large. A shadow of an old, bent oak cast on the bedspread.

I almost reached over and picked up the phone to call Jack. Like a reflex. I'd spent so many nights in this bed, talking to him through the night. Sometimes I'd drift off, only to hear his voice through the receiver saying, "Norma, Norma, good night, hang up."

I'd wanted to talk to Suzy about Jack and Chuck, but she hadn't asked me a question about my life. We had spent the whole time talking about her life, her fling with Ty, her impending marriage to Sammy, her mother.

I shifted on my pillow. Dad's snores drifted up through the vent. It was like here, in Auburn, I was expected to be exactly who I was before I went away to college. Like I was stripped from the four months in the dorms, like all the people and experiences were a dream.

Grandma and Grandpa came for Christmas. The Christmas tree bent at a strange angle at the top, and Mary wasn't with us, but other than that, we did Christmas like usual. We went to midnight mass, and the next morning we all gathered in the living room and opened stockings, then presents. I settled into the familiarity like a sleepy baby into her bassinet.

We drank eggnog and played board games while Mom cooked, wearing her denim "Yay E.R.A." apron. Grandma beat each of us at Yahtzee, over and over. Grandpa finally gave up and read the newspaper. Dad played classical music on the stereo.

As usual, we had a turkey and ham dinner in the afternoon.

"Norma, tell us all about college," said Grandma, as she poured gravy over everything on her plate. She was a small woman, and I knew she'd eat only a few bites of the mound in front of her. Dad and Grandpa were digging in. They were so focused on eating I figured they wouldn't be good for much conversation.

"Well, it's great." I said. "It's fun."

Grandpa cleared his throat, something he did every few minutes, and poured himself some wine.

"What about your classes?" asked Grandma.

Chewing, everyone looked at me.

"Well, the semester's over, and I'll have new classes next semester." I liked the way that sounded, like I was an expert using specialized vocabulary about universities and fresh starts, an expert who sequestered herself away in libraries and turned page after page under golden light. What a lie. "But last semester, I really liked English." I took a bite of green jello salad, to stall.

"Tell us why you liked English," said Grandma, in her teacherly voice. She used to be a fifth-grade teacher.

"I had a great teacher. Linda."

"Linda?" said Grandma. "You call your professor Linda?"

"Yes, she asked us to."

"Well, I'll be. Okay, so tell us about this Linda."

"She had us write papers based on stuff in the newspaper, current events, things that interested us." I could feel the interest I'd had in the class resurging, accompanied by regret for being such a lousy student. I had never before been a lousy student, but now I'd proven one had lain dormant in me for eighteen years.

"Can you believe it, Mother?" said Mom, looking pretty in her red velvet blouse and silver earrings. "She didn't have to read any novels. In English class. Just the newspaper. That seems odd."

"What current events did you write about?" asked Grandma.

"The first one was on" . . . I tried to recall how Linda had talked about it so my grandmother would be impressed . . . "the irony of the media's focus on weddings. You know, like the, um, glorification of the wedding of Luke and Laura on *General Hospital*."

"You wrote about a soap opera in your English class?" Mom seemed genuinely irritated now. I was wondering if she was thinking she should have forced me to go to U.C. San Diego instead of Sac State.

"Yes. I got an *A*. And Linda read it to the class as an example of a really good paper."

"Bravo," said Grandma, clapping her tiny hands. "What were some of the topics of your other papers?"

I'd only written two others—one about myself and my interests, and the one about LSD. I took another bite of food, chewing, swallowing.

"Well, one was about drugs, and how they're bad and things."

Mom narrowed her eyes at me. Sometimes I felt like all the reading she did helped her see through things that fooled other people.

"I'd like to read that paper," Mom said.

"Okay," I said, as nonchalantly as possible. "It's in my dorm room, but I'll bring it home and show you some time."

Coming through the front door after shopping for white wedding shoes with Suzy, I heard my parents talking in the kitchen.

They were sitting at the table. Mom held a piece of paper in her hands. I knew right away something was wrong.

"Norma, please sit down," said Dad.

"What's going on?"

"Your grades came," said Mom.

My heart sank. I knew they had to be bad.

"Oh." I could feel my face blanch and my pulse race.

"I just can't believe this," said Mom, pushing the paper toward me.

C-minuses in English and Tennis. The rest F's.

"What's going on?" she demanded. Her voice shot up an octave. "Norma, answer me."

"Barbara," said Dad, placing his hand on her arm.

"You've never even gotten a C before!" Her eyes looked bloodshot.

"I know, I'm sorry." My skin was cold and clammy. I shivered.

"Is that it? You're sorry?"

"Barbara," said Dad.

Mom looked over at him, and then down at the table. I looked out the window at the big ghost pine, green against the gray sky. I'd never been such a failure. I couldn't explain the feeling, but I felt both like an ashamed little girl and a defiant grown-up. I'd made a mess of things, yes. But by messing them up, I was, oddly, claiming them as mine— mine to mess up, if I chose.

"Norma, now, please tell us, what's going on," said Dad.

"I don't know. It's all just so new. Everything's so different." I didn't know what I meant. Everything I could entertain saying felt partly true, partly false.

"We figured there'd be an adjustment period, moving away from home," said Dad. "But these grades. It's just not like you." He paused. "It's more like me."

"Stan. This isn't funny. At all. She's on academic probation. One more semester like this and she's kicked out of college."

We sat silent for a moment. I shivered again. It felt like my body was being shot through with a surge of electricity, like when they try to restart someone's heart. Dad began lightly drumming his fingers on the table. Thump, thump, thump—my heart.

"Did you ever find out who stole your typewriter?" asked Dad.

"The R.A. said he was working on it."

We fell silent again. A gust of wind blew, and tree limbs scraped the window.

"Norma?" said Dad.

"I'll do better, I promise," I said, cutting to the chase in hopes of ending this conversation as soon as possible. "I will. I promise." I thought of Linda saying, *Don't promise me, promise yourself.*

"How will you do better?" Mom asked. "What's going to change?" That was always Mom's move: *I have grave doubts about your promises.*

"I'll go to the library every day to study. It's just too loud in the dorms to concentrate. I promise. I'll go every day. I'll do better. I want to do better." The more I said it, the more I was beginning to convince myself.

"And call us," said Mom. "Every weekend."

"Okay," I said. "Okay, I will."

The French Lieutenant's Woman. Sophie's Choice.

I scanned my mother's bookshelf. It was New Year's Eve. My parents were at a party. I had been hoping to spend New Year's with Suzy, but she and Sammy flew to Seattle to visit his brother. I called a few other friends—Karen, Kay, Sheila—but they were out of town too.

Roots. The Exorcist. Jonathan Livingston Seagull.

Mrs. McMahon, our neighbor, had asked if I could baby-sit, but I'd lied and said I had plans. My parents had invited me to come with them to their party, but I had no interest in hanging out with a bunch of people my parents' age.

The Thorn Birds. Princess Daisy.

I pulled *Princess Daisy* off the shelf, fingered the gold embossed letters on the cover. I turned it over and read the back.

Men desired her. Women envied her. Daisy's life was a fairy tale filled with parties and balls, priceless jewels, money and love. Then, suddenly the fairy tale ended.

I put it back on the shelf.

How to Save Your Own Life, the sequel to *Fear of Flying*.

I grabbed it, thrilled. I hadn't known there were more of Isadora Wing's adventures. I poured a coke over ice and added a splash of rum from my parents' bar, then sat on the couch in my mother's spot overlooking the windows to the deck. The pool lights were on, illuminating the blue water in the dark night. I pulled an afghan over my legs and settled down to read.

Isadora had a lot of sex with a lot of different men. Sometimes several at once. And then she thought her husband was having an affair and was upset about it.

Isadora was writing a book about a woman who had sex with a lot of men.

Now Isadora was really upset. Years before, her husband had pressured her into taking his name when they'd gotten married. And now she realized if she divorced him, she could never completely shake him—his last name would always remain printed on the covers of her books.

He owned her, I thought. Is that what Suzy was getting herself into? But this wasn't the 1950's or 60's, I reminded myself. Times had changed. Marriage could be more equal, couldn't it? You didn't even have to change your name anymore.

Whooping and hollering filtered through the night from far away. Shouting, whistling. I looked at the clock. Midnight. It was now 1982.

I set down the book, stood and stretched. Picking up the phone, I dialed Jack's number.

You've reached Jack's. Leave me a message. Ciao.

We hadn't talked since the night we'd had sex on my birthday. He hadn't called me since, and this was my first attempt to contact him. It was almost a relief to get his machine because it felt good to slam down the phone on his voice.

Wrapping the afghan around me, I pulled open the sliding glass door and walked out on the deck. The cold night air stung my face. A half moon and thousands of stars shone in the clear, black sky. Dark leaves floated on the lighted pool water. Somewhere people whistled and banged pots and pans. A few firecrackers popped.

I thought of all the hot summers I swam for hours in this pool with my friends, my sister, and sometimes alone. I'd pull myself up out of the water then lie on the hot deck, the warm wood heating up my cool skin.

It seemed I always knew how to swim. I didn't remember learning. But I had a wisp of a memory of my father teaching me—not to swim, but to jump into the pool. I'd been afraid to do it. I'd always sat at the edge and dropped in, or walked down the steps.

I stood looking down at him, my father, water up to his waist, dark hairs thick on his chest, gleaming. My toes curled over the edge of the pool. He held out his arms to me.

Jump in. Jump in, Norma. You'll be fine. You know how to swim. I'm here. I'll catch you. Jump.

Chapter Fifteen — The Best Place in the World

Smoking a joint, Liz sat on my bed in white pants and a white blouse, wiggling her toes that stuck out of a battered, dirty knee-length walking cast.

"Aren't you ready yet?"

"The more you bug me the longer it's going to take," I said. I typed another sentence of my Psychology assignment. The professor hadn't asked for it to be typed, but I wanted to make a good first impression.

Liz held the joint to my lips and I took a hit. She sat back and continued to wiggle her toes. Music and voices screeched from the Billy-Goat Room.

"Jesus, aren't you overdoing it?" Liz demanded, more than asked. "It's only the first week of the semester."

I didn't answer, just continued typing. I was determined to resist Liz's attempts at derailing me, as much as they made me feel favored.

"What's this?" She lifted a paper off my desk and flipped through it. "You wrote a paper on doing LSD? And you got an *A*?"

She sat on my bed and read through it. The music from next door cranked up a notch.

"Finished!" I typed the final period.

Liz looked up from my paper on LSD. "Shit, girl, this is great. You make me want to drop acid."

"I can't believe you've never done it before."

"The idea freaks me out. I thought if you did it, next thing you knew you'd be in an alleyway begging someone to pay you for sex so you could get your next hit."

"How'd you know what I've been doing all winter break?" I joked.

"Very funny." She threw the paper at me and took another hit of her joint.

"Maybe Paul could get some for us," she said. "I could talk Benny into it. The four of us could do it together."

"Chuck's not talking to me." As soon as I said his name, a mix of frustration and desperation hit me.

Liz rolled her eyes. "God, when is he going to get over it? Have you seen him since break?"

"No," I said. "He's never in his room. It's like he's avoiding me."

"Maybe he'll be at the party," she said.

"I doubt it. He doesn't go to those things."

"Benny either. He just plays those damn videos on that Atari, I mean Re-tardi."

Liz and I joined the Quarters game in the Billy-Goat Room. I sat on the orange carpet, while she sat in Billy's chair, her cast propped up on his bed. I wanted to be there, to flaunt myself, to let Billy know he didn't intimidate me— even though he did a little. But he wasn't around. Goat was sitting next to me, when he sat. He kept jumping up to change the album, or to grab some more beer, or to dance a little jig when his quarter hit.

The drunker I got, the more I thought about Chuck. I wondered what he did over winter break. Did he go back to L.A.? I knew almost nothing about his family, except that he was an only child and his parents were divorced. When Chuck and I hung out together, he talked a lot—mostly about movies. But I didn't know much about what was deep inside him.

I thought I saw him across the room and almost stood up to go over to him, but it was some other guy in a baseball cap.

Liz had gotten up to hobble to the bathroom, or so she said, but she hadn't come back. That must have been over half an hour ago. I decided to go see if she was with Benny. Maybe Chuck would be there too.

When I stood up, Goat said, "Where're you going, Norma?"

"To find Liz."

"I'll come," he said, jumping up and almost losing his balance but catching himself agilely, like a cat.

I walked quickly out to the hall, hoping to lose Goat, but he caught up with me and grabbed my arm. I was dizzy.

"Norma," he said, his bloodshot eyes looking up at mine. He was two or three inches shorter than me. He buried his face in my neck and started kissing me, reaching under my shirt and stroking my breast.

"Knock it off," I said, trying to push him off, disgusted at him—and at myself for the twinge of guilt I felt at rejecting him. I had every right to say no.

"Why Norma? Come on." He pulled me to him and rubbed himself against me, burying his face in my neck and pulling at my hair.

"Stop it, Goat," I said, continuing to push at him. At the moment, I only wanted Chuck.

"I love it when you call me Goat," he said.

I pushed as hard as I could, and he fell backward, tripping over his feet like he was doing a new version of one of his jigs. He fell against the wall but remained standing. I ran as fast as I could down the hall and into the girls' bathroom. Someone was kneeling in a stall, retching.

My heart racing, I leaned against a sink. The retching stopped then started back up. In the mirror, my red hair looked wild, my eyes puffy. I washed my face then ran my wet fingers through my hair.

Two girls I didn't recognize came in, their arms around each other, laughing. They stood in front of the mirror and watched themselves laugh.

I opened the bathroom door and looked both ways down the hall, then shot out and ran up the stairs. I needed Chuck more than ever. At the top, a guy and a girl sat smoking.

"Hey," they said.

"Hey," I said, my best attempt at casual.

I knocked on Chuck and Benny's door. No answer. I tried the knob. Unlocked. I pushed the door open, slowly. It was dark. But I could hear what Liz and Benny were up to so I quietly shut the door.

On my way back down the stairs, I felt tears welling up in my eyes. Where was Chuck? What was he doing? Stacy had claimed she'd been invited to a party in another dorm. Was she with Chuck? I missed him. I missed him terribly. I missed our backgammon marathons, our spontaneous dancing, the way he let me sleep in the crook of his arm. I missed his soft skin, the way he smelled. I even missed watching black-and-white movies with him.

When I was almost to my room, Kirk greeted me in the hall.

"Hey Norma, *que pasa?*"

"Hi Kirk."

"Hey, wanna come smoke a doobie?"

I looked at his green eyes and thought about the cozy cave of his room. I wouldn't have to go back to my empty room, covering my head with a pillow to block out the sounds of the Billy-Goat party.

"All right."

In his room, Al Jarreau on the stereo, Kirk handed me a baggie of weed and the rolling papers. While he opened two beers for us, I tried to roll the joint, but the pot kept falling out, and then the paper tore.

"Here, I'll do it," he said, and took over, probably thinking that I was no Liz.

When he lit the joint, took a hit and passed it to me, I asked him, "So where's the best place you've ever been?"

"In the world?"

"Yeah, the best place in the world." I wanted him to tell me stories, to weave worlds of travel that I could participate in vicariously.

As he shifted next to me on the couch, his gold chain sparkled in the dim light and the alligator disappeared in a fold of his shirt.

"That's a hard one," he said. "Narrow it down."

"In Europe," I said. "The best place in Europe."

"That's tough."   White smoke drifted from his nose. "But I have to say, one of the most amazing places I've been is Mykonos, Greece. It's an island, a paradise."

"Warm blue water and white sand?" I asked.

"You know it.   Amazing topless beaches.   Fucking incredible.   You drink all day on the beach and party all night at the discos.   And the Greeks, man, they know how to live.   They're not all uptight like Americans.   It's looser. Anything goes."

It sounded like a Greek version of the dorms.   While I understood the enticing appeal of partying with foreigners, that wasn't the Greece I wanted.   I wanted the Greece of ancient ruins, of fragrant, hushed museums, of spirited cafes where I'd sit with my notebook and watch people.

I leaned my head back on the couch.   After all the drinking I'd done, and now smoking pot, I was suddenly very, very tired.   I wished I was in my own room, in bed, but I was too tired to get up.

We listened to Al Jarreau for a while, continuing to pass the joint back and forth, our feet up on the coffee table.

"Hey Norma."

"Yeah?"

"So does Liz like me?"

"I think so."

"I mean, is she into me?"

"I don't know."   I wished I could say yes, but it seemed cruel to bolster his hopes.

He took a hit of the joint then lay his head on the back of the couch, like mine.   White smoke drifted up.

"Is she really seeing that dorky guy with the glasses on the second floor?"

I closed my eyes and felt myself drifting, like I was a kite and someone else held the string.

"Norma? Is she?" His voice sounded far away.

"Kind of," I whispered.

It was quiet. Something clicked, soft music flooded my head, a man's voice. I was drifting, drifting.

Lips on my lips. Kissing. Soft, nice, warm kissing. Chuck.

Kissing, soft kisses, a body, warm, on mine, hands, soft. Chuck, Chuck.

It was dark. I blinked. Blinked again. A little light. A little more.

I was naked in a bed under soft sheets. I sat up. I could now see the outlines of the room, the bed, the bedside stand. I reached for the lamp and switched it on. Kirk's bedroom. I was alone in Kirk's bedroom.

I got up, accidentally knocking over a bong on the floor. An acrid stench shot up as the bong water spread over the carpet. I found my bra, my underwear and reached for them, my head throbbing as I bent down. In the living room, I found my jeans and blouse on the couch.

As I dressed, I kept expecting Kirk to appear. In his kitchen, I found a glass and drank some water. Where was he? Maybe doing rounds. I was relieved. I didn't want to pretend around him, to feel compelled to kiss him goodbye, or even to say *see you later*.

The hallways were quiet. In my room, my green digital clock read 3:30. Stacy made a little humming noise and rolled over as I undressed and climbed into my bed.

Chapter Sixteen — Vertigo

The third week of the semester, I was in my room, typing up the last page of my English paper, when my door flung open.

"What fresh hell is this?"

Chuck's voice filled the room. I turned around. Chuck stood with Benny in the doorway. My body flushed and my heart picked up its pace. I wanted to jump up and throw my arms around Chuck, to kiss his Charlie Brown face all over. But I restrained myself from acting in a way I normally wouldn't. Chuck was standing there like nothing had happened, like I'd never betrayed him. I thought it was best to duplicate his bearing. I couldn't believe he was standing in my room and talking to me, and I didn't want to risk scaring him away.

"Hi Norma," said Benny. His hair had grown back so well it almost looked the same as it had before the shaving incident. Chuck was wearing his usual baseball cap.

"You're doing homework on a Friday afternoon, Norma Jean?" said Chuck.

"I've turned over a new leaf."

"Eew, why would you want to do that?" Chuck grinned. He pulled three cigarettes from his pocket and lit all three, handing one to Benny and one to me. "So, we're on our way to San Francisco for the weekend. How would you like to join us? Two's company, three's a crowd, and we like it crowded."

Benny drove his family's old yellow Ford LTD that Chuck named Lurch. I was in heaven, sitting up front with Benny, Chuck sprawled out in the back, smoking. I took in every word we said, every look on Chuck's and Benny's faces, like someone who'd been lost in the wilderness and was recently rescued and given my first warm meal in weeks.

"Did you know James Bond had a Scottish mother and a Swiss father? That's one reason Connery, a Scot, was the best Bond."

"Well, what's Roger Moore?" asked Benny.

"Ee's a stinkin' Englishmun," said Chuck in a Cockney accent.

"And what about that guy you told me about," I asked, "the other one who played Bond once in, what was it, 1969?" I remembered Chuck telling me that the first night we'd met when he'd invited me into his room.

"Ding ding ding, you win the prize Norma Jean for a great memory! Yes, 1969 George Lazenby. He's, ugh, Australian."

"What's wrong with Australians?" asked Benny, peering up at the road signs.

"They're brutes," said Chuck.

I froze, remembering that word, "brute." It was what Chuck had called Jack after Jack barged into my room on my birthday. My face flushed, but as Chuck kept prattling on about James Bond trivia, I relaxed. Could he really have fully forgiven me?

As we drove over the bridge to the city, the fog was rolling in. The buildings of San Francisco rose up in the distance.

"Look, there's the Ferry Building," said Benny, "the pointy one with the clock. See it? See how small it is?" We peered out the windows. It was dwarfed by the other buildings on the skyline. "My mom says that was the tallest building in San Francisco when she was a little girl."

"This is so not L.A.," said Chuck. "Gray sky, not yellow." He rolled down his window. Cold air and traffic noise rushed in. My hair flew all around. "And smell that, children!" he yelled over the roar. "That's the smell of this thing called the ocean. We have one somewhere in L.A. too, I've been told!"

"It's the Bay!" yelled Benny.

Chuck leaned his body out the window, his arms spread. His cigarette flew out of his fingers, and his baseball cap flew off.

"And we're crossing the Golden Gate!" he screamed.

"The Bay Bridge!" corrected Benny.

"And this place has its own song! Hit it, Norma!" he shrieked.

It took me a second but then I broke out singing, with all my might, *When the lights go down in the city, and the sun shines on the Bay* . . .

"No, no, no!" yelled Chuck. His face was pink from the wind. "Tony Bennett, my dear, Tony Bennett!"

And so I sang, with a joy spreading out to my toes and fingers, as though I were sprouting feathers: *I left my heart in San Francisco . . .*

Benny's house was one of those prototypical San Francisco Victorians, squeezed in a row of other Victorians painted pastel pinks and blues and yellows, perched on a steep hill. Mr. and Mrs. Moss seemed thrilled we were there. They put Benny and Chuck in Benny's room, and me in the guest room.

"So tell us," said Mr. Moss, his bald head shining in the dining room light, "does Benny have a sweetheart in his life?"

I looked at Chuck and took a bite of rice. Mrs. Moss had cooked us Mexican food for dinner, complete with virgin Margaritas.

"Dad," said Benny, blushing.

"Our friend Liz is pretty hot for him," said Chuck.

"Liz?" said Mr. Moss, grinning his gentle Grinch grin.

"You're embarrassing your son," said Mrs. Moss, sliding another cheese enchilada onto Benny's plate.

"No, Benny doesn't mind, really," said Chuck, sipping his virgin Margarita. "Wow, this is great, Mrs. Moss."

"Call me Rita, please." She smiled at him, tucking her dark hair behind her ear, a small diamond earring flashing.

"You'd love Liz like a daughter, Rita. She would have come with us, but she had a sorority event to attend."

"Oh, a sorority girl," said Mr. Moss. "A sorority girl." He dipped a chip in salsa.

"She's not what you think," said Benny, pushing his glasses up the bridge of his nose. "But she's really nice."

Chuck kicked me under the table. I looked down at my food and suppressed a smile.

"What do you mean she's not what we think? What makes you think we think something?" said Mr. Moss.

"What I think Benny means," said Chuck, "is that she's rather outgoing. A pistol, in fact. A nice balance to your shy Benny."

"My Benny, shy?" said Mrs. Moss. She giggled. "He's just got his face buried in a video game so often that you forget he has things to say. But he's not shy."

"Would you all please stop talking about me like I'm not here?" Benny said, a force to his voice I'd never heard before. He was perched on the edge of his chair, a salsa stain on his white tee-shirt.

"To change the subject," said Chuck, "one of my favorite films of all time was made in this city."

"Which one?" I asked.

"Guess."

"*Vertigo*," said Mrs. Moss. "Alfred Hitchcock."

"A lady after my own heart," said Chuck, grinning at her.

She tilted her head and smiled back. Was it my imagination, or was she flirting with him?

"Have you been to Mission Dolores, Paul?" she asked. "That's where Carlotta Valdez's headstone was, until they removed it because, well, too many tourists. Not very respectful to the dead."

"I can't believe you didn't tell me your mother is a film buff, Benny!" Chuck took a vigorous swig of his virgin Margarita. "No, Rita, I haven't been to Mission Dolores. It's tragic. I've only been through this city, and quickly I might add, a few times before. Perhaps tomorrow you could take us on a tour? To Mission Dolores and the California Palace of the Legion of Honor, where Kim Novak so hauntingly stares at the tragic painting of the beautiful Carlotta Valdez?"

"Oh, I wish we could," said Mrs. Moss, her voice suddenly sounding much younger, like that of a girl's. "But we're attending Benny's cousin's wedding tomorrow, remember? That's why we asked him to come home this weekend."

"Ah yes," said Chuck. "Alas. Well, another time, then?"

"It would be my pleasure." Again she tucked her hair behind her ear.

Mr. Moss clapped his hands. "How about a game of Monopoly, everyone?"

Chuck kicked me under the table again.

"That sounds delightful," Chuck said, "but I'm exhausted. I've been up every night this week, studying. I'm taking a monster Chemistry class."

"You are?" asked Benny.

"Yes, speaking of monsters, with the lab hours alone you'd think I could create Frankenstein's monster by the end of the semester."

"Well, we did have a late dinner," said Mrs. Moss. "Look, it's almost 9 p.m. You children must be exhausted from the drive. Frank, we can play tomorrow night."

In Benny's room, Chuck opened the window and rolled a joint. We all sat on Benny's bed and smoked and talked. Soon I looked over and saw Benny had fallen asleep.

Quietly, Chuck and I moved to the floor. We sat cross-legged, facing each other on top of his sleeping bag.

"I think Mrs. Moss has the hots for you," I whispered to Chuck, who was rolling another joint.

"She certainly seemed rather frisky," he said. "She's probably ravishing Mr. Moss now as we speak."

"Eww, thanks for the visual." I crumpled my mouth like I'd just eaten a lemon.

Benny made a sound and turned in bed.

Chuck lit the joint and we passed it back and forth in silence. Benny's room had a desk, dresser, and a bookshelf sagging with books. Towers of comic books leaned on the floor at the foot of his bed.

Chuck's hair had grown back in almost as well as Benny's. I remembered the first time I'd seen Chuck in the hallway last semester, how he'd been wearing his baseball cap and had invited me in for a glass of wine. At the time I'd thought he was cute. But since then he'd grown handsome, now that I knew his quirks and his ways of talking. I knew what made him angry, and that he had compassion enough in his heart to forgive my huge, stupid mistakes. I'd never known anyone like him. I knew he had depths that he'd only allow a someone special to see. I wanted to be that someone special. I wanted to get lost in his depths.

I leaned forward and kissed him. He kissed me back, his hands in my hair. He tasted and smelled smoky. The essence of Chuck.

When we pulled back from the kiss, he whispered in my ear, "You better get to bed, Norma Jean."

"Can't I just sleep here with you?" I whispered back.

"I don't think that's a good idea."

Reluctantly I stood and walked down the hall to the guest room, passing Mr. and Mrs. Moss's bedroom. Smiling at the thought of her ravaging her husband, I thought I may have heard a little noise coming from behind the closed door, but I wasn't sure.

"So this is Coitus Tower," said Chuck.

"Coit Tower," I corrected him.

"Hitchcock said he included it in background shots of *Vertigo* as a phallic symbol, so I think it deserves the name Coitus Tower."

"Whatever you say," I said gleefully.

Inside, we walked around, gazing at the Depression-era murals.

"Now these are strapping, muscular people," said Chuck, commenting on the stylized paintings. "Their appendages are grotesquely well-developed. If they weren't clothed, it would probably be frightening."

At the top of the tower we stared at the view of the blue and white city below. It was a clear, windy day. As I looked down the hill, down at the city, down to the bay, I felt a familiar twinge of something in me—something that irrationally prodded me to jump, as though I could fly through or float in this lake of a sky. I thought of my father standing in the pool. *Jump, Norma, jump.*

"What a city, Norma Jean!" Chuck shouted. "Top O the World!"

Two tourists on the other side of the tower, a man and a woman, looked over.

I grabbed his hand. "Shh, Chuck, you can't go screaming all over San Francisco."

"What a shame," he said, pulling on my hand, taking me back to the tiny, creaky elevator run by an old guy with no teeth. As we exited, Chuck said, "I wouldda tipped him a nickel, but he couldn't have bitten it to see if it was real."

At Fort Point, we stood on the rocks and stared up at the Golden Gate Bridge.

"This is where Kim Novak jumps into the water, and Jimmy Stewart saves her. Water-soaked blouse, now that's a time-honored tradition. Her bazooms get star treatment, let me tell you."

The wind whipped my hair in my face. I gathered it with one hand and imagined leaping into the water, my hair flying.

"I don't know Kim Novak. Is she beautiful?"

"Is the Golden Gate Bridge golden? Actually, it's more orange than golden. Well, you get my drift." He took a drag on his cigarette.

"Why is it," I said, "someone gawky with a long neck that looks like it can barely support his head—Jimmy Stewart I mean—why can he be a movie star, but the women have to have big tits and perfect faces?"

"That's not at all a fair description of Jimmy Stewart."

"And wasn't he kind of old by the time *Rear Window* was made—too old to be Grace Kelly's boyfriend? Why don't you ever see older women with younger men?"

"What about *The Graduate*?"

"But that's what the whole movie was about! They made a big deal out of it. It's not made a big deal when the man's an old geezer and the woman a prom queen."

"Norma Jean, you are quite the astute feminist critic. Now quit spoiling my favorite movies, and let's go have a drink."

Bundled up in our coats, we sat in an open-air restaurant, eating clam chowder and drinking beer. Just like when I'd come to the city with Jack, Chuck and I weren't carded. I wondered about that—that somehow being with a man made people think I was older. I hadn't thought about Jack while being with Chuck, but now being near Fisherman's Wharf was forcing memories on me: Jack and me eating sourdough bread, him buying me a key chain, and us making out in the car in the parking garage. Foolish. I pushed the memories aside.

"Chuck," I said. "Where have you been lately? I come by your room all the time, but you're hardly ever there."

Taking a sip of soup, he looked at me over the spoon. "I made some off-campus friends. I met them in one of my classes. They have a house downtown, and we hang out and party there."

"Oh," I said. I was hoping he'd say he'd take me there some time, but he didn't. I wondered if one of these "friends" was a girl he had a thing for. Or maybe he took Stacy with him. I felt raw, vulnerable. I was too afraid to probe.

"The dorms get old, sometimes, Norma Jean. Don't you think? The same parties, the same dramas, all within the confines of that oppressive, dreary building. I mean, my god, the carpet is orange."

"I know. It shocked me when I first saw it," I said. "The college must have gotten a deal on it."

"No doubt."

We sat in silence, sipping our beers, watching people and cars go by. Pink-cheeked tourists bustled about in the cold, rubbing their hands together.

"What's your mom like?" I asked.

"What do you mean?"

"Well, is she nice? Do you get along with her?"

"She pretty much leaves me alone, and I leave her alone. It's an unspoken agreement." His voice was clipped and tight. It was clear he didn't want to talk about this.

I finished my beer and looked at him. He was staring out into the street. I wanted to know more, but I didn't know what else to ask or how, without upsetting him.

"Oh my god," said Chuck. "Look at the leather queens."

"The what?"

"There, on the motorcycle."

Two men wearing all black roared by on a Harley dressed in studded leather jackets, chaps, and big heavy boots. I wouldn't have thought anything about it if Chuck hadn't said something. I'd never heard men called "queens" before. The idea of a male queen was comical to me; I pictured a bearded man wearing a tiara.

"Fags," he said. "Now we've had the complete San Francisco experience."

Chapter Seventeen — Buzz Kill

"Now Norma, don't get upset," said Stacy the minute I walked in the door Sunday afternoon, returning from the San Francisco trip. She was wearing her bathrobe, her hair up in a towel.

"What?" I said, my eyes going right to my typewriter. It was there and seemed fine.

"Well, look."

She pointed to the full-length mirror on my closet door. Someone had etched "WHORE" into it.

I sank to my bed and put my head in my hands.

"I'm just so sick of this," I said quietly.

"I know, I know," said Stacy. "And it's my fault, I'm so sorry. I forgot to lock the room when I left to go to the movies on Saturday night. When I came back, I saw it. I reported it to Kirk. At least there's nothing as horrible as pee on the bed or a missing typewriter."

"Gee, always look at the bright side, huh?" I heard the sharp edge to my voice: defiant, ashamed, and deflated at all once. Stacy flushed. "I'm sorry," I said. "It's just that this is getting really old. Really, really old."

"I know, I know."

"I'm going to do something to that asshole."

"Who?"

"Billy."

"It's not Billy," she said.

"How do you know?"

"I asked him."

"You asked him? And you thought he'd just come out and tell you the truth? 'Uh, Stacy, I'm sorry, I'm a burglar and a thief, and I like to destroy people's property and reputations.'"

She sat on her bed and pulled off the towel, her wet hair draping her shoulders. "Not exactly. But I told him someone was doing something very hurtful to you. He admitted he's not your biggest fan—"

"Oh great."

"But listen. He swore up and down he had no idea what I was talking about, and I believe him. I do. And there's more."

"How would he like it if I wrote up posters about his outrageous dick size and hung them all over the halls?"

"His what?" Stacy's eyes got big.

"His outrageously huge dick," I said, savoring the reaction I saw in Stacy's expression. "I slept with him once. Stacy, he's a monster."

She broke out into convulsions of laughter. "Really?" she shrieked. "Really?"

I looked down at the floor, pleased yet ashamed at sharing such a confidence. "I shouldn't have told you that. Don't tell anyone else, okay?"

"Scout's honor," she said. "Now listen, you didn't let me finish." She paused. "How huge is 'outrageously huge'?"

"It wouldn't fit all the way in."

"Oh my god!" She laughed and laughed, and finally I couldn't help it, I joined in. I'd never seen her laugh like this before. Her face bloomed pink. Finally she stopped and wiped her eyes, smearing her mascara. "Okay, well here's the thing," she said. "Billy told me he was going to do me a favor and ask around to see if he could find out who's doing all these things to you."

"He did?"

"Yes, but don't tell him you know. He said he's doing it for me, not for you."

"Great. He probably wants to get into your pants."

"Well, that's already been established," she said. "But I'm not interested, and he knows it. We're friends, that's all, just friends. And with what you just told me about—well, about how he's so well-endowed, sounds like a good thing." She giggled. I was surprised to hear her joke this way and to speak so matter-of-factly about sex. She usually didn't say much about sex. Maybe with my crack about Billy I'd opened the door, inviting our friendship to move to a deeper level.

She stood and began combing out her hair.

"Is that what you are with Chuck, too?" I asked. "I mean, Paul."

"What?"

"Friends. Or are you more?"

She glanced at me then turned to her mirror, as though she were avoiding my eyes, as though the door I thought I'd just opened slammed shut. Something, it seemed to me, was going on.

"Just friends," she said.

I tried to focus on reading and highlighting my textbook, but music from the Billy-Goat Room was thumping, and people were shouting and laughing. Irritated by the noise, Stacy had taken off somewhere. I knew I should pack up my stuff and go to the library, but I figured I couldn't focus anyway as agitated as I was about being called a "whore," and about someone actually going to the lengths of engraving it on my mirror. I imagined a man's thick, hairy hand taking the time and effort to push a knife into my mirror, carefully carving out each letter. It felt violent, beyond threatening, like someone truly wanted to do me harm.

"Norma, come join us, the party's fun! People are dancing!" shouted Liz, as she came into my room, a beer in her hand. "Even Benny and Chuck are there!"

"They are?"

"Yeah, I talked them into coming. We're having fun." She looked at herself in Stacy's mirror then grabbed Stacy's brush and ran it through her hair.

"But I don't want to be around either Billy or Goat," I said.

"They're not there," she said. She set down the brush and pulled lip gloss out of her pocket, rolling it on her lips. "They took off with a couple of chicks. Come on! But here, take one of these first." She put the lip gloss down and dug into her pocket for something else. She handed me a yellow pill.

"What is it?"

"I'm not sure. Kirk said they're kind of like Quaaludes, but better. He just handed them to me. Let's each take one."

If it would help me stop obsessing about a knife carving into my mirror, I was all for it. We drank them down with her beer. Then I brushed out my hair, changed my shirt, and joined her.

The music was so loud in the Billy-Goat Room, I didn't hear Chuck yell "Norma Jean!"—but I could tell he had by the way his lips moved. People were jumping on Goat's and Billy's beds and dancing all around. Chuck stood in a corner with Benny. I went up to them and kissed them both on the cheek.

"I had a great time in the city, thanks!" I yelled.

"What?" said Benny.

"She had a great time!" shouted Chuck. "She's thanking us for taking her to San Francisco."

"You're welcome!" yelled Benny. His eyes wandered over to where Liz danced with Kirk. I grabbed both Benny's and Chuck's hands and began dancing with them. I saw Kirk leave the room, and soon, Liz joined us, handing us all bottles of beer.

We danced together, laughing and drinking. The pill I'd taken was washing warm through my body. I felt light, like my body was a cloud you could pass your hand through. I looked at Liz and Benny and Chuck and realized my birthday wish had come true—that we'd continue to be together, loving each other. It had just taken some turmoil and a little time.

"Whoo hoooo!" yelled a bunch of male voices.

I turned around and saw a girl with short blonde hair and a denim mini-skirt dancing on top of Goat's desk.

"Take it off!" yelled a couple of the guys.

The girl continued to dance, gyrating her hips, and then slowly she peeled her shirt off over her head. The guys went crazy, yelling and grabbing at her legs. She lost her balance for a second and they backed off. She kissed the air in their direction and kept dancing in her lacy bra and skirt.

"Take it off!" yelled the guys again.

She peeled off her skirt and danced in her underclothes, smiling down at the guys grabbing at her. A guy jumped up on the desk next to her and pulled off his shirt, revealing a barrel chest. He moved his body against hers. They gyrated together and he ran his hands up and down her body.

Then he reached around and unsnapped her bra and pulled it off, waving it over his head, whooping with the guys below. The girl stopped dancing and stepped back, her hand over her breasts. The barrel-chested guy threw her bra to the crowd then wrapped his arms around her. She tried to push him away.

"Oh shit," I said, anxiety pulsing through me.

The barrel-chested guy bear-hugged the girl and pulled her off the desk, a group of guys surrounding them.

"This is not good," said Chuck. By now the guys had formed a clump that made it hard to see what was going on. Chuck squeezed through the crowd and ran out of the room and in seconds reappeared with Kirk.

Kirk muscled into the ring of guys. The roaring music snapped off.

"Now guys, can't you see she's had enough?" said Kirk, pushing up next to the girl and putting his arm around her. Her face was white, her hair clinging to her sweaty face.

A minute ago, the guys looked like a pack of lions going in for the kill. Now, to my surprise, they backed off. Someone handed the girl her shirt and she held it to her chest, eyes down. Kirk put his arm around her and led her out.

"Asshole," said the barrel-chested guy, shoving Chuck backward.

"Peace," said Chuck, putting up his hands and backing out of the room. I ran after him, Liz and Benny in tow.

"Chuck! Are you okay?" I asked.

"I'm fine," he said.

"You were great!" I reached over to touch his arm.

"See why I don't go to these fucking parties?" he said, jerking his arm away.

"Are you mad at me?"

"No, no." He leaned over and kissed my forehead. "I'm going to bed, Norma Jean." To my disappointment, he didn't invite me to join him, just took off upstairs. Benny followed him.

"That's a buzz-kill," said Liz. "Although I'm definitely still buzzing. Look, I can't feel a thing." She slapped her arm. "Can you?"

I pinched myself and didn't feel it.

"How strange," I said. I slapped my leg, my arm, my face. Nothing.

"Pinch me," said Liz. "On the arm, right here, hard as you can."

I did. "Anything?" I asked.

"Nope."

She did the same to me.

"Wow, I could fucking have surgery right now!" shouted Liz, laughing. "Follow me!" She moved quickly down the hallway, limping on her now cast-free leg. I ran after her, my head floating. It was the oddest sensation to run without feeling my feet.

Liz picked up her pace and slammed right into the wall at the end of the hall. I followed suit.

"Holy crap! This is amazing!" she yelled.

We slammed our whole bodies into the wall some more. Over and over.

"Follow me!" Liz said.

We ran through the lobby, past the bone-crushing vending machine, past the white guy and black guy playing Space Invaders, and out the glass doors, into the dark night air, past the lawn and to the asphalt walkway.

"Take off your shoes!" she shouted. We did, and threw them down. We ran along the lighted walkway like wraiths, twisting around the dorm buildings and over to the main campus. A few streetlights spotted the dark college grounds.

We ran building to building, punching the walls, slapping the lamp posts, not feeling a thing. I was breathing hard, but I felt light as a feather, a kite.

"Whheeee!" shouted Liz as we rounded the corner of the gym. We stopped at a chain-link fence surrounding the pool. The dark water sparkled, illuminated by the moon.

"Want to?" she asked.

"Why not?" I answered.

We scrambled over the chain-link fence, threw off our clothes, and dove into the pool. For a few seconds, it felt like flying.

Then the cold February water seized my chest, taking my breath away. I tried to say something, but I couldn't. I swam to the side of the pool and watched Liz take a lap to the deep-end.

She did a swimmer's flip, pushed off the side, and swam lap after lap. I held my breath and plunged down into the dark water, weightless in the foreign quiet. When I surfaced, Liz's splashes sparked up like fireflies in the black night.

The next day, Liz and I were so bruised and sore from the soles of our feet to the tops of our heads that we stayed in bed all day. Stacy brought me two sandwiches and a diet soda. I asked her if she'd bring one of the sandwiches to Liz. When she narrowed her eyes at me but agreed to do so, I knew that she hadn't forgotten what Liz had done, but she had forgiven her.

That night, Liz hobbled downstairs and leaned next to me on my bed, propping her swollen ankle on pillows. Chuck hooked up the Betamax, and Benny brought white wine, and, along with Stacy, we watched *Vertigo*, Chuck reciting the best lines and pointing out each San Francisco location he and I had visited together.

Chapter Eighteen — Sleep of the Dead

"How can you say there are no good topics to write about?" said Linda, waving a newspaper in her hand. She was frustrated with the class because students had been complaining that they didn't know what to write about.

I was taking her for my second semester of English, in part because I wanted to prove to her, and myself, that I was better than a C student. I tried to follow her advice, to promise myself I'd do better, but I couldn't get my parents' disappointment and anger out of my head. Whenever I thought about homework, I heard their words and saw their pinched faces across from me at the kitchen table. The only way to push that memory away was to imagine myself alone on an airplane bound for another country, the wing lights blinking blue in the night.

"When you say there are no good topics, you're saying the world is boring. The whole world!" Although we had to write more pages this semester, Linda assigned similar papers—to write about an event in the world and talk about its significance and how it connected to us.

"How many of you knew that in December, the first American test-tube baby was born?"

No one raised a hand. I had seen something about that in the paper, but I didn't raise my hand either. Linda's intensity scared me a little, although it fascinated me at the same time. I wanted to watch her in action, but I didn't want to get in the middle of something that could turn into a battle.

Linda's chest rose and fell, her big gold earrings rocking back and forth, the armpits of her baby-blue blouse darkening.

She pointed to a lanky Asian guy in the front row. "What do you think of test-tube babies?"

"Well, I don't know," he said.

"If two people can't have a baby, do you think science should get involved?"

"I don't know. Maybe." I felt for the guy. I wouldn't have known what to say either. I wondered if everyone else in class was as relieved as I was that they weren't the person Linda was picking on.

A girl near the window raised her hand. "I think it's against God," she said. The way she said it made me feel that she knew something I didn't.

"Okay!" Linda looked relieved. "Say more!"

"Well, if a woman gets pregnant, it's God's will. If she doesn't, that's God's will too. Science shouldn't mess around with what God has planned for people."

I wondered how this girl knew God's will. It seemed like she was God's therapist, that she knew His mind forward and backward.

"Okay, thank you," said Linda. "Now does anyone disagree with that?"

A few hands shot up. "Hey, not everyone believes in God," said a girl in the back. I wished I'd said that—although I wasn't sure if I believed in God or not. It seemed strange to believe or disbelieve in another being. That being either existed or didn't—my belief had nothing to do with it.

"Or maybe," said another, "God made scientists to help out people who can't have babies." The logic of this comment appealed to me—using the God-girl's lingo against her. I thought that Chuck would laugh at that one.

"Okay," said Linda, pointing to the God-girl who was slumping in her chair, frowning. "The idea that science should not interfere with procreation—you could write about that. It's a strong topic. You could probably make a very good argument. And how do you do that? You think about the people who disagree with you—someone who says," and she pointed to the atheist-girl, "not everyone believes in God. You'd address that—how?"

"Well, God's everywhere," said the God-girl, "like on our money, in our Constitution. He's always been part of our laws and always should be."

The God-girl was getting on my nerves. She was like God's cheerleader, all peppy and happy, ignoring His possible faults—but I didn't know enough about God to say anything.

"Good!" exclaimed Linda. "The only way to make a convincing argument is to take into consideration the other side. Address it and argue against it."

"Do we always have to argue?" asked the lanky Asian guy. "I mean, what if we just want to write?"

"On what, for example?" Linda handed him the newspaper. "Find something. Anything."

He glanced at the paper, turned a few pages.

"The 49'ers. I think it's cool that they beat the Bengals in the Superbowl. What about that?"

"Well, who cares about football?" said Linda. "Isn't it a waste of time and money? Don't the players get paid way too much? What's the big deal about a bunch of guys trying to run each other over?"

"That's not what football's about," he said, sitting defensively back in his chair. "It takes, I don't know . . ."

"Skill?" asked Linda. "Perseverance?"

"Yeah."

"You have to realize that not everyone cares about the things you care you about. So help us understand why they matter. But what's more important is that you do care about something. In fact, that's your homework for tonight. Write a list of ten things you really care about, off the top of your head—anything: family, friends, events. Then take a look at the newspaper, and write down ten events in the paper that matter to you. Anything. Just show me that you give a damn about something, okay?"

"Help me!" I shouted. Stacy looked up from her bed, startled. She was leaning against her pillows, filing her nails. "I have to write a list of ten things I care about, and I don't know what they are. What do I care about?"

"What are you doing?" she asked.

"My English homework."

"That's weird. You have to write a list?"

"And all I have so far is, my family and friends."

"Maybe you should say your dad as one, your mom, and your sister. Then list out the names of seven friends, and you're done."

"Argh!" I clicked my pen up and down.

"What about partying? You seem to be pretty into that. Fiddling around with your consciousness."

"Very funny." I put my head on my desk. "Besides, I already wrote a paper last semester on taking LSD."

"Hey, turn it in again!" said Stacy.

"Same teacher. I can't. Besides, she wants a list, not a whole paper."

"Oh." She was silent for a moment. "Well think about things you like. What do you like?"

"Friends, movies, books, blah blah. I'm a nothing. I'm boring. I have no life."

"I think you care about love," she said.

I turned my head, laying the opposite cheek on my desk so I could look at her out of the corner of my eye.

"Love?"

"Yeah. Think about it. You're searching after the right guy."

"I am?"

"That's why you've been hanging onto Jack for so long. You believe in love. The perfect love. The one."

I felt a little stung when she said I'd been hanging onto Jack. I sat up. "That's gross," I said. "Just gross." I hated to think that guys were the center of my existence. Was that really how I acted?

She set down her nail file and picked up a bottle of nail polish and shook it. "I think that's what everyone cares about, really. Finding the right person. We all think there's someone out there who can complete us, make us whole."

"A woman doesn't need a man to make her whole," I said. "I don't think. Maybe. Shit, who knows."

"I believe there's someone for everyone," said Stacy.

"Is that guy who went to the East coast school—do you think he's the one for you?"

"Ted?"

"Yeah."

"No. I really don't."

"You sound so sure."

"I am."

"How can you be so sure of anything? I think I stay with Jack, not because I believe in love, but because I don't have a clue if I do or not. I'm sure about nothing. In *Vertigo*, Jimmy Stewart was sure that Madeline was the one for him, he was certain—he was obsessed—and look where that got him."

"That's a movie. Don't tell Paul I said so—I wouldn't want to burst his bubble—but movies aren't life."

"Yeah, life is affairs and high divorce rates and spousal murder," I said, thinking about everything I'd been reading in the paper lately as I perused articles for Linda's class.

"Norma," said Stacy, stroking the pink nail-polish brush across her thumbnail, "you are way too young to be this cynical."

I gave up on the list and left the room, not sure where I was going—just allowing myself to escape my homework for the first time this semester. I wasn't sure what felt better: finishing homework or willfully abandoning it. I wandered the halls, peeked into some open rooms, waved at a few people who were sitting around. In the lobby, I watched the black guy and white guy play Space Invaders. I bought some potato chips from the evil vending machine. Then I walked upstairs to Chuck and Benny's room.

Benny looked up from his video game.

"Hey Norma."

"Hi Ben. Where's Chuck?"

"Don't know. Haven't seen him all day. Want to play Frogger?"

"No thanks," I said.

He pushed a button on his video controls then looked up at me. "Norma, can I ask you a question?"

"Okay."

"Does Liz like me?"

"Of course she likes you, Benny."

"How much?"

"I think she likes you a lot. What do you think?"

"It's hard to tell sometimes."

"Yeah," I said. "I know what you mean. Can I ask you a question?"

"Okay."

"Does Chuck like me?"

"Of course," he said. Benny blushed. Crimson crawled up his temples and down his neck. At first I tried to ignore it. Then I tried to see if I could figure out what it meant. But it was like trying to read a palm. I knew nothing about life-lines and had no idea how to decipher such a message.

The week before Spring Break, Liz insisted the four of us drop acid together. We sequestered ourselves in Chuck and Benny's room, and Chuck dimmed the lights and opened the beers.

"I may not find out the meaning of the universe, but this is certain to raise some questions," said Liz. "Quote unquote, Norma Rogers."

"Wow, it feels good to be quoted," I said, smiling.

"What's this music?" asked Benny.

"*Inna-Gadda-Da-Vida*, the best tripping music in history," said Chuck. "Scientifically verifiable."

We sat on the floor on pillows in a circle. Settled in and ready for another amazing acid trip, I wanted to light candles, but Chuck said that wasn't a good idea unless we wanted to end up in the Burn Unit.

"I'd probably get kicked out of the Delta Thetas if they knew I was doing this," said Liz.

"You would?" I asked. "Why?"

"They have their rules. No drugs, for example."

"No drugs! But what about pot? And Quaaludes? And those yellow pills?"

"Nope. They don't know about any of that. The only thing they know about, because they pass it out, is speed. All the girls take it. Helps with dieting, you know."

"How is that not a drug?" I asked.

"Diet pills, dear. What you call them is what they are."

"How long does this take?" asked Benny.

"Are we there yet, Dad?" said Chuck simulating a bored child's voice. "Here, have a cigarette, Ben. Relax. Enjoy." Chuck lit two cigarettes and handed one to Benny.

"Whoa," said Benny. "Do you all see the tip of the cigarette, the way it snakes red in the air like that?"

"You're already seeing trails, Benny," I said. I moved my hand in front of my face. I wasn't.

"Scratch your scalp," said Chuck. We all scratched our scalps.

"Oooh, amazing," said Liz.

"What, what?" I asked.

"Don't you feel it?" she said. "It tingles all over. More than tingles. It's like a rainfall for your head."

I tried it again. Nothing.

"Can you ever get a bum hit, one that doesn't work?" I asked Chuck, worried I wasn't going to be able to experience this trip with my friends.

"Relax," said Chuck. "It'll happen." He lay back on his elbows, staring off into space. The long drum solo played like a heartbeat. I could feel the rhythm in my spine. Liz lay back on the floor, her head on the pillow.

"Wow," she said.

Everything felt soft. The air was soft, my skin, the drums. The floor began to ripple. I was on a magic carpet, floating. Up high, higher and higher.

A huge face loomed over me, a gun emerging from the shadows, pointing at me.

"Oh shit," I said, or thought I did. Everything echoed.

I held up my hand, against the gun. My palm spread, my fingers grew, faster and faster, looping together, hanging like dead flesh. I shook my hand, which felt like a long, drooping glove. I looked away. The ground rippled and crawled.

I had to get to Chuck. He was so far away. I had to creep to him. I creeped and crawled, creeped and crawled, holding onto the undulating floor.

"Chuck."

"Norma—" he said, but the wind blew the words away. Everything echoed and echoed and echoed through me. I was a shell, hollow.

Chuck, Chuck. I crawled to him, his face, his face, melting skin, skull, skull, his blue hollow eyes, his red hollow eyes. Turn my head, turn my head, look away, streaks of orange.

Liz, Liz, where are you, find you, crawl to you, shaking ground, caving in, crawl and crawl and crawl to her. Liz, flat, crushed, run over, crushed.

No, no, no. No, no, no, no . . . .

My roaring head lay in Chuck's lap. He stroked my hair.

"Norma, how are you feeling?" he whispered.

"I don't know." I was shaking, shivering. "I'm cold." I felt I'd fallen into a mine shaft or a well and had just been pulled out.

He reached back and took a blanket off the bed and spread it over me. The blanket streaked through the air with a soft, reverberating whoosh.

Liz and Benny lay on Benny's bed, asleep.

"What time is it?" I asked.

"4 a.m."

I tried to think for a minute. Patterns like amoebas shifted in the air.

"Ten hours?" I said.

"Yeah. You had a bad time."

"I know." I'd seen his face as a skull and Liz crushed flat as though a truck had run over her. "Did you?"

"No, I was okay. You freaked out Liz a little, but I told her to think of blue flowers, and she relaxed."

"How could you do that when you were tripping?"

"Experience."

"And look, they're asleep," I said. "I'm so wired right now there's no way I could sleep."

"You had a bad trip. Happens sometimes. And I blew it. I forgot to face Bond to the wall."

"That's okay," I said, my skin tight with the leftover creepiness that haunts you after a nightmare. Somehow it seemed like the bad trip was my fault—that it was part of the accumulation of things I was doing wrong. I nestled into the shelter, the comfort of Chuck's lap. "I think it was me. It was just me."

I was still jittery when I went back downstairs around noon. Walking into my room, I encountered Jack leaning back in my desk chair, his legs crossed. He was wearing a brown velour shirt, jeans, and cowboy boots. I should have been shocked to see him, but I wasn't. His appearance seemed normal, like an emerging wisdom tooth that pinches and pinches at your gums and then, one day, you see it's come through.

"Norma," he said.

"Jack." I smoothed my hair with my hands. "What are you doing here?"

"Your roommate let me in. But she had to take off. She said I could wait. Man, why didn't you tell me you had such a hot roommate?"

I sat on the bed, facing him. Something seemed strange, and I realized it was that we hadn't kissed or even touched each other. Even when it was months since we'd seen each other, we always greeted each other with a kiss or hug.

"How long have you been waiting?" I asked.

He looked at his watch. "Not long."

"What's going on?"

"I wanted to come tell you myself," he said. "I would have called or written a letter, but I didn't want to be a chicken-shit."

My head echoed with memories of the acid trip, reverberations, hallucinations, Chuck's and Liz's distorted faces, Chuck's warm hand smoothing my hair. Jack's and my voices had an odd quality, like I'd been swimming and had water in my ears or had spent all night at a deafening concert.

"What's going on? Are you okay?" I asked, rubbing my eyes. All I really wanted was to get into bed. I realized with a little kick of surprise that I was asking Jack these questions as though they were part of a script. I wasn't sure I cared what was going on. I wasn't sure I cared if he was okay.

"Yeah, I'm okay. I just have something to tell you, Norma. I'm getting married."

I blinked, rubbed my eyes again.

"You are?"

"Yeah."

I almost said "Congratulations," but that didn't seem quite right. In my state of mind, I couldn't trust my words. "I don't know what to say, Jack. I feel strange right now. I—I've been up all night." I reached down and unlaced my shoes and kicked them off my feet to the floor.

"I'm sorry I didn't tell you sooner," he said.

"What do you mean?"

"Well, I should have told you, that's all."

"How long have you known her?"

"Since September."

I jumped up from the bed, but the movement seemed false—the scripted, hyperbolic response of a bad actor.

"September? Am I hearing this right—September? When I moved in here?" I sat back down and sighed, exhausted. "Is it Peggy?"

He rubbed his hands on his thighs. "Yeah."

"She didn't sound too happy when I called."

"Well, yeah."

"Jack. I hate to put it this way, but you don't seem like the marrying type." Even though that was a cliché, it felt like the first clear, true thing I'd said to him since I walked in the door. Or for months, for that matter. To my surprise, he looked a little flushed, as though he agreed with my point. For the first time, I felt something shift between us—as though for once I was the one who could teach him something.

"Norma, she's pregnant."

"Oh." I crossed my legs on the bed and put a pillow in my lap. "Well, this isn't the 1950's when unmarried pregnant girls had to slink off to dark allies or homes for unwed mothers." I heard a new authority in my voice. I was relishing the feeling that Jack was for the first time closer to my equal—if not my subordinate.

"She's not exactly a girl. She's 32."

I looked at him and smiled. "You're shitting me."

"Next month. In fact, we're getting married on her birthday."

He leaned forward in the chair, his face moving close to mine. With his eyes and lips right there, I felt a little surge like I always did. But this time the erotic quality of that surge had an oddly objective quality, as though our chemistry were impartial. I noticed the sexual tension, as though it had nothing to do with me, and let it pass—like a moth fluttering by.

"Do you have a beer?" he asked.

"Maybe. Check."

He turned and opened the mini refrigerator. "You have two. Want one?"

"Okay."

He opened them both and handed me one. I held up my beer and said, "Well, I don't know if this is appropriate, but fuck it if it's not. Congratulations." He sat still, watching me as I clinked my bottle against his.

"You know, you're really something, Norma," he said.

"What do you mean?" I asked, digging for the compliment, knowing inside that he meant something good, something strong. Perhaps another, deeper sense of "womanly."

"You're just really special. There aren't many girls like you. If we would have met at a different time, you older, maybe, me—I don't know, me something—well, maybe it would be you I'd be marrying."

I drank a long swig of my beer. I knew the words that were coming to me, long before they emerged from my mouth.

"Jack," I said. "I'm glad it's not me."

When Jack left, I climbed into bed without taking off my clothes. I slept all day, the sleep of the dead. The good thing about the sleep of the dead is, if you wake up, you're reborn.

Chapter Nineteen — Devil Woman

Sitting in the backseat of Lurch, Benny's car, I was the highest I'd been in months, and I wasn't drinking and hadn't taken any pills. I'd taken a hit or two of the joint that passed my way, but that wasn't why I was high.

I was high because—well, I wasn't sure why. It wasn't just that Stacy sat next to me, and next to her sat her stepsister, Tabitha. It wasn't just that Benny was driving, Liz sitting between him and Chuck. It wasn't just that I was surrounded by my friends on this drive through the mountains, past thick rows of pines and blinding white snow, all under a completely cloudless azure sky. It wasn't just because we had the music up loud and were singing to any dumb song that came on the radio. And not just because it was spring break—and we were headed to a cabin together. Or because I had almost no homework over vacation. Or because I felt free from Jack. Perhaps it was none of these things, or a combination of all of them, that made me feel like I could drift out of Benny's car like a helium balloon and float up through the remarkable blue sky.

"Benny, pass this semi, for god's sake," said Liz. "Every second you drag your ass, we miss out on spring break. Time's ticking. Tick tick tick."

Benny gunned Lurch's engine and pushed the car into the passing lane.

"What a man," deadpanned Liz, kissing his neck, which immediately bloomed red.

"Hey girls, anyone?" asked Chuck, turning around in his seat to pass the joint. He grinned at us under his red baseball hat.

Tabitha took the joint and inhaled. Her dark hair drifted around her face in the wind generated from Chuck's window, which was cracked open.

"'I love this one!" shouted Tabitha, almost every time a new song came on. We sang as much as we could from each song.

Let's get physical, physical . . . .

We're an American Band . . .

Celebrate good times, come on! . . .

Dancing Queen, feel the beat from the tambourine . . .

We sang and sang. When most everyone stopped at a particular lyric, I'd keep singing. Stacy looked to me when she didn't know the words.

"How do you know all these lyrics?" she asked.

"She's a Cyborg," said Chuck.

"Ooh, I love this one. Turn it up, Benny!" said Tabitha.

"Me too!" shouted Stacy.

And we sang, *Sexual Healing . . . I want some, Sexual Healing . . .*

Liz ran her hand through Benny's hair.

Sexual Healing, I want some . . .

Chuck turned around and serenaded us. He looked at Tabitha, then me, then Stacy. I kept trying to catch his eye again, but he stared at Stacy, and she at him, as they sang and sang. As I watched them, I felt my high begin to wane. That was it, I decided. I needed to get to the bottom of this, soon. This weekend, in fact. I had to steel myself, to draw on the strength I'd had with Jack and to get the guts to ask Chuck once and for all: *are you in love with Stacy?* I cringed inwardly. What if the answer was yes?

I stopped singing and looked out the window at the emerald trees rushing by, tipped in snow.

The cabin had only one bedroom that Liz claimed right away for herself and Benny. Stacy said I could have the fold-out couch in the living room, but I insisted she and Tabitha take it. Chuck and I set up our sleeping bags on the living room floor.

"Let's get up early tomorrow to ski," said Benny. "The slopes are going to be busy."

"Early? Ski? What fresh hell is this?" said Chuck, pouring margarita mix into the blender.

"I brought some extra gloves for you," said Benny.

"Kind of you, dear boy, but I'm not masochistic enough to actually hang out in the snow for longer than it takes to walk from a warm car to a warm bar."

"Chuck, you're not skiing?" I said, disappointed. "Come on. It's fun."

"Unlike you, Norma Jean, I didn't grow up in a town with gun racks on the trucks."

"But Benny didn't, either. I mean, he's from San Francisco—there's not exactly snow there."

"Come on, Paul," said Stacy. "You should give it a try."

"Absolutely not."

"I'm with you, Paul," said Liz.

Benny put his arm around her. "I don't think so," he said. "You're coming skiing with me." It was the first time I'd heard him say something like that to Liz.

"Listen, Benny, I'll do whatever the fuck I want."

Benny dropped his arm and took off his glasses, cleaning them on the hem of his sweater.

"Skiing's a blast," said Tabitha. "I can teach you a move or two."

"Well, maybe you could teach me some moves some time, but not on the slopes," joked Chuck, raising his eyebrows ala Groucho Marx.

"Chuck, Liz, you're really not going to ski?" I asked.

Liz kissed Benny on the cheek. "Well, maybe I'll give it the old college try."

"Weak woman," said Chuck. "I'll be sipping a hot toddy and ogling the babes in tight ski sweaters while you mindless children strap wood on your feet and flail ridiculously down icy hills."

"Skis aren't made of wood anymore," said Benny.

"Thanks for the technological update," Chuck said, and flicked on the blender to a roar. He poured margarita into six glasses.

"Come on, someone, make a toast. I'm worn out from pushing the button on this machine."

"Here's to surviving our first year in the dorms," said Liz, holding up her glass.

"That's a tad premature," said Chuck.

"God willing," Liz added.

Mildred Pierce!" exclaimed Chuck. He'd been flipping through the channels, sitting on the floor in front of the television. Stacy, Tabitha and I lay back on the bed, folded out from the couch. Benny and Liz had gone to the bedroom.

"1945, Joan Crawford, Ann Blyth. Look." He pointed to Joan Crawford on the screen. "Mildred's one tough broad, a self-made businesswoman, an entrepreneur. She owns three restaurants. And she," he pointed to Ann Blyth, "is her ungrateful 17-year-old daughter. The little bitch. All she wants to do is spend her mother's money, sing, and bed men she can blackmail." He took a drag of his cigarette.

"Look at those eyebrows," said Tabitha.

"And that hair!" said Stacy.

"And those shoulders. What's up with her shoulders?" I asked.

"Girls, girls. Joan Crawford was one classy broad."

"Did people think she was beautiful?" I asked.

"Absolutely."

Stacy giggled. "I think she looks frightening."

"But her daughter's pretty," said Tabitha. "Except, what's up with that corsage on her dress? Looks like she's going to the prom, and she's just standing around."

"You girls have no appreciation for this era," said Chuck.

"Why should we?" asked Tabitha. "This is 1982, end of the twentieth century. Get with the times, Paul."

Chuck took another drag of his cigarette and blew a few smoke rings. His eyes were red. I realized he didn't say anything in response to Tabitha's remark. It was unusual. Usually he'd have a witty comeback. But he just kept staring at the T.V.

I was about to get up from the bed and go sit next to him when Stacy did exactly that. She walked across the floor, her long blonde hair swinging, then sat cross-legged next to him, and lay her head on his shoulder. He handed her his cigarette and she took a drag, white smoke rising. Jealousy crept up my spine.

I looked over at Tabitha. I couldn't tell if she was watching Joan Crawford or staring at Stacy and Chuck as they sat there, Stacy's head on Chuck's shoulder, sharing a cigarette. I wanted to go sit next to him, to put my head on his shoulder, to drape my arm around him. But it was like they had a wall of invisible protection around them, one I couldn't penetrate if I tried.

Later, as Chuck and I lay side-by-side in sleeping bags, and Stacy and Tabitha slept on the couch-bed, I realized Chuck hadn't said much that evening after Tabitha had teased him about getting with the times. He seemed sad, distant.

I whispered to him, "Are you okay?"

"I'm fine," he said.

"Are you sure?"

"Yes. Good night Norma Jean."

"Good night."

I closed my eyes and saw Ann Blyth yelling at her mother, Joan Crawford. Joan looked baffled, her dark eyebrows like question marks. Ann was incensed, her white corsage puffed up at her neck.

"Chuck?" I whispered.

"Yeah?"

"What's your dad like?"

"He's a real estate agent."

"No, I mean, what's he like?"

"Tall, at least 6'1."

"Chuck."

"What?"

"What's his personality like?"

"He's a fucking blast," said Chuck. "Life of the party. Yes, for him, life's a big fucking party."

I was afraid to push it any further. I moved my head over to Chuck's pillow. It seemed he was comforting us both when he reached out his arm and pulled me in. I lay my head on the warmth of his chest and listened to his breathing change from quick and shallow to slow and deep.

Benny transformed on the slopes. Strapping on his skis, he looked different—taller, poised, dignified. At the top of the lift, he pushed off with ease, winding down the hill, crouched low, his poles in perfect position. At the bottom, he stopped with a swoop and turn, the powdery snow shooting up next to Liz and me.

"See, you just need to relax your body," said Benny. "And bend your knees."

"What I need is another joint," said Liz. "How the fuck can I relax? I feel like I'm in concrete shoes and the mob is about ready to dump me off a bridge."

"I think this may be too fast," I said to Benny. "Look, Liz, just walk like this up part of the hill." I side-stepped in my skis. "And then do the snow-plow. Spread your skis apart at the back, like this, tips together." I snow-plowed slowly toward her. "See? Just try this. Then when you get off the lift, you can slowly snow-plow down."

"I feel like a total idiot. I think I'm going to go join Paul."

"Come on, Liz," said Benny. "Just try it a little. It's really fun. Really."

"Why don't you two go up on the lift? I'll just stand here and watch one more time."

"You promise?" said Benny. "You won't take off?"

"Shit," said Liz.

"Promise."

"God, I promise. Now go."

At that moment, Stacy and Tabitha skied up.

"Hey you guys!" said Stacy, her cheeks bright pink, her long blonde hair flowing out of her knit cap. I saw myself distorted in her dark sunglasses and wondered how I could like her so much and be so jealous of her at the same time. The feeling was disorienting, like doing an underwater somersault and for a split second not knowing which way is up. "Are you taking the lift up again?" she asked.

"They are," said Liz. "Why don't you just head up together, a happy foursome?"

"Don't move," said Benny. "Promise?"

"Fuck, what did I say? I'll stay right here. Now go. I'm freezing my ass off. I'll watch one more time then I'll try it, okay? Go!"

The chair lift came along and swooped up Benny and me first, then Stacy and Tabitha. Benny's and my skis swung under our feet. The sky was crystalline blue, the snow blinding white. As I always did, I marveled at the concept of the ski lift. No seat belt. One little move forward, and you could drop down through the sky to the ground.

"How'd you learn to ski?" I asked.

"My family came up here every winter since I was a kid," he said. "How about you?"

"I was in ski club in high school."

"Wow, ski club," he said. "I wish we had that. I was in bowling club."

"Bowling club?" I laughed. "Really? Are you a good bowler?"

"I've thrown 300 a few times."

"You have? A perfect game? Benny! You are more talented than I ever knew. What other sports are you good at?"

"Frisbee."

"What?"

"Yeah, I can do some Frisbee tricks."

"You can? Why don't we know this about you?"

"You never asked."

"What else?" I asked. "What other sports?"

"Rugby. My team went to the finals."

I looked at him. The rugby players I knew were huge guys. They said it was the most brutal sport there was.

"Are you kidding?" I said.

"Yes. But just about the rugby." He grinned. "Gotcha."

I playfully poked him in the ribs and he giggled.

We lifted the tips of our skis as the top of the hill approached, met the uplift of packed snow and pushed ourselves away from the chair, shoving off hard, leaving the ski lift behind to ski down the hill. The icy air bit my face. Benny skied circles around me, but I did okay.

Liz kept to her word and was waiting at the bottom. In a minute, Stacy and Tabitha joined us.

"We want something harder," said Stacy. "You guys want to go to the diamond lift with us?"

I could tell Benny wanted to.

"Benny, go with them," I said. "I'll hang out with Liz."

"Yeah, she'll teach the retard how to ski," Liz said.

"No, it's okay, I'll stay," he said.

"Go Benny," said Liz. She kissed him quickly on the lips. "God, go. Have fun."

The minute the three of them left, Liz said, "Let's go have a drink."

"I don't think so," I said.

"I just hope Benny doesn't drool all over them. I think he has a thing for Stacy. And Tabitha's such a sphinx she's intriguing him, I'm sure."

"What guy doesn't drool over Stacy?" I said. "They can't help themselves. But come on, Liz, he doesn't have a real thing for her like he does for you." I knew I was a hypocrite for trying to talk her out of being jealous of Stacy. But I wanted Liz to like Stacy. I wanted my friends to get along.

"Don't be so sure."

"No, really. I think Benny's in love with you."

"Now you're really making me gag," she said. "I need a drink."

But I talked her into giving skiing a try, and she wasn't bad, after all. In fact, she ended up actually enjoying herself it seemed, as we floated up the hill on the lift, then progressed slowly down the hills. She even laughed when she fell into a soft bank of powder and playfully threw a handful of snow at me. I never would have guessed she had it in her.

Sitting on the green shag carpet, I pulled my sweater off over my head. Underneath I had on a tee-shirt. Tabitha and Stacy were both down to their bras and underwear. Benny was wearing only his pants, and Chuck had on his tee-shirt, boxers, and socks. Liz had on all her clothes, having lost two rings and her earrings. In spite of being permeated by the numbness of drink, I felt a little electricity in my veins, something I always felt when playing this game.

Benny tried hard, but he couldn't keep his eyes off Tabitha's and Stacy's bodies. Every time I looked at him, he was staring at their lacy bras. Liz noticed too, I thought, which suddenly made me nervous. Maybe playing Strip Quarters with this group wasn't the best idea.

I took the quarter and bounced it on the table. It tumbled into the glass. I pointed my elbow at Chuck. He grinned, handed me his joint, then drank the beer and removed his tee-shirt. I took a hit of the joint then handed it to Benny.

Liz bounced the quarter on the coffee table. It hit the edge of the glass then bounced off, falling to the table. She shrugged, drank the beer in the glass then removed her necklace.

"Come on, that's not a piece of clothing," said Tabitha.

"It all counts," said Liz, glaring at Tabitha with red eyes. Liz's words were thick, as though her tongue were swollen.

"I don't think so," said Tabitha.

"Who died and made you queen?"

"No one."

"Well quit telling me what's what, then." Liz took a swig of her margarita.

"Relax, Liz," I said.

"Who is she to tell me what to do?" There was a hysterical edge to her voice.

"She's just saying it's not fair," said Stacy. "Some of us don't have on jewelry."

"That's not my fault," said Liz. "Why don't you just tell me the truth—you can't wait to see my boobs." Liz jumped out of her seat and yanked her shirt off over her head.

"Now Liz," said Benny.

"Are you that twisted?" Liz yelled, glaring at Tabitha and Stacy.

"Liz, knock it off," said Chuck.

"Here," she said, reaching around to the back of her bra. "Let's just get it over with."

I couldn't believe Liz was going off on Stacy again— and this time, Tabitha, too. The nightmarish memory of my aborted birthday party instantly engulfed me.

Chuck jumped up and tried to grab her, but she ducked out of his way.

"Why even bother with this stupid game?" she yelled, unsnapping her bra and pulling it off. She sling-shot it across the room. "I mean, if we want to all see each other naked, why don't we just do it?" She pulled her panties down and kicked them off. "There!" she screamed.

"Liz," said Chuck. He approached her, and again she ducked away, running to the other side of the room. She crouched, naked, by the couch like a zoo animal in the corner of its cage. We all sat there quietly for a moment. I was baffled and a little nauseous. My skin was crawling.

"Okay, Liz, have it your way," said Chuck, stepping back from Liz. "You're right. You're absolutely right." He pulled off his socks then wriggled out of his underwear, dropping them to the floor. To my amazement, he stood there, hands on his hips, his penis dangling in its blond fur. He looked silly and vulnerable, and I felt the deepest respect for him at that moment. He was trying to save us—just like he'd saved the girl at the Billy-Goat party who was surrounded by crazy guys. "Come on, who's next?"

Benny's eyes looked bigger than ever behind his glasses. Liz was still crouched by the couch like a panther, her face flaming red.

"Come on, Norma Jean," said Chuck, holding out his hand. I walked over to him and took his hand, kissing it. Then I curtsied. My heart was racing. I knew Chuck was right—that together we could fix this. Together, we could make it all better.

To the song on the stereo, I began singing, then stripping.

She's just a devil woman, with evil on her mind
Beware the devil woman,
She's gonna get you from behind.

Chuck moved his feet to the music as I took off my clothes. When I was naked, I stood next to him, giddy, feeling like one of the characters in *Hair*. Chuck crooked his finger at Stacy and Tabitha, beckoning them over. Slowly they stood and came to him, grinning. After peeling off their bras and underwear, they danced in a circle with us, naked. Both Stacy and Tabitha had long, thin legs and small breasts.

Stacy had what looked like a brown birthmark on her flat stomach. We were like a tribe, dancing around the fire to bring on the rain.

When the song changed to Donna Summer, I went over to Liz. Reluctantly, she let me pull her up on her feet over to the circle. She closed her eyes and swayed with us to the music:

Bad girls, bad girls, talking about bad girls, beep beep.

Benny never got up from his seat at the table, but that was okay. We needed an audience.

I woke in the middle of the night. Chuck lay snoring next to me in his sleeping bag. After our naked dance, we'd all gotten dressed and watched *Saturday Night Live*. Liz had passed out on the couch, and Benny carried her to bed. When Stacy and Tabitha had turned out the lights and climbed into the converted sofa, Chuck lay on his side, his back to me. I had curled up behind him and, warm, fell asleep.

I wished Chuck had made love to me. I wondered if he didn't because Stacy was there, a few feet away. Or maybe he never would again. Maybe whatever we might have started was over. Maybe he'd be my friend but, deep down, he would always hold a grudge. That was my fear. Maybe that's why I couldn't ask him if he loved Stacy or me. I was too afraid to hear the answer. I had never known anyone like him. I was in awe of the way he'd defused Liz, the way he'd steered the Titanic away from the iceberg.

I opened my eyes. It was very dark. I needed to get up to go to the bathroom, but I was so warm, and the air outside the sleeping bag felt like ice on my face. I blinked, trying to get my eyes to adjust. A little moonlight through the window scarcely illuminated the room.

Slowly and quietly, I pushed off the sleeping bag and stood, chilled in my short tee-shirt, my bare legs pricking in the chill. Looking down, I tried to avoid stubbing my toes on the stuff strewn on the floors—shoes, duffle bags, beer bottles. I also didn't want to hit the edge of the sofa bed.

I heard a soft noise, a murmur, an exhalation, maybe Stacy or Tabitha dreaming, or sleeping fitfully? I glanced toward the bed. Something was moving, the shadows of the bed oddly shifting. A moan. Were they okay? Was one of them sick?

I took a step toward them, my eyes adjusting to let in more light. I stepped over a shoe, peered at the bed.

And that's when I saw it.

Did I see it? Was I seeing right?

Tabitha was moving on top of Stacy, their long hair mingled and spread on the bed, Tabitha's bare shoulders silver in the moonlight.

My heart thudded in my chest. I asked myself again, Was I seeing right? I blinked. I blinked again. No question.

I felt an intense pressure in my bladder. I needed to pee now more than ever, but I worried that if I slipped by their bed they'd see me. Then what? It was too dizzying to imagine what might happen if they knew I'd seen what they were doing.

I turned around and crept down the hall to the side door. I slipped out the door into the black and white night. Immediately my socks soaked up wet snow, and my lungs tightened in the piercing cold. Crouching behind a shrub, I peed on the ground, more stars than I'd ever seen twitching in the slate-black sky. My heart was leveling out, calming down from its frantic pace, but my mind was pulsing at warp speed. Tabitha and Stacy? Stacy and Tabitha? No one would believe it. I had seen it—and I wasn't sure I believed it. There had been a rumor in high school that Evelyn Gorlich and Mrs. Vayer, the P.E. teacher, were in love—that they sat next to each other as the bus took the basketball team to away games, that Mrs. Vayer had love notes from Evelyn in her desk drawer. But I hadn't taken the rumors seriously. I'd just laughed with the others behind Evelyn's back at her funny walk and her gawky, makeup-less appearance. I felt bad for her, though. The summer of my sophomore year I said hi to her at the town swimming pool. She said hi back then ran up the stairs to the high dive and did the most graceful swan dive I'd ever seen. After that, whenever I'd say "hi" to her at school, she'd say "hi" back, but she never tried to say anything more than that. Neither did I.

My mind like an anthill of swarming images and feelings, I slipped back into the house and peeled my soaked socks off my ice-cold feet. I went back to my sleeping bag and lay down, cold but sweating, my pulse hammering in my head. Part of me wanted to wake up Chuck and tell him what was going on. But what would happen then? Would he tell me to mind my own business and lose respect for me? Would he jump up and confront them—a scenario that both thrilled and terrified me? How could this be? Stacy and Tabitha? Was everything Stacy told me about Tabitha a lie? What else had she lied about? I'd never been so confused, so torn. All the nice things she did for me were not an illusion. Was this?

I strained beyond the push and pull of Chuck's breath to see if I could hear anything. Nothing.

I curled up against Chuck again, shivering, trying to bury myself in him, in his heat. Soon I was drifting off to sleep, part of me working to convince the other part that what I'd seen had been a dream.

Chapter Twenty — Multitudes

When we came back to campus, spring had burst open in Sacramento. Trees and flowers bloomed, fuzzy stuff floated in the bright air, birds raucously rustled and shrieked. People hung out in bathing suits on the circular lawn outside the dorm, tossing footballs and Frisbees. Some leaned against trees, reading thick textbooks, others napped in the shade. We felt the freedom of summer in our bones, so it was hard to go to class—and when we did go, it was hard to take anything seriously. Even Linda lightened up a little by changing an assignment. We didn't have to write about an issue. Instead, we had to write a poem about anything of our choice. To get us started, she read aloud some Walt Whitman:

> *Come closer to me,*
> *Push close my lovers and take the best I possess,*
> *Yield closer and closer and give me the best you possess.*

I raised my hand. "Did you say lovers or lover?"

"Lovers." She closed the book on her finger. "Why do you ask?"

"It just seems strange. A love poem for more than one person."

A few students laughed.

Linda opened the book again, flipped back a page or two, and read,

Do I contradict myself? Very well then, I contradict myself.
I am large . . . . I contain multitudes.

She looked at me, her large gold earrings sparkling. "That was Whitman for you. Everything was plural, everything abundant. He believed in the *merge*, in the one being the many, the many being the one. He wasn't about *but*. He was about *and*. In fact, one of the words most used in *Leaves of Grass* is *and*."

As I walked out into the bright afternoon, I thought *and, and, and, and*. I liked the idea of *and* not *but*. Maybe I'd start my poem with the word *and*.

I looked around for Chuck, hoping he'd be meeting me after class, but he wasn't there. I hadn't said a word to him, or anyone, about Stacy and Tabitha. Besides, I wasn't sure what I'd seen. Had it really been what I thought? I entertained the idea that I hadn't gotten out of bed, that the whole thing had been a dream. Still, I'd thought about telling Liz or Chuck, just to see how they'd react, but we'd all been a bit surly and hung-over the next morning, so having a heart-to-heart talk about anything at all had no appeal.

And since we'd come back to the dorms, I hadn't seen much of Chuck other than one late-night backgammon session while Liz and Benny sat on Benny's bed, Benny teaching her how to play Tetris. No time had seemed right to reveal what I thought I knew about Stacy and Tabitha, the secret swirling inside me like the Tasmanian Devil.

I walked across the campus toward the dorms. I needed to talk to my parents. I needed to tell them that next year, I wanted to get an apartment with Liz. It had been Liz's idea. She'd thought about moving into the sorority house but decided it would drive her crazy to be All Sorority, All the Time, as she put it. Besides, she said, she thought with the way I organized my schoolwork binder and typed all my assignments, I'd be a good influence on her.

My dorm room was open. Stacy sat on her bed, reading *Cosmo*.

She was good, I thought, really good. She displayed all the props of a regular girl—the right magazines, the pink fingernail polish, the long blonde hair, the flirting and dancing with guys. She had fooled everyone. Everyone. Chuck didn't know how right he'd been when he'd said, upon first meeting her months ago, that she'd make a good actress. She could win an Oscar for this performance. I wondered what else she'd lied about. Maybe she knew the identity of my secret hater. Ever since she'd supposedly talked to Billy (I was now doubting everything she'd ever told me that I hadn't witnessed first hand), nothing else had happened to me. No mysterious, mean signs on my door. No more stolen or damaged property. Maybe Billy had, in reality, admitted his guilt and told her he'd stop if she wouldn't tell me the truth. Or maybe my secret hater was just bored and had moved on to another silent victim.

"Hey Norma," Stacy said, flipping the page of her magazine.

"Hi Stacy." I dropped my backpack to the floor and flopped down on my bed. In spite of everything, I still felt affection for Stacy, remembering the ways she lay the washcloth on my head and brought me 7-Up when I was sick, the way she pulled my urine-stained comforter off my bed and washed it. She was the most complicated person I knew, and my feelings about her matched in complexity.

"What are you up to?" she asked.

"Not much. You?"

"Not much."

I sat up on my bed and crossed my legs. I ran my hands through my hair to sweep it off my face. "So where are you and Tabitha getting an apartment next year?" I asked. "Liz and I are thinking of that complex over on Monroe. It's got a pool."

"Actually," she said, looking up from her magazine, "we're getting one in Portland."

"Portland? Portland, Oregon? What do you mean?"

"I'm transferring up there, to Oregon State. Tabitha wants to move up there to be close to her dad."

I watched her turn a few more pages of the magazine. I wondered if she and Tabitha were moving for other reasons—maybe someone else had found out about them.

"Well, why are you going with her? I mean, you have a whole life here, friends, school." I swallowed. My throat was tight. I wondered if she was going to tell me the truth. Part of me wanted her to, but part of me didn't. What would she say anyway? "Lesbianism" seemed like an impossible admission.

"She's my best friend," she said.

"It seems odd," I said. I could feel myself pushing it, and I didn't really want to, but I couldn't help myself somehow. "I mean, lots of girls have best friends, but they don't go moving with them everywhere. My best friend Suzy stayed in Auburn when I came here. She didn't leave her boyfriend or anything to come follow me around. I mean, what about Tabitha's boyfriend?"

Stacy turned a few more pages of the magazine. My words reverberated in the air, and I didn't like the way they sounded. I wished she'd hurry up and say something to erase my insolent tone.

She turned another page then set the magazine down on her pillow and looked at me.

"Right before my mom died," said Stacy, her voice like a nun's speaking judiciously to a catechism class, "she told me that the two most important things in life are family and love. Family and love. Tabitha is my step-sister, my family. I love her. I love her very much."

That was the closest she ever came to telling me the truth.

And the leaves on the trees were voluminous.

And the men and the women were, too.

I put down my pen and watched Goat spin around speedily on the lawn then throw a yellow Frisbee. It sailed across the green expanse to Billy, who unfolded his long paper clip of a body to reach up and snatch it.

I looked back at my poem and wrote more:

And they lay and jumped on the emerald

grass, which, if not trimmed like a crew cut, would

grow and grow and grow and grow.

"What's up Norma?" Liz plopped down next to me. She was wearing white shorts, a white tank top, and long silver earrings.

"Just writing a poem for class."

"Let me see." She read it to herself quickly, moving her lips silently. "I don't get it."

"What don't you get?"

"The whole thing. I hate poetry. Why doesn't it just say what it means?"

"Some things are better that way, I guess," I said, wondering if that was true.

"Whatever." She took a drink of her diet soda. "God, I can't believe we only have two more weeks of school. Thank god."

"What are you doing this summer?" I asked.

"I don't know. Nothing, I hope. I just want to do nothing for a while."

We watched Billy and Goat throw the Frisbee back and forth a few times. Even though I wasn't fond of either of them, it was oddly pleasurable to watch them having fun, flying that piece of plastic through the air, their bodies doing what some young guy bodies can do—nearly defy gravity. I wondered if they noticed me watching them.

"Norma," said Liz after a few minutes. "I'm glad we're going to get a place together."

"Me too," I said, genuinely excited about the future as usual. "I can't believe all we've been through this year. I'm so glad I know you."

"Okay, enough," she said. "Don't get sappy on me." But she had the same look in her eye that she did when we were skiing together and throwing snowballs at each other— a soft look that conveyed the opposite of her prickly words.

"Liz, can I tell you something?"

"What?"

"You have to promise you won't tell a soul."

"Okay, I won't tell a soul."

I looked at her. "I mean it. Promise. You can't tell a single solitary person."

"I promise, I promise."

With a sting of guilty pleasure, I could see I'd whetted her curiosity. She sipped her coke and handed me the can. I took a sip and handed it back.

"Well," I said. "One night at the cabin, I got up in the middle of the night to go to the bathroom." I paused and took a deep breath.

"And?" she said.

"You have to swear you won't tell anyone."

"I swear, I swear. Geez, Norma, what the hell is it? You've got me in total suspense."

"Well, I saw Tabitha and Stacy in bed, and they were. Well."

Her eyes widened. "I knew it, I knew it!" she yelled.

"Shhhh!"

"I knew it!" she whispered fiercely. "What did you see? Tell me what you saw."

"I'm not sure," I said. "Maybe nothing."

"Norma, don't pull that shit with me. You saw something, and you know exactly what it was."

"Well, I think I saw them, I don't know, doing something. Tabitha was naked, on top of Stacy."

"Oh God!" yelled Liz.

"Shhhh! Come on Liz, calm down."

"So what did you do?"

"I just went back to sleep."

"You didn't say anything to them?"

"No! Of course not. What would I say?"

"Did you tell Paul?"

"No. You're the only one. And you better not tell a soul."

"Norma," she said. "You have to tell Paul."

"I do?"

"Absolutely."

"Why?" I knew where she was going, but I played dumb. I wanted someone to convince me so I could feel less responsible for my actions. Hypocritical, I knew.

"Because you want him to know, don't you?"

"Maybe."

"Don't play that game with me," she said. "You have a thing for Paul, right?"

"Kind of."

She arched her thin eyebrows at me.

"Yes," I said.

"You love him. You're in love with him."

I swallowed. "Yes." Saying this out loud felt like a roller-coaster plunge. Goose bumps sprouted on my arms.

"And we both know he has a thing for Stacy."

"I think so."

"So if he knows that there's no hope, well . . ." She took a sip from her coke, her long earrings sliding back across her neck. She handed me the can. I tipped it to my mouth but it was empty.

"Norma, do it."

"I don't know," I said. "I don't know." Meaning, *I know, I know.*

"Norma, go upstairs right now. Right this minute. I'll go with you."

"But you can't be there when I tell him," I said.

"Of course I won't be there when you tell him. I'm going with you so I can grab Benny and get him out of there. Then the two of you can be alone."

Benny was playing Tetris when we walked in.

"Hey Norma, hey Liz, want to play?"

"Where's Paul?" demanded Liz.

"I don't know," he said.

"When was the last time you saw him?"

Benny pushed his glasses up the bridge of his nose. "I don't know. A day or two ago."

I looked at Chuck's bed. It was so neat, everything tucked in. I looked at his desk. It was dusty. When was the last time he'd been here? Why was he gone so often? Who were these off-campus friends? In this burst of truth-telling, I suddenly had to know. I wasn't going to take "I don't know" for an answer anymore.

"Benny," I said, adopting Liz's exacting, insistent tone. "Have you ever met Chuck's off-campus friends?"

"No."

"Has he told you anything about them?"

"Not really," he said.

"What are their names?" I asked.

"I don't know."

"He's never mentioned a name?"

Benny thought for a second. "Well, maybe Vince?"

I sifted through the papers on Chuck's desk, opened a drawer, pulled out pens, papers, matchbooks. A little green address book. I thumbed through it. There were entries in pencil and pen on most of the pages, some crossed out, scribbled through, girl names, guy names.

"Vince Salazar," I said, noticing my palms were sweating, belying my confident tone. "10th Street. Is that it?"

"I don't know," he said.

"Liz, can I borrow your car?"

"Absolutely, sister," she said, digging into her purse and tossing me the keys. They rang through the air and landed in my hand.

With the window rolled down to cool the hot car, I drove downtown. Huge leafy trees shaded the street. Most of the houses were small bungalows with tiny manicured lawns. I passed a girl and a guy riding bikes. I passed a park, festooned with shiny balloons for what looked like a child's birthday party. I passed a dirty guy in tattered clothes pushing an overloaded shopping cart.

At 10th street, I turned right and slowed down, looking at the numbers on the houses. 1225, 1227. There it was, 1229, a little blue house with a huge purple hydrangea in bloom by the front door. The house looked like a grandmother's, not like the party house of a bunch of college guys.

As I got out of the car, I could feel the heat from the asphalt rise up my legs. A gray cat padded along the sidewalk then plopped down on her pudgy side in the sun. I stepped over her and walked up the walkway. The blinds were drawn. It didn't look like anyone was home.

I knocked on the door. And waited. Nothing.

I rang the doorbell. It had an old-fashioned chime. I rang it again.

Inside, I heard something stirring, a little noise, a voice, some footsteps, the chain unlocked.

The door opened to a Magnum P.I. look-alike in a silk bathrobe and bare feet. Tall and stocky, he had thick black hair, a mustache, and a five o'clock shadow. At the minimum, he was thirty years old. I was sure I was at the wrong house.

"Yes?" he said in a baritone voice.

I took a step back. "Oh, I'm sorry, I was looking for Vince, and Chuck, I mean Paul . . . I'm sorry."

"I'm Vince," he said. "Do I know you?"

"You're Vince?" I asked, confused. There must have been some crazy coincidence at play.

"Yes."

"Paul's friend?" I asked, expecting him at that point to tell me I had the wrong house.

"Yeah. Oh, you're a friend of Paul's. Paul!" he yelled. "Someone's here for you!" He opened the door wider. "Come in."

I took another step back, dizzy and disoriented. "No, that's okay," I said.

And then I saw him. Chuck squeezed up next to Vince. He was wearing pajama bottoms. No shirt, no shoes. His hair was mussed, and like Vince, he was unshaven. A grown-up Charlie Brown.

Oh, I thought. Oh.

And it all came together. Like one of those books you read where suddenly all the coincidences that seem disconnected congeal at one moment, and everything makes sense. You know the writer knew it all along, and that some of the characters did too, but you, the reader, and one clueless character, didn't until that moment. And this was it.

I had come to tell Chuck that Stacy was gay, but he knew it the whole time. All the times I'd walked into my room to find Chuck and Stacy engaged in intimate conversation on her bed flashed through my mind. All the ways they looked knowingly at each other, mouthed words to each other, sang to each other.

Chuck knew Stacy was gay.

And Stacy knew Chuck was gay.

And me, I knew nothing. Nothing. I was just a big empty nothing, a big zero. I was the blank line created when an eraser is swooped over a writing-filled chalkboard. It was the feeling I got at the ocean, a vast expanse of nothingness. I was nice Stacy, mischievous Liz, witty Chuck—in other words, I was a mirror. And without anything to reflect it, the mirror is nothing.

"Norma Jean," he said in a new voice. A voice filled with sex.

I looked at his blue eyes, his thin, blond hair, his round face. My eyes felt so dry and blank I couldn't blink. I stared. A bird swooped from a tree, screeching.

Something echoed over and over in my head: *Who are you? Who are you? Who are you?* But the question wasn't so much directed at Chuck. Or Stacy. It was directed at me.

I turned around and started walking back to the car.

"Norma Jean," I heard him say.

I stopped and turned around like a remote-control toy.

They hadn't moved. Chuck was still standing in the doorway next to Vince, as though to reinforce that he'd chosen him. Not me.

"Norma Jean. Why don't you come in? Have a glass of wine."

I felt an odd sensation, like I was leaning forward looking at him from a great height, like peering over the edge of Coit Tower down onto the city—as though if I took a step forward I'd plunge or fly.

I felt something pushing against my ankle. The gray cat, bumping against me, purring.

"Come on, Norma Jean. Come in."

As though the remote control had been pushed again, I turned around. I had no mind, no brain—just this shell of a body that somehow walked to the car, opened the car door, inserted the keys, started the engine.

As I drove away, I caught a glimpse of Chuck and Vince in the doorway, framed by purple flowers.

Stacy was gone when I got back to my room. If she'd been there, what would I have done? Maybe I would have channeled Liz and screamed at Stacy: *you fucking liar, how dare you play with people's lives.* But that imagined scream seemed far away, like a canyon echo. I was zeroed out, dizzy, light as a kite. I needed to tie a rock to my swaying string. I sat on my bed and dialed the phone.

"Hi sweetheart," said Dad. "Hold on a minute. Barbara! Norma's on the phone."

"Hi Norma," said Mom, picking up the extension.

"Hi. How are you guys?" I asked, my throat clenching. All I wanted at that moment was to sound—to be—normal.

"We're fine, honey," said Dad. "How are you? Are you okay?"

I blinked back tears. "I'm fine," I said. "What have you guys been up to?"

"We canvassed some neighborhoods today, posting fliers for my school board bid," said Dad.

"That great," I said, trying unsuccessfully to swallow. "How many other people are running? Do you think you have a chance?"

"Well, there are two seats, and four of us are running. So, fifty-fifty."

"That's a math problem even I could figure out," I said, channeling Johnny Carson reading a joke from a cue card.

"Glad to hear it," he joked back.

"What else is new?" I asked, my sole intention to keep them on the line.

"We cleaned the pool. It's all ready for summer," said Mom. "I was thinking you could have some of your friends over, kind of last hurrah for Suzy."

"A bachelorette party?" I said, tears welling in my eyes.

"No strippers though!" She laughed.

"Darn, too bad," I said, silently dabbing at my tears with the corner of my pillowcase.

"And we talked to Mary," Mom said. "She said her ankles are so swollen she can hardly stand it. As soon as the baby's born, we'll be going down there for a week or two."

"Can I come?" At that moment I wanted nothing more than to be in the predictable circle of my family.

"Well of course you can if you want to," said Mom.

"I want to," I said. "I really, really do."

When I hung up the phone, Liz barged in. "I thought you'd never get off the phone. So what happened? How'd it go?"

I wiped my eyes with the back of my hand and looked at her.

"Not too well, huh?" she said. "Was he upset?" She sat next to me on the bed. I put my head on her shoulder.

"Liz," I said, softly. "It's not what you think."

"What are you talking about?"

I was tired. If I could have fallen asleep on her shoulder without telling her a thing, I would have. It seemed like it would take a huge effort to spit out the words, to explain to her what had happened. It was like explaining a dream—or a nightmare. I decided to try for economy. "Chuck's off-campus friends?" I said.

"What about them?"

"They're not friends. It's a friend. One friend. One male friend. One man, in his thirties, in a bathrobe."

She pushed my head off her shoulder and faced me.

"What in the hell are you talking about?"

"Chuck," I said, "is gay."

"What? You're confused," she said. "You mean Stacy's gay. What are you talking about?"

"Listen carefully. Chuck doesn't want Stacy, just as Stacy never wanted Chuck. They are friends, gay friends," I said in a monotone, as though reading aloud *Fun with Dick and Jane*. "They've been having long heart-to-hearts about it. Here in this room. On this bed. They've poured out their souls to each other, leaving the rest of us in the dark."

Liz stood up and paced the floor. Music started up in the Billy-Goat Room, a deep thumping bass vibrating the wall. She paced back and forth, her feet tromping to the beat of the music. After a minute or two, she turned to face me, her hands on her hips, her silver earrings swaying.

"Okay," she said. "I've thought about it. And I have to say, after contemplation, I'm really not surprised. Paul always seemed like a bit of a queen to me."

It was just like Liz to make her rash decision sound like a deeply felt insight. I lay back on the bed and closed my eyes. *Look at the leather queens,* Chuck had said that day in San Francisco. *The fags.* As though he were a tourist.

"Think about it," she said. "All that movie stuff. Seems a little fruity when you really think about it."

While I cringed at her choice of words, her jabs felt a tad cathartic. With my eyes still closed I said, "But we had sex."

"Yeah, so, that's how guys are. They're animals. They can get it up no matter what."

"Thanks a lot," I said, meaning, is that all I meant to Chuck, really? Was he thinking about guys when we were together? Did he really never even care about me? But even in the heat of my dejection, I knew that couldn't be completely right—because of how he'd been so hurt when I'd chosen Jack over him.

"What are you doing, Norma?" She grabbed my arm and pulled me up to a sitting position. "Are you going to lie around and mope about one fish in the sea? Come on, let's go next door. Now's a great time to party. It'll make you feel better."

"I need to sleep," I said.

"No way, come on."

"Really, Liz," I insisted.

"Okay, just a little nap." She glanced at her watch. "I'll be back in an hour. You'll feel better. Then we'll have fun, okay?"

I could see she was trying to be a good friend. But a few minutes after she left, I got up, opened my door, looked both ways, then took off down the hall, through the lobby, past the black guy and white guy who didn't look up from their game of Space Invaders, and through the glass doors into the warm early evening.

Chapter Twenty-one — Who Are You?

As I walked across the bridge that connected campus to town, it felt like something was squirming in my veins—like my blood had changed directions. The school year played through my mind as though my brain, impatient with the programming, incessantly flicked the channel changer station to station. Stacy and Tabitha in togas on Stacy's bed. Chuck holding out his arm so I could snuggle in the crook to sleep. Liz swimming across the dark pool. Benny, morphing from awkward to unruffled as he skied. Chuck laughing about his bald head. Jack holding out flowers to me, Chuck in my bed. James Bond pointing his gun at me. . .

A mosquito buzzed at my ear. As I stopped to smack it, I looked from the bridge down to the river. The water shimmied, reflecting the red and gold of the setting sun, lapping at the gray and black bank of rocks. I heard far-off voices, punctuated by laughter that might have been coming from a distant cluster of trees. The air was at the mid-point between hot and cool, the kind of air you can't feel your skin in. Or maybe I was just numb. Not numb enough, though, to avoid that familiar pull that I always felt at heights, the sensation to leap and fly. I reached up and grabbed the high railing, which still radiated heat from the ephemeral sunny day. The railing was high enough to discourage a spontaneous leap. Not that I'd ever really jump. I had no desire to die—just to fly, as though a knowledge of flight lay dormant inside me. With all my strength, I gripped hard and bent my knees, allowing my feet to dangle off the ground. I dangled there for a few seconds, imagining I was hanging over the water. I thought of riding across the Bay Bridge with Benny and Chuck, Chuck hanging out the window commanding me to sing. I thought of Jack and me on the Golden Gate Bridge, smiling as a stranger agreed to take a picture of us with our camera. I had seen the Golden Gate from a different perspective when Chuck and I had roamed the city—at Fort Point, we'd looked up from below to its orange buttresses. This small, gray Sacramento bridge was so different from the Golden Gate it was hard to believe they had the same dictionary definition. The metal was digging into my hands. I let go, my feet landing back on the bridge, my palms as red as the crimson sky.

I didn't know where I was going. I didn't know what I wanted except to be away from the dorms. I walked across the bridge and down a street lined with apartment buildings. Barbeque smoke drifted from a balcony where a group of tanned, shirtless guys stood, talking and drinking cans of beer. One of them whistled at me and yelled "Hey baby!" followed by a chorus of male laughter. I tried not to flinch, just kept on walking, knowing I should feel offended or flattered or irritated, but my feelings drew a blank.

The voice that had invaded my brain earlier came back, echoing over and over, *Who are you?*

As I walked through the apartment-lined neighborhood, dusk settled into early night. A sliver of moon pierced the dark blue sky. Two cars drove slowly past, their headlights crawling ahead of them. I turned a corner and faced a cluster of flat-topped buildings, lit up. A hardware store. A Mexican restaurant. A bookstore.

As I opened the door to the bookstore, the moldy scent of old books surged out. A guy behind the counter looked up at me and then back down at the magazine spread out in front of him. He was very round, with at least three double chins and oval glasses, like the worm with the hookah in *Alice in Wonderland*.

"We close in twenty minutes," he said, his eyes down.

The Who played over the sound system: *I've had enough of being nice . . . of trying to love my brother . . .*

I wandered through the dark, sagging shelves of fragrant books, pulling down a few ragged paperbacks at random, leafing through the pages. I could feel myself filling up with something—with the fondness I had for books, for stories, for the print on the page. I hadn't read a complete book in school, front to back, all year. How could that be? I liked Linda, and writing in English class was good—but why weren't we reading books? I wondered if she thought there was something wrong with books—or if she didn't want to deal with students complaining. No, that wasn't it. They complained anyway.

I pulled down a few novels with titles and authors I'd never heard of and chose two by their prices: twenty-five cents each. I continued to walk down the aisles, gliding my fingers across the book spines, moving along from literary fiction, to romance, to American history, to autobiography, to self-improvement.

The Who were now singing, *Love is coming down on me, love is burning, teaching, turning out in me . . .*

In a dingy corner, a title caught my eye. I pulled the dusty book off the shelf: *Loving Someone Gay.* The words an indictment, a promise.

As I stood at the counter, the silent worm-guy gently placed my books in a stained paper bag while Roger Daltry sang, as though serenading to me my very thoughts, *Who are you . . . who the fuck are you?*

In the Mexican restaurant, I sat eating a quesadilla and reading *Loving Someone Gay.* I'd broken the book's spine so the book lay perfectly flat on the table, the cover hidden. The writer said that it was dangerous for gay people to call attention to themselves. "We are not conformists," he wrote. "We break rules to express our love."

It was that word that hit me the hardest. *Conformist.* I felt the itch of something crystallizing in me. Maybe that was what drew me to Stacy and Chuck. And even to Liz and Benny. They weren't conformists. At least not entirely. Maybe they sparked in me things I liked, helping me to try on personalities to form my own: Stacy's niceness (not conforming to the popular harsh, flippant put-downs of others), Chuck's humor (not conforming to a way he "should" see the world), Liz's candidness (not conforming to good manners expected of girls), Benny's nerdiness (not conforming to what's cool).

As I read, I thought that maybe Stacy's and Chuck's gayness couldn't be separated from them, from what I liked about them. I didn't know how to put my finger on it, but maybe they hadn't lied to me after all. Perhaps keeping something to yourself wasn't lying. Perhaps their secrets made them freer to be non-conformists. Is that what the book was saying?

And what about me? Was I a conformist? What if I never got married? What if I lived like the writing Isadora Wing—but with no regrets? What if I lived in multitudes, like Walt Whitman—with a lover and a lover and a lover? What if I were the female Jack London or Jack Kerouac? These thoughts filled me up with a fluid warmth, a sense that I could be these very things.

The bell on the restaurant door jangled, and I looked up from my book. A man and a woman entered. They were my parents' age, maybe a little older. His arm around her, he guided her to a table. They sat and talked over their menus. I couldn't hear exactly what they were saying, but the familiarity of their intonations cleared out a space in me. The filled-up feeling I'd had imagining all of my non-conformist possibilities was joltingly replaced by a gap, a splinter of emptiness. It didn't matter what the man and woman were saying. They were connected through years of being together, of sharing something.

I thought about my parents, about all their years together—married, monogamous, as far as I knew. It was hard to imagine otherwise. Raising their daughters in our small town, our big house of shag carpets, California King bed, swimming pool. A mother swapping books with her daughter. A father teaching his daughter how to jump into the pool. *I'll catch you* he'd said. As though he meant: *I'm here to guide you, to help you, to make you feel safe.*

When I got back to the dorm, I headed to the Billy-Goat Room, hoping Liz would still be there. I wanted to talk to her, to see if I could put into words some of my swirling, conflicted thoughts. Sometimes Liz could help me untwist my brain with the punch of her brisk logic.

The hallway was quiet and empty, the door to the Billy-Goat Room ajar. I heard the murmur of male voices as I approached. Then I thought I heard my name. I froze. Were Billy and Goat talking about me? With a sinking feeling, I inched forward, closer to the door, straining to hear.

"Holy fuck, man." That was Billy, speaking in his I-don't-know-a-girl-is-listening voice. A less restrained, more jovial voice.

"Yeah, Norma and Sonja and even Clarissa." I could tell Goat had been drinking. That's probably why he was oblivious to the fact that their door was open. Or maybe he didn't care. I sank to the floor, sitting cross-legged on the carpet just outside the door where they couldn't see me. And if they did—well, if they didn't care, neither did I, I told myself, even though my heart was racing.

"Fucking A," said Billy. "What about Trish?"

"That chick with the long black hair on the second floor? Yeah."

"Fucking A." Billy laughed then abruptly stopped. Maybe he was drinking a beer or taking a hit of a joint. "Me too."

"What?" Goat screeched at a hysterical pitch that made me jump.

"Every single one of them."

"I figured Norma, but Clarissa?" I was stunned that they were gossiping. I thought only girls gossiped.

"I told you about Norma," said Billy. "You have a shitty memory, dude."

"Fuck you, and no you didn't," said Goat cheerfully.

"You sure got your head up your ass," said Billy, an amiable quality to his voice. "You need to cut back on the drinking, dude, it's killing your brain cells."

"Good one," laughed Goat.

I was struck that they sounded so companionable, as though they were true friends. I hadn't thought much about that before. In fact, I'd never seen them interact much beyond throwing the Frisbee to each other on the lawn. At their parties they were hooked up with other people—girls, usually. But of course they'd had nights like Stacy and I had—nights when they lay alone in their own beds, talking just before sleep or chatting while doing their homework. I felt a little envious at how chummy they sounded—they were joking together, telling each other their secrets as though they were equals. I'd always felt Stacy was my superior, like a mother who took care of me. And of course she didn't tell me her deepest secrets, not even close.

"What a whore," said Goat. My throat clenched. *A whore.* Just like the note. Was he my secret hater? Or maybe it was a coincidence. Why did he think he could just throw that word around? And against me? I tried to alleviate my burning shame by thinking, *Fuck him. He's a whore himself, the male version.* It kind of helped, kind of didn't.

"That's a little harsh, don't you think?" asked Billy, his voice dropped low and gentle. And it was then I could tell they weren't necessarily equals. Billy was being like a father to Goat—trying to teach him something about humanity. For some reason, I wasn't that surprised that Billy had that kind of father/teacher in him. I remembered our one night together, how he had taken out his guitar and played for me. We'd sung together. He'd shown me he could be kind. Of course, he wasn't that sensitive. Still, that was why I'd been so irritated with him. I wanted more of his kindness. And now I was getting it. Inadvertently—but I'd take it anyway.

"I mean, come on, man," said Billy.

It was silent for a moment. Maybe they were sipping at their beers. Maybe Billy was giving Goat some space to think about what Billy was saying. Finally, Billy spoke again. "I mean, man, she's a human being."

"Yeah, man. You're right. It was harsh," said Goat, perhaps disingenuously but with what could have been a tinge of regret.

That night I sat on my bed finishing *Loving Someone Gay*, the first complete book I'd read all semester. How odd. I'd imagined myself reading book after thick book in college, engrossed in a dim library or in a brightly-lit Student Union, or on a lawn under a tree with broad leaves. Instead, I'd been assigned to read no novels, only the newspaper and chapters from textbooks. The mismatch between fantasy and reality seemed like something to pay attention to, to learn from. Was there a way to make my fantasies a reality?

For the first time in a long time, my room felt like a refuge, like a place I wanted to be. I had left the hallway soon after Goat and Billy had shifted the conversation to their summer plans. I'd been tempted to barge into their room so they could know, or wonder if, I'd heard them talking. But I'd been through so much in the last twenty-four hours, I didn't have the energy. Maybe Goat was my secret hater. Or maybe it was someone else—someone random, like the Meteorologist, or even some girl. Although it was doubtful a girl would pee on my bed. She'd have to stand on it, couldn't aim like a guy. Anyway, my secret hater hadn't pulled anything in months—and school was almost out. I was leaving this place soon, so it didn't really matter. At least that's what I told myself, to keep calm the small part of me inside that felt rubbed raw with the sandpaper of my secret hater's anger.

I still felt a little sting from Goat's words about me, but the balm was Billy. He had stood up for me. He had chastised Goat. He was nicer to me behind my back than to my face. It was pleasing to leave it that way, as though Billy and I shared a secret.

I was just about ready to turn out my light to sleep, when Stacy came in.

"Hi," she said, setting her purse and backpack on her desk. "Long night at the library. Cell biology final this week." I realized she was probably telling me the truth—that all the times she said she was at the library, she probably was. She was studying. While Chuck was with Vince. A new image entered my mind, Vince and Chuck in bathrobes watching an old movie in the cozy little house encircled by beautiful lavender flowers. Maybe they were more like two husbands than two leather queens.

"What are you reading?" Stacy asked, pointing to the paperback I still held in my hand. I hesitated then I held it up for her to see the title.

"*Loving Someone Gay,*" she said. "I guess you found out about Paul." She dropped her gaze and opened a desk drawer, pulling out her hairbrush. I'd never seen her brush her hair before bed—she looked like those 100-strokes-a-night girls, but I knew she wasn't one. She was brushing her hair, I believed, to keep her nervous hands busy.

"Yes, I did," I said. "And you knew? He told you?" I tried to sound surprised.

"Yes," she said. Brush, brush.

"Why did he tell you and not me?" I was pushing it with her again. If I could have taken back that question, I would have. The compassion in *Loving Someone Gay* haunted me. Stacy was a non-conformist. It might not be safe for her to tell me, I reminded myself. For whatever reason.

"I have a gay uncle," she said, throwing her head upside down and brushing the underside of her hair. "I mentioned that to Paul, so maybe that's why. He knew I wouldn't judge him."

"Did he think I'd judge him?" I asked, meaning, *Do you think I'd judge you?*

"I don't know," she said through her wall of hair. "Maybe not you, but you're such good friends with Liz. And, you know, she's pretty judgmental."

I wasn't about to deny that.

"So did he just come out and tell you?" asked Stacy. I wondered if she was curious how she might tell me, or someone else, about herself.

"Well, no . . ." I said, suddenly realizing what a bind I was in. I couldn't tell her I'd sought Chuck out, bearing the news about Stacy. "Or yes. I mean, it's kind of complicated. As you can imagine. I mean, we did sleep together."

Stacy flipped her hair up over her head and looked me in the eyes. "I know. I'm sorry. I hope finding out didn't hurt you too much, Norma."

My first instinct was to guard myself against Stacy's generosity. Hurt? I wasn't hurt. But of course I was. Very hurt. And also something else. Many other things. I was clearer, like someone had washed my psychic windshield. I was weaker—and stronger. I was a whole bunch of things at once. And that, I felt, had to be okay.

I groped for the most honest words I could find. "It was kind of like a hammer to my heart."

Stacy's eyes pooled with sensitivity. I thought she was about to come over and comfort me, but I jumped up first. For once, I wanted to be the one to initiate our coming together. I imagined, based on the unspoken aspects of this conversation, she needed as much comforting as I did.

I sat next to her on her bed and hugged her. It didn't matter that she was a lesbian. Or maybe I had a little bit of a funny feeling hugging a lesbian, but I knew that was about me, not her. Inside my heart and brain, I could hear Roger Daltry singing his jubilant question, *Who the fuck are you?*

The flight attendant set three bags of salted peanuts and a plastic cup of ice, along with a coke can, on my tray. The flight was only half-full, so the cheery flight attendant gave us extra snacks and extra pillows. She encouraged sleepy passengers to stretch out to sleep on empty rows, even though the flight was just two hours. I wasn't tired, though. I was wide awake.

I was on my way to San Diego to join my parents and my sister, who gave birth to a little girl the day before, on my last day of finals. They named her Miranda.

Everyone thought I was coming down to visit and that I'd be driving back up to Auburn with my parents in a week. But as the plane was taking off, pushing up and up and up into the sapphire sky, I felt my own flight, my wings. I was leaving Sacramento—leaving behind the town where I'd gone away to college just an hour from my own home. I was leaving Jack and his soon-to-be wife and child. I was leaving Liz to her sorority sisters, and Chuck to his new love. I was leaving behind Benny and his video games, and the Billy-

Goat Room. I was abandoning my secret hater to his own demons. Like Stacy taking off with Tabitha to Portland, I was taking off with me, myself and I to San Diego.

When I got there, I'd take up Mary on her Thanksgiving offer to stay with her for a while. I knew she'd love to have extra help with the baby. And I'd transfer to San Diego State. It wasn't the prestigious U.C. San Diego that my parents had hoped for me, but I wasn't into prestige. I was a non-conformist. At least a little.

I was sure Liz would blow a fuse when I told her I wouldn't be her roommate. But like she always did, she'd get over it and maybe even be happy for me.

Crunching on salty peanuts, I watched the white wing of the plane push through the blue sky above a bulge of white clouds. Filled with the optimism of new beginnings, I planned to write Liz voluminous letters. I planned to take literature classes where I'd be assigned novel after novel to read. I planned to walk along the beach, sometimes with my sister and the new baby, and sometimes alone—to face the ocean's vast nothingness, to try to listen to what it might teach me.

Chapter Twenty-two — Heart Breaker

"Hello, I'm trying to reach Norma Rogers."

"This is Norma Rogers."

I'd been unpacking my suitcase when the phone rang. I had to do some laundry and then re-pack the suitcase since I was leaving again in three days. My house plants looked droopy. I'd need to ask Miranda to water them for me.

"Norma Rogers, who used to go to Sac State, back in the early 80's?"

"Yes." I held the phone with one hand. With the other, I pinched a dead leaf off my fichus plant.

"I can't believe I found you. I've been trying for months. This is great."

"Who's this?"

"It's Dan, Dan Wasserman"

"Who? I'm sorry, I'm drawing a blank." I walked into the living room and sat on the couch. My cat, Woolf, jumped onto my lap.

"I lived next door to you in the dorms."

"Goat?" I said, the anachronism of his name jarring me.

"Yeah, Goat," he laughed. "It's been twenty years since someone's called me that."

"Goat," I said, trying to force my brain to manifest a picture of him. I remembered his nickname but not his face. "Is it really you? Unbelievable."

"Yeah, it's me. I'd heard through the grapevine you were living in Santa Cruz. You must be loving life there, huh? The beach and all?"

"It's great," I said, "but I'm not home much. I travel a lot for my work."

"What do you do?" he asked.

"I write for a travel magazine."

"Very, very cool," he said.

"What do you do?" I asked, feeling the elusive awkwardness of this conversation press on my chest. Vaguely, I had a strange feeling about Goat.

"I'm a house painter. I own my own business. Dan's Your Man House Painting."

"That's clever."

"Yeah, lots of people like it," he said. "It gets attention." He paused, cleared his throat. "So, Norma, I'm calling for a specific reason."

"I thought you might be." Running my hand across Woolf's black and white fur, I wondered if Goat was selling something—if he'd attended a weekend sales seminar and was told by the enthusiastic huckster of a pyramid scheme to contact every single person he knew in his past. No contact was too old for a potential sale.

"Well." He cleared his throat. "I'm calling to apologize."

"What do you mean?" I asked then it all came flooding back, the vague bad feeling about Goat crystallizing. The typewriter, the notes on the door, spaghetti in my mailbox, urine on my bed. It had been him. Had I always thought so? I wasn't sure.

"I did bad things to you. I stole your typewriter, for one. And I threw it off the river bridge one night. I was drunk. Very drunk."

"Off the bridge?" Memories seeped into my mind of floating on a raft one hot afternoon under that bridge, of standing atop it looking down, of walking alone across it one evening at sunset. "My parents gave me that typewriter as a graduation present," I said, the hurt teenager that apparently still resided in me peeking out through the crack in my voice.

"I know," he said. "I'm so sorry. And there's more. I wrote those cruel notes about you and, I know it was disgusting, but I peed on your bed. I put spaghetti in your mailbox."

"And my mirror?" I asked, knowing full well what his answer would be.

"Yeah. I'm so sorry," he said. "And then that time in the hallway, I grabbed you."

I tried to think back. He grabbed me?

"And put my hand, you know. Well I'm sure you remember. Norma, I was totally plastered each time I did those things. But I remember them. And drinking so much—that's no excuse."

"We all drank so much," I said.

"Exactly," he said. "But I never stopped. I couldn't stop. And now I'm—well, I'm in a 12-Step Program. This is part of it, making amends. When I knew I needed to do this, you were the first one I thought about. I thought, I need to find Norma Rogers."

I continued to pet Woolf, who was purring like crazy. I didn't know what to say. I'd virtually forgotten about what had happened, and here it had been haunting him all these years.

"Why did you do it?" I asked.

"I don't know. I was an idiot. A drunken idiot."

"Well, thanks," I said, admiring his forthrightness, his honesty. It struck me that we were only eighteen years old then. Kids. I believed he was sorry. He was a man now, a human being who had made mistakes. "I accept your apology," I said, smiling as I suppressed the desire to tell him to say ten Hail Mary's.

"Thanks, Norma. That's very nice of you. I didn't know if you'd scream at me or hang up, or what."

"I never expected a call like this."

"Yeah." He paused, silent, as though he didn't want to hang up.

"Well, if I ever need my house painted . . ." I began.

"I'm in Tucson," he said.

"Oh." I laughed. "Hey, are you still in touch with anyone from the dorms?" All the memories his call sparked felt like a tickle in my throat, dredging up curiosity about the past.

"Billy and I talk once in a while," he said.

Surprisingly, I felt myself flush, recalling Billy's guitar, the awkward night in his bed, the echo of his words to Goat, *She's a human being.* Maybe some messages take a long time to sink in.

"He's in North Carolina," Goat continued. "He teaches math, at a high school, has three or four kids now."

"That's great," I said. "I hope he's happy."

"He seems like it, I guess," said Goat, sounding for all the years like a boy who doesn't quite know how to interpret the world. "What about you? Are you still in touch with anyone?"

"You remember Liz?" I asked.

"Oh, yeah, that wild Asian chick?"

I smiled. "Uh huh. And Benny?"

"The nerdy guy, big thick glasses?"

"Yes. They're married."

"No way!"

"Ten years now, I think. They split up after college but then found each other again in a surprising way, as software engineers at the same company."

"No way!"

"Yes. They took a trip to Las Vegas to reconnect—and they came back married."

"Wild," said Goat.

"And now they have two kids, two boys. They live in San Jose."

"Anyone else?" asked Goat.

"No."

"Isn't it weird," he said, "that we all lived together, partied together, did all kinds of other stuff together . . ." He paused awkwardly. "Well you know what I mean, I mean almost everyone saw each other naked, it seems. And now, we're all strangers."

"I hadn't thought about it that way," I said. "You're right, it's odd. Life is surprising and strange."

"You said it."

"I have another question for you," I said. "Why did everyone call you Goat?"

"Billy started it. He said I looked and moved like a Goat. And I'm a Sagittarius, you know the goat-archer, so it stuck."

"I'm a Sagittarius, too. November 25."

"No way!" he said. "That's my birthday, too."

Flickers of memory came to me—pot brownies, Liz in a cast, my other friends and me dancing in a circle in the middle of my room.

"Too bad I didn't know that," I said, smiling at the coincidence. "I would have invited you over to blow out the candles on my birthday pot brownies."

He laughed. "Birthday pot brownies. Wow, we were relentless, huh?"

"Hi, Auntie Norm," said Miranda, as she let herself into my front door with her key. I stood from where I'd been sorting through my mail to help her with the overstuffed bags she balanced in her arms.

"What's all this?" I asked.

"Just my things. I mean, I'm going to need two weeks worth of stuff."

We set the brown paper bags on the table. A black boot and a paperback book tumbled out. She sat at the table and tucked her long brownish-red hair behind an ear that sparkled with five silver earrings. Wires hung down from her ears to the iPod in her shirt pocket. I wasn't leaving for two days, but she said she wanted to bring some of her things over early or she'd have to make two trips in one day.

"Don't you have a suitcase, my dear?" I bent down and kissed her head. Her hair was thick and bristly like mine.

"Probably somewhere," she said, pulling the earphones from her ears and setting them on the table. "But these bags are fine. When I come back Friday I have to bring all my paints, my canvasses and sketchbooks."

"You're just a few miles away. You could go back whenever to get whatever you need." I walked into the kitchen and poured iced tea into two glasses. "You won't be a prisoner here!" I shouted toward the dining room.

"To the contrary, Auntie Norm," she said as I walked back into the dining room and set down the iced tea, two spoons, and the sugar jar. "This is freedom. Campus housing is like prison."

"Is it really that bad?"

"God," she said, rolling her hazel eyes. "You should know. You lived in the dorms, didn't you?" She added four heaping spoonfuls of sugar to her glass of iced tea and stirred.

"Only for a year," I said. "And that was at Sac State, not U.C. Santa Cruz. You're up there in the beautiful mountains and pine trees, with the deer walking all around. And all the really cool people."

"All those really cool people just get drunk and stoned in the beautiful mountains and puke and trip out in the pine trees," she said.

"Is that so?"

"Yeah, don't tell Mom or Dad I said that, though. I think it would freak them out."

I remembered my walk with Miranda's mother, my sister Mary, along the beach one Thanksgiving so many years ago, telling her about my life in the dorms. And then living with her, while I went to San Diego State, when I shared more of my dorm stories. My real dorm stories. I was surprised she sent her own daughter to live in dorms. But the University representative had told her that living on campus was an important part of the college experience.

"And the deer?" said Miranda, her voice raising in its Southern California lilt. "Yeah, they're pretty cool. But wherever there are deer there are mountain lions. You know, you've seen those warning signs posted all over campus. Some kid in my Queering the Arts class came across one the other day on the path to the library."

"What happened?"

"He did what he was supposed to do. He stood still, yelled and screamed, held his backpack over his head to make himself look big and tall. The mountain lion slinked away, he said."

"Wow, that's amazing," I said. "I don't think I'd have the presence of mind to do that."

"Tell me about it. I think I'd shit my pants, or turn and run, which you're not supposed to do or the lion thinks you're prey."

I sipped my tea. "Miranda, you know you can come live here with me."

"Thanks, Auntie Norm," she said, "but some of my friends and I are talking about renting a house closer to the beach. We all want to be able to wake up in the morning and catch some surf before class."

"That sounds great."

"But it'd be sick if I could still use your place when I need, you know, my privacy once in a while. I can be your house-sitter any time. It's good, it gives me time to get centered."

"Sick?" I looked at her face, her freckled complexion, the fine gold hoop threaded through her nose.

"Yeah, you know sick, cool, great, awesome, whatever."

"Okay, right." I smiled. "And if you want to, you can have people over here when I'm gone. Just not too many. Don't let it get out of control."

"Nah, I don't think so. Maybe I'll have Davy over for a night or two, but I need some alone time."

I felt like I was looking at someone who knew so much more than I did at her age. I didn't remember being okay with being alone at age eighteen. And she had the opportunity to have her boyfriend over every night for two weeks, and she'd just have him stay a night or two? Admiration for her, and pride in her, swelled in me. I had, after all, been like a second mother to her the three years I lived in San Diego.

"And," she said, "I'm really behind in my Expressive Drawing class. I'll use the time to catch up. Where's Woolf? Maybe I'll draw a whole series of the fattest cat alive."

Woolf must have heard her name because she came padding into the room. Miranda bent down and lugged the cat up onto her lap. "God, you're so disgusting you're cute," she said, petting the cat's back. "What was it like when you lived in the dorms?"

On the heels of my conversation with Goat a few hours earlier, I felt her question permeate me, like diving into a cold swimming pool on a hot day. I had no idea how to begin answering her question.

"Well, it sounds similar to what you've described," I said.

"Oh, lovely." She sneered. "How did you stand it?"

I realized that if I were the same age as Miranda right then, living next to her in the dorms, she probably wouldn't have liked me. I was glad I was 38 to her mature eighteen.

"It was okay," I said. "I met some fun people. But, as you know, I moved out after a year to go down to San Diego. When I was in the dorms, my grades suffered. Grandma and Grandpa were mad at me."

She shifted Woolf on her lap. "That's what Mom says, that Grandma and Grandpa were strict. It's hard to imagine that now. They're just so cool."

My parents were crazy about their grandchildren — Miranda and her younger sister, Virginia. My parents traveled to San Diego often to visit them, and two summers ago they took them on a cross-country train trip. They all returned tanned, rested, and loaded down with Old Faithful key rings and Grand Canyon coffee cups. Mary was thrilled to have some time to herself since raising two teenaged girls alone was a challenge. After she and Hal divorced, he moved to the Southwest, seeing the girls only on holidays. But while my parents had the girls for the summer trip, Mary hadn't stayed alone long. She'd met a cardiologist in her yoga class and married him after getting pregnant. The girls now had a one-year-old baby sister, Tessa. Miranda loved Tessa but wasn't too thrilled with the cardiologist's attempts at eleventh-hour fatherly discipline, so instead of attending U.C. San Diego, she came up to Santa Cruz.

"I'm glad you love Grandma and Grandpa," I said, aware of how calling my parents *Grandma* and *Grandpa* felt familiar yet foreign. My own grandparents had both died — Grandpa first, of a stroke, then Grandma five years later after heart surgery. Many people of all ages came to her funeral, people we didn't know. Turned out they'd been her fifth-grade students over many years.

"Yeah," Miranda said, lifting Woolf off her lap and putting her on the floor, where she wobbled then lay down at Miranda's feet. "And I like that Grandma and Grandpa take us on trips or come down to see us, not making us come up and stay in Auburn. What a boring town."

"You think so?" I said, feeling a surprising jab, a little protective, somehow, of my hometown.

"Yeah, there's no ocean, nothing to do, and it's small, everyone's in your business."

"It's true that your business is everyone's business in Auburn," I said. I told Miranda how it had been such a huge scandal when Suzy didn't show up for her wedding to Sammy. We were all dressed, waiting in the church festooned with flowers, and the bride never showed. After most people had left, a group of my friends and I sat in the church's basement under sagging streamers, each drinking our own bottle of champagne. We found out later that Suzy had run off with Ty Villanueva, to Reno, getting married that day in a casino.

"Geez, what happened then?" asked Miranda.

"Their marriage lasted ten days," I said. "Suzy came back to Auburn, annulled the marriage, then married Sammy in a civil ceremony. They divorced after four years when Suzy ran off with a guy she met at a religious retreat. I don't know where she is now."

"Was she a good friend?" Miranda drained the rest of her iced tea, the ice clinking against her teeth.

"A very good friend."

"How sad to lose touch with a good friend," she said.

As I cleared the glasses from the table, I thought about how the attrition of certain friendships seemed normal to me, how it seemed natural as a cliff's erosion, occurring so slowly over time that it was easy to overlook.

While I told Liz and Benny the story about Goat's call, Liz broke out into hysterical laughter. She said "Holy crap!" over and over, tears running down her face.

"Why do you think it's so funny?" asked Benny. We were standing in their kitchen and he was tossing the salad. He wore wire-rim glasses and a blue button-down shirt. "I mean, the guy had a problem, obviously. He's trying to clean up his act."

"Dan's Your Man House Painting?" said Liz, wiping the tears from her eyes with a kitchen towel. Her black hair, shining with glints of blue, grazed the shoulders of her white blouse. "Making amends? The typewriter got thrown off the bridge?" She broke out into laughter again. When she finally calmed down and caught her breath she said, "Jesus, that's great."

"I think I was in shock that he called," I said. "And I couldn't believe all the details he remembered."

"Especially if he was as toasted all the time as he says," said Liz. She poured red wine and handed me a glass. "I don't think that was it."

"What?"

"I think he had the hots for you and was pissed off that you wouldn't sleep with him."

I sipped my wine. For a second I got a bodily rush, a full-body memory of Goat on top of me, his little mustache pressing into my face as he kissed me.

"Who said I didn't sleep with him?" I said, anticipating with pleasure Liz's outburst which was sure to follow.

"What?" screeched Liz.

"Did you really?" said Benny, his wire-rim glasses glinting under the kitchen light.

"Yes. Once."

"Maybe he was pissed off that you were sleeping with other guys but that you wouldn't sleep with him a second time," said Liz. "Why only once?"

"It was just one of those things," I said, realizing that Liz was probably right. Goat wasn't just drunk. He'd been angry with me. No matter. He had told me the truth of what he'd done—and it was so many years ago.

"Yes, one of those things," said Liz. "One of those drunken things. Those were the days. All party, all the time—no responsibilities."

"Liz, you ought to have your head examined," said Benny. "I hated every minute of living in the dorms." He took a sip of wine then began cutting French bread on the cutting board.

"You did?" I asked, not completely surprised. Although at the time I didn't think of it this way, I now saw that I loved and hated the dorms. Equally.

Some shouting came from the other room.

"Boys!" yelled Liz. "If you can't share that goddamn video game, I'm going to throw it out the window!"

The shouting stopped.

"They fight over everything," she said. "It's maddening."

"Why'd you hate the dorms, Benny?" I asked.

"Where do I start? Bathrooms full of puke? No privacy? No silence? And not to mention the unsolicited haircuts."

"You make it sound like getting your head shaved while you were passed out happened every-other-day," said Liz.

"Once was more than enough."

"But there was something good about the dorms," said Liz. "You met me there." She un-tucked his shirttail and ran her hand up and down his back. I always enjoyed watching Liz cozy up to Benny. Their love, their connection, their spiky bantering warmed me.

"But I might have met you at ZeroNet anyway," said Benny. "I don't think I had to suffer the dorms because of you."

"Well, you got lots of ass from me in the dorms. Doesn't that count for anything?"

"I could have gotten lots of ass other places," he deadpanned.

I laughed.

"You take that back, Benny Moss!" shouted Liz, pulling her hand out from under his shirt and slapping his arm.

"Okay, okay, I take it back," he said, smiling, obviously enjoying whatever it was that he enjoyed the most in Liz — her forceful playfulness, perhaps. He moved to the sink and turned on the water.

"Goat. I still can't believe that little twerp called you," said Liz, refilling her wine glass. "And I can't believe you slept with him. What else didn't you tell me? I thought we were friends."

"I told you the most important things," I said. "I told you about Stacy and Chuck."

"God, what a shocker. Every time I go to the Pride Parade in San Francisco with my sister, I keep wondering if I'll see either one of them there."

"Why don't you take me this year?" I asked.

"Norma, you know it's a special thing between me and Sandy. The sister bond and everything. I'll go with you when she finally gets a girlfriend who will take her. I wonder when the hell that will be. I think she's so crabby because she doesn't get enough pussy. Maybe that's Benny's problem." She laughed, shooting Benny a look, clearly pleased with her equal-opportunity joke.

"I didn't say it," said Benny, grinning.

"When Sandy and I go together, I'm sure everyone thinks we're a couple," continued Liz. "*C'est la vie.* Anyway, why don't you just go by yourself or with some other friends?"

"Maybe I will," I said. "I've always been curious. Benny, aren't you curious about it?"

"I watch it on T.V.," he said, as he chopped a tomato. "Always looking out for Liz and Sandy. But I never see them."

"Why don't you go with me?" I asked.

"There are thousands of people there. I'm not big on crowds."

"I can't believe you both had gay roommates all that time," said Liz, "and you didn't know."

"Why would I know it?" I said. "Stacy never did anything to hint. I mean, all the guys wanted her. I just thought she was, I don't know, a very nice person—very mature, in a way, almost motherly. It never would have crossed my mind."

"What's your excuse?" she asked Benny.

"What do you mean?"

"Didn't Paul ever give a gay vibe to you? Ever?"

"I don't know what a gay vibe is," said Benny.

"And he never tried to make a move on you?" asked Liz.

"I don't think I was his type. According to Norma, he liked big, burly guys."

"I wonder if he still does?" I said, my skin prickling at the thought of him, as though he was standing next to me with his sweet Charlie Brown face.

"Norma, you should find him," said Liz. "I bet you anything he lives in San Francisco. I mean, gay Mecca, Alfred Hitchcock, et cetera et cetera. At least look in the fricking phone book. Or no, I have a better idea."

She ran into the other room and came back with her laptop. Online, she typed in Chuck's name.

"Look," she said. "There are two 'P. Fellows' in the city. I bet you anything he's one of them." She wrote the two numbers down on a piece of paper and handed it to me. "Now what was Stacy's last name?"

"Bly," I said.

She typed in, "Stacy Bly."

"Hm, hm," she said. I looked over her shoulder. "Surprising, not much. A Stacy Bly ran a marathon in Seattle."

"That's got to be her," I said. "She liked to run, and she moved to Portland. Anything else?"

"Nope, that's all I can find. No S. Bly's or Stacy Bly's in Western phone book listings. Oh, here's one, no two S. Bly's in Florida, and another three in Chicago. And here's a bunch in New York. She could be anywhere."

The first number Liz had written down on the slip of paper was him. I heard his voice on the answering machine: *You've reached Paul and Steve. Leave a message, darling.*

I left a bumbling message and spent the next hour packing. Then the phone rang.

"Norma Jean? Is it really you?"

"Hi Chuck." My heart was racing. His voice sounded exactly the same.

"I'm thrilled beyond words, I can't tell you! Norma Jean, Norma Jean. It's been so long. Are you married? Pregnant and barefoot? Babies? What, do tell?"

"None of the above," I said, feeling that old-but-immediately-familiar sense that he drew out the droll repartee in me.

"Oh, you must have juicy stories then. Let's get together, okay? Where, when?"

We agreed to meet that evening for a drink at a restaurant in Palo Alto, the halfway point.

I couldn't decide what to wear. Almost all my clothes were black. Didn't I have any color? I thought about calling Liz for advice but decided against it. She'd just use my jitters as an excuse to tease me. I settled for black pants and a black and white sleeveless blouse. I brushed my long wavy red hair and put on some mascara. My palms were wet and my heart beat crazily like I was going on a blind date or meeting my secret love. Silly, I thought. Silly.

Chuck was seated at the bar, a glass of wine in front of him. When he saw me he shouted, "Norma Jean!" and came up to meet me. We hugged, and I felt in my body all those nights of sleeping warm and safe in the crook of his arm.

"You look stunning," he said.

He was almost bald. He was wearing jeans, a white madras shirt, and small round blue-tinted glasses.

"So do you, just like a movie director."

We sat. "Well, I'm not one of those," he said. I asked the bartender for a glass of white wine. "I teach film at City College. You like the hairdo?" He patted his head. "Just like the old days," he said, "when strangers entered my abode and shaved me clean."

"Did you ever find out who did that?" I asked.

"Not a clue."

I told him about Goat's phone call, about his 12-Step Program and making amends.

"Ah, the sins of the past. The glorious sins of the past." He sipped his wine. "Norma Jean, you really are stunning." Already warm from his presence, I blushed. "And you're single?" he said. "I find that hard to believe."

"I travel a lot with my work. I write travel articles."

"You must have a man at every port, then, huh? Do tell."

"Well, kind of. There have been a few." I smiled into my wine glass like I was flirting with him. "And I still see Jack once in a while."

"What? That brute?"

A blush crawled down my neck. How could I ever have done what I did—told Jack in Chuck's presence, right after we'd made love, that Chuck meant "nothing" to me? I'd done my best all these years to shove down that shameful memory, but sometimes it surfaced—and now the shame returned to punish me. "Chuck, I'm so sorry . . ." I began, but he interrupted me.

"No one here is in a 12-Step Program."

"But . . ."

"Really, Norma Jean. That was twenty years ago. Tell me about you and the brute."

I took a deep breath, relieved. He was right. It was a long time ago. "You know *Same Time, Next Year*?" I asked.

"Alan Alda, Ellen Burstyn, 1979."

"We're kind of like that."

"You get together once a year for a week to ball your brains out?"

I laughed, surprised that I was feeling a little shy. I almost never felt shy. "Sort of. It's not actually that planned, or regular. Sometimes more, sometimes less. What can I say? He's been married three times."

"Well why doesn't he marry you? The brute."

"He asks me every time I see him—even when he's married to someone else. I always say no."

"Norma Jean. Sounds like you're still quite the feminist."

"Maybe. I don't know," I said. "Maybe I'm just a non-conformist."

"Join the club, sweetie," he said.

We sipped our wine. The bar lights dimmed, and a man with a guitar began playing in a lit-up corner.

"So who's Steve?" I asked.

"Only the love of my life," he said. My heart dropped a little. Silly, I knew, but it did. I had no control over my heart. "We've been together ten years."

"Like Benny and Liz," I said.

"You still know Liz and Benny? That's amazing. I know no one from the dorms."

"Not even Stacy?" I asked, hoping he still knew her. I would have loved seeing her again.

"No, that little Grace Kelly vixen—she dropped off the planet when she moved to one of those weird non-California states. But—Benny and Liz? My god, how are they?"

"Married with two little boys."

"Good for them. With the way they were always hopping in bed, you'd think after all this time they'd have more than that."

"Well, they didn't see each other for ten years," I said, telling him their story.

"Ah, true love," he said, bumping his shoulder against mine. "They found each other again."

To my disbelief, my eyes began to brim with tears. I turned and said, "Excuse me, I have to use the bathroom," and found my way, in a blur, to the woman's restroom. I leaned against the sink and let myself sob. I didn't fully understand what I was crying about, but it felt good to just let it happen. My mascara had smeared so I washed my face and reapplied it.

It was strange, and strangely wonderful, to realize Chuck was out there, sitting at the bar, sipping his wine, waiting for me. I went back to him.

As though he knew I'd been crying, he smiled kindly at me as I settled back into the seat next to him. We sat in silence for a moment, sipping at our drinks, listening to the guitar.

"So what ever happened to Vince?" I asked, his name conjuring up his Magnum P.I. face in my mind.

"Ah, young love," he said. The bartender put down peanuts in a silver dish. Chuck threw a handful in his mouth and crunched thoughtfully. "Well, what can I say? I moved to the city and broke his heart."

"You're terrible," I said, knowing exactly what I'd say next, knowing that I would be talking not just about what happened to Vince but what happened to me. "You're the biggest heart-breaker."

"No," he said firmly, "you are."

We were quiet again for a few moments. He reached over and took my hand. Our hands felt warm together. Gently, he rubbed his thumb up my palm. Then he put my hand to his lips and kissed it. I reached over and kissed his cheek. Warm and soft, just like I remembered it.

"Want to come for dinner tomorrow night at our place?" he asked, still holding my hand. "Steve makes a mean California roll with a special wasabi sauce. And bring the lovebirds. If they can get a babysitter. I don't want little kiddies breaking our valuables."

"I'd love to. But I have to take a rain check," I said, both relieved and disappointed. I wanted this amazing man back in my life, but I needed a little space and time to fine-tune myself, to learn how to love him a new way. This would be a familiar, but brand-new, relationship. "I'm flying out in the morning to Brussels."

"Brussels?"

"To do an article on the beer capital of the world."

Chuck let out a laugh. "Norma Jean, some things never change."

Bonus Preview of Kate Evans'

Complementary Colors

Coming from Vanilla Heart Publishing-Summer, 2009

What happens when a 31-year-old straight woman falls in love with a lesbian? *Complementary Colors* tells this story. It's 1993, and Gwen Sullivan is agitated. She's been married and divorced and is now living with her scientist boyfriend who loses himself in dark moods. Her job at a tutoring center and her work on the Bill Clinton-for-President campaign leave her vaguely dissatisfied. She hopes taking a night class in poetry might help. In the poetry class, the allure of two lesbians takes her by surprise. She can't get them out of her mind. This prompts her to question who she is—and who she wants to be.

Soon, Gwen cannot deny her intense attraction to one of the women, Jamie. The feeling is mutual, but Jamie, too, is in a long-term relationship—with a woman minister. As Jamie and Gwen become more and more entwined, Gwen must ask herself who she is and what she wants from life. She begins to see gender, sex and sexuality differently. And as she feels compelled to "confess" her love for Jamie to her women friends, she is continually surprised by their complex reactions. This leads her to make one of the most important decisions of her life.

Chapter One: Beautiful

I was craving something, but I wasn't exactly sure what. I wanted something new. I wanted something beautiful. My life was at a strange stand-still, stagnant as the smoggy San Jose air. So I'd signed up for a poetry class. I'd been looking forward to it all week, but now as I sat in a university classroom, waiting for class to begin, I thought maybe I'd made a mistake. The students leaned on their desktops, talking to each other in the circle of desks, casual and comfortable in their jeans, while I sat stiffly in my work clothes: black blazer, pink blouse, dark nylons and black heels, my long brown hair pulled back in a clip.

Sitting in the circle with us was Professor Alameida. I knew her name because it was printed on my class schedule. She had long gray hair and a craggy face, and the sleeves of her denim jacket were rolled up to reveal silver and turquoise bracelets. When she opened a folder, silence descended on the group.

Just then, the classroom door creaked open. In walked two people, two women. They were unlike any two women I'd ever seen. They both had short dark hair, gelled into spikes, and they wore black leather jackets, baggy jeans, and black boots. It's hard to explain now why I didn't think "lesbians" right away. Or "dykes." But I didn't. It was 1992; why would I know any gay people? Or I should say lesbians. I did have an old college friend, Manny, who was gay, or so I assumed. He now lived in Massachusetts; he'd moved there with a guy I assumed to be his lover. But my life, not unlike most people's lives, was mostly filled with people like me: in my case that meant straight people, in their twenties and thirties, who were dating, or engaged, or divorced. The lesbian world might as well have taking place in Massachusetts, while I lived my straight life in California. Until that moment, of course.

I wasn't the only one staring at them. It seemed everyone did. The two women had made a rather dramatic entrance, coming in late on the first day, walking in like they were one person split in two. For women, they took up a lot of space, with their spiky hair and bulky leather jackets and big boots shining with silver buckles. They sat in the two empty seats right next to the professor. The desks seemed too small for their bodies, their energy. They leaned back, knees apart, feet planted like men.

"Sorry," said the taller one, three silver earrings glimmering in one ear, and a smear of a tattoo on the back of her hand.

Professor Alameida looked over at them, half-smiled, and placed her hand on the desk of the woman closest to her. She handed them each a syllabus with a certain ease, a sense of familiarity.

"It's okay, we just started," she said, leaning forward in her desk and crossing her feet at the ankles. "I'm Vanessa Alameida. Please call me Vanessa. Not professor. I don't like that stuff." Her voice was so low and gravelly I had to strain to hear her. "This class is about poetry, poetry, poetry. You will write a poem most weeks, beginning next week, as it says here." She tapped her finger on the syllabus. "You will bring copies for everyone. I don't want you to write a poem at the last minute. You should be writing it and thinking about it all week. A poem is a living thing. If you dash it off and bring it in dead, we'll know." She put her fist over her mouth and coughed a deep cough, her silver bracelets jangling.

Anxiety grew in me. I'd have to write poems and bring them in, fresh and vulnerable as kittens with their eyes sealed shut. I looked at the blank piece of paper in my notebook in front of me. If I put my pen to it, thinking "poem," would a whole bunch of words emerge, words put together in such a way as to create something new, something that at this moment didn't exist? I used to think about that sometimes when I'd begin to write a journal entry—that in a few minutes, I'd be to the bottom of the page even though I didn't know when I was starting what would propel me, what would get me there, and what it would be like to finish. My living time wouldn't have passed unnoticed; I'd have created something. Could I do this with poetry?

The most I had ever written was when I'd recently lived in Japan for a year. But aside from some journal-writing, most of the writing had been letters. Writing to people I knew helped alleviate my dizzying culture shock. Could I now write something artful, something that would surprise me and take me to new places? Could I be hopeful? I didn't know exactly why I needed hope. The idea of hope seemed to feed something elusive in me that was hungry.

"Now here, let's read this," the professor said, handing the person to her left a stack of papers. The stack continued person to person, around the circle. The leather-jacketed woman with the tattoo on her hand leaned over to the other one and whispered something in her ear. They both quietly laughed. I found myself curious about what she said, and oddly, a little embarrassed, as though maybe they were making fun of me. I knew that was crazy—they hadn't even looked at me. They were probably oblivious of my presence. Yet something about having them in the room, dressed alike and sharing secrets, made me feel a little inept and eager, like I used to around the popular girls in middle school.

When the paper came to me, I saw that on it was a poem by Louise Glück. I'd heard the name before, but I didn't know her work. Maybe I'd read her work ten years before when I'd been working on my undergraduate degree in English. That was the thing that always surprised me about having a degree in English: how much literature there was in the world, and how little of it I really knew.

Vanessa read the poem aloud, slowly, as though chewing each word:

Messengers

You have only to wait, they will find you.
The geese flying low over the marsh,
glittering in black water.
They find you.

And the deer--
how beautiful they are,
as though their bodies do not impede them.

Slowly they drift into the open
through bronze panels of sunlight.

Why would they stand so still
if they were not waiting?
Almost motionless, until their cages rust,
the shrubs shiver in the wind,
squat and leafless.

You have only to let it happen:
that cry—*release, release*—like the moon
wrenched out of earth and rising
full in its circle of arrows

until they come before you
like dead things, saddled with flesh,
and you above them, wounded and dominant.

When Vanessa was finished, we sat, quiet. I didn't really understand the poem. But I felt it. I felt it inside me, like it was about something very real that I couldn't articulate, like it was a fish swimming around in my veins. The poem, it seemed to me, used words to get at something beyond words. The deer, the geese, the shrubs. I knew exactly what she meant.

Vanessa uncrossed then re-crossed her legs. A guy with dreadlocks and ripped overalls sniffed. A young woman with short blond hair shifted in her seat. She wore baggy shorts with sandals, and one of those olive green sweaters that looks like the most comfortable sweater in the world, the kind that pretty actresses with tousled hair wear in beach movies. She looked like she'd stepped out of the "casual wear" pages of a high-end catalogue.

The sun was getting low out the window. I could see the dark edges of a tree and the corner of a dirty white concrete building across the way.

"Well," said Vanessa. "What do you think?"

I felt myself flush, as I often did when students don't answer a teacher's question. It seemed to be my fault, that I should have an answer for her. I wanted to say something, but I worried I'd sound like a fool. I wanted to say, "I feel this poem in my veins." But that would sound completely idiotic. As a student with a degree in English, I thought I should instead say something about the images, the metaphor, the use of repetition.

Out the window, the tree was completely still. It was a warm, summer-becoming--fall evening. I became aware of the florescent lights overhead as the balance of light outside shifted to dim and the room brightened.

"I think it's beautiful," said the tall, leather jacketed woman with the tattoo on her hand. She had dark eyes and thick eyelashes, almost as thick as my boyfriend Matthew's. And a delicate chin that curved up, just slightly, and a small scar on her forehead. She had taken off her leather jacket to reveal a black tee-shirt and a necklace on a long silver chain.

Her words had given me permission to speak. "Me too," I said. "I think it's beautiful, too." I could feel the eyes of the class on me. I swallowed and looked down at the poem, seeing if I could find a line I especially liked, but then a guy who looked Vietnamese was talking, saying, "What does she mean, 'wounded and dominant'?"

"What do you think she means?" asked Vanessa.

I lost his answer, though, because as soon as I looked up from the poem, I glanced over at the tattooed woman, and saw that she was looking at me. When my eye caught hers, she didn't look away, just smiled. The girlishness of her smile surprised me. She had a mouth full of movie star teeth: large, straight, and bright white. I smiled back, trying to say with my smile that I liked her comment on the poem, that I appreciated the way she had spoken up and given me room to do the same.

Then she said something to me, silently exaggerating her mouth movements, so that I might be able to read her lips. I couldn't figure out what she was saying. I tilted my head and looked at her quizzically, shrugging my shoulders, so she'd try again. She held up the poem and pointed to it.

Then, slowly, she mouthed two words, pausing between. She mouthed the words one more time, very slowly. A surprising tingle scuttled up my spine.

I saw that she was saying, "Yes, beautiful."

Photo Credit Brenda Jamrus

Kate Evans is the author of a poetry collection (*Like All We Love*, Spirit/Q Press) and a book about lesbian and gay teachers (*Negotiating the Self*, Routledge). Her stories, poems and essays have appeared in more than 40 publications, including the *North American Review, Bellevue Literary Review, Santa Monica Review*, and *ZYZZYVA*. Her work has been nominated for a Los Angeles Times Book Prize, a Lambda Literary Award and two Pushcart Prizes. A California native, she teaches in the Department of English and Comparative Literature at San Jose State University.

Readers can learn more about Kate Evans and her writing at www.beingandwriting.blogspot.com.

Printed in the United States
151377LV00002B/47/P

9 780982 115077